Acknowledgements

For me a work like this book is never done in a vacuum. St. Paul uses the analogy of the human body to describe the community of men and women who work together to achieve and reach a certain goal or task. In the twelfth chapter of his first letter to the Corinthians, he compares the need for each person to cooperate with one another as the body.

By the same token I must tip my hat to those who have greatly helped me give birth to this project. Each of these following saints has also given this work legs.

To my lovely wife, Alice, who through her profound patience and understanding has created a sanctuary for me to partake in this journey.

To my gentle and loving sister, Irene Staropoli, who introduced me to the Carpenter, the mender of broken dreams.

I must recognize Joseph Caracciolo for his insight and creative talent; for dressing 'Caper' and placing much needed meat on its bare bones.

I would like to heartily thank Reine Bethany for her insight and editing skills.

A special nod goes out to Jeanne Bifulco for her skillful photography;

To Detective Bernard Marshall (Retired) and Sergeant Timothy Hagan of the NYPD Blue for their technical assistance in this project;

And to Maggie Marshall-Hagan for her editing and technical support.

Chapter 1

Why do I always listen to Peg? Is it because she's so sweet? Or because she's so pretty? Maybe 'cause she smells so good! Maybe all of the above. The thought of her made him smile. *Whatever her hold is on me, she's the reason I'm heading to Bayville. I sure wouldn't be going to this thing on my own account.*

Michael Ryan thought as he maneuvered his '64 Mustang along Glen Cove Road, sparring with the hectic Friday night traffic. Good Friday, yet people up this way didn't think much about holiness.

But Mike himself wasn't quite into charity functions. Nonetheless, he was headed for a fund raiser at the home of a famous evangelist, all on account of Peggy.

The town of Bayville is a hamlet on the famous Gold Coast of Long Island, where mansions sit along the shore on expansive manicured lawns recounting tales of wild revelry once hosted by the likes of the Roosevelts, the Fitzgeralds and the Vanderbilts.

Waiting impatiently for the light to change, Ryan glanced at the headline from the copy of *Newsday* lying on the seat beside him — the basketball bad boy of the week got busted for drug use and sexual misconduct. *Well, surprise, surprise. Couldn't they come up with a more important lead story than that? What a waste of paper. Waste of time too.* The light changed.

Ryan was going to meet his partner, Peggy. They worked out of Nassau County's Eighth Precinct. They were cops — plain-clothes detectives. For the last four years she had been his partner and a good friend to him and his son.

Peggy was a born-again Christian. Mike had no problem with that. After all, Mike himself believed in God; though he sometimes wondered whether or not his answering machine was working because the Big Man didn't return any of his calls.

Peggy had been bugging him to go with her to some kind of service by a woman named Tamara

Steele, a sort of evangelist whose thing was healing. *Oh yeah, Peg corrected me about that. The Steele woman doesn't actually do the healing; she is only God's instrument. God works through her. He does the healing.*

Well, Peggy had finally worn him down. She was very persuasive. He agreed to go with her to see this new Oral Roberts.

"It would be great for Jamie, too." Peggy's eyes shone like the neon lights in Times Square when she heard him say he would go.

"Wait a minute! I'm not bringing my son to a freak show!" He had crossed a line.

"*Freak show?*" she snapped. "You think I would subject Jamie to anything that was weird or could hurt him in some way? I love Jamie as if I had carried him in my own womb."

She shocked him by her passion.

"No, I'm sorry," he said. "Of course you wouldn't hurt Jamie. But you know how sensitive he is. Since Katie's murder even the slightest thing can set him off."

"I know, Michael. Maybe you're right. But I only want what's best for you and Jamie." Her commanding hand, usually firm when performing her duties, was surprisingly soft as she placed it on his arm.

"Okay, Peg. But Jamie has a cold, so he won't be able to come anyway." Mike didn't exactly lie; Jamie did have a slight cold, and when a bug entered that kid's chest, he always had a difficult time shaking the darned thing.

Mike's son, Jamie, was born with cerebral palsy, and when he was just nine days old, he caught pneumonia. The boy was strong and he survived, but the damage to his lungs would affect him the rest of his life. And although it was obvious as he grew that he was as sharp as a tack, he had problems articulating because of the CP. He also had ambulatory problems, and often tripped over his own feet.

And now, as if that wasn't enough, Jamie was haunted by the memory of seeing his mother brutally cut down by a seventeen-year-old punk trying to knock over a convenience store. Mother and son were in the wrong place at the wrong time. Ever since then, whenever Jamie saw someone with a tattoo he would get spastic, and it often took two hours or more for him to calm down.

Mike had vowed to get the young creep who killed his wife, no matter how long it took.

The twilight turned pitch black as Mike made a left onto Bayville Avenue. You can't see your hand in front of your face on the North Shore at night, but that didn't slow him down any as he turned onto Perry Avenue. It took a while to find the gates to the private road on the right. As he entered he put his brights on just in time to avoid careening into an embankment. He slowed down. The winding drive seemed endless. The final curve was very sharp, and as he rounded it the silent blackness exploded with the glare of revolving red lights.

Mike recognized the aging patrolman directing traffic away from the brilliantly lighted mansion. Uniforms were everywhere.

"Hey, Dave, what's with all the blues?" he asked. "It looks like a patrolman's convention." Five squad cars were parked on the mountainous lawn, forming a circle, their revolving lights creating a psychedelic scene.

"All I know is Sally called all available cars to the Gold Coast, and here we are. Detective Younger is inside with the lieutenant."

"Man, this has to be big to get Dunbar out. What's going on?"

"Don't know yet," the patrolman shrugged. "Hey, Detective Ryan, looks like I'm movin' up. This is the North Shore. Is an old Irish cop from Flatbush like me allowed to enter these pearly gates?" He grinned.

Although he laughed as he left the old guy directing traffic, Mike was apprehensive. *What the heck is going on?*

He took the broad marble steps that led to the mansion's front door two at a time, noting the Grecian statues of gossamer-clad beauties that stood silent on each side, cool and undisturbed by the commotion all around them as he passed. He was greeted at the iron-clad door by a butler wearing a waistcoat. Before the man could protest his presence, Mike flashed his badge. The butler slowly bowed, moving out of his way.

As Mike passed through the foyer, the main staircase to the second floor caught his attention. . . *more marble of course. . . and winding*. It reminded him of an old 1940's flick. *It probably took all the gold in Fort Knox to pay for this spread*, Mike thought. *I would bet a whole month's salary that old man Steele didn't lose one night's sleep worrying about the cost.* Mike couldn't help but notice the golden chandelier dangling from the ceiling of the main hall.

The burly man with his back to Mike finished scribbling in a little notebook, turned around, and stopped short.

"Detective Ryan, to what do we owe the honor?" sneered Dunbar. There was no love lost between Mike and his lieutenant — civility on occasion was the best they could manage. Apparently this was not to be one of those occasions.

"I was supposed to meet Detective Younger here. She asked me to come with her to her friend Tamara Steele's fund raiser service. I figured I'd check it out."

"Well, you're a little late." Nausea unsettled Dunbar's face for an instant, but he controlled his features. "I'm afraid Miss Steele could use some healing herself. Her body is about as cold as yesterday's meatloaf. Seems like someone got bored with her sermons, so they plunged a knife into her to shut her up. Blood is splattered all over her bedroom." Dunbar stopped, drew a breath, and continued, "Since you're here I might as well put you to work. Come take a look at the body." The lieutenant led him to a spacious room with a plush vanity chair and expensive dressing table opposite the canopied four-poster bed.

Mike reached into his overcoat pocket for some surgical gloves. His hand hit something hard. He pulled out a computer game.

"Detective, one of your amusements?"

"No, it's my son Jamie's." Mike felt a sheepish smile forming.

"Well, maybe when you're done playing games you'll allow us to get on with the investigation."

Mike fumbled with the game and shoved it back into his trench coat. He felt like an idiot. *I want to brain that kid.* Then he smiled to himself, remembering Jamie's glee when he trounced Mike at one of the computer games. Thinking of that always made him chuckle.

His chuckles died as he surveyed Tamara Steele's bedroom. He approached the canopy bed and examined the once beautiful body, now engulfed in a pool of blood. He waded through a squad of cops from the Special Victims Unit who were examining her fatal wounds. They were taking snapshots with their digital cameras, and bagging evidence they hoped would point to the killer.

"Mike! Mike, you heard?" It was as much a statement as a question from his partner as she emerged from the adjoining bathroom. Peggy Younger stood about five foot six, and she toyed with her long single braid as she spoke.

"Dunbar just told me," said Mike. "Man, she must have really teed somebody off. I'm really sorry, Peg. I know how much you admired Miss Steele."

"You know," intruded Dunbar from the bedroom doorway, "old man Steele is very rich, very influential and very sensitive. And he's used to having his own way. One slip-up and somebody's gonna have to answer to 1550 Franklin, and it's not gonna be me!" The Nassau County Seat on Franklin Avenue in Mineola was a place most cops avoided like the plague; those politicians were nothing but trouble. "If we don't handle every aspect of this case with kid gloves, Steele's gonna have it plastered all over the front page of *Newsday*, and we really don't need the publicity."

Lieutenant Dunbar was a typical civil servant, a man constantly looking over his shoulder—a guy with little or no ability, just a good test taker — like so many others, who milk their connections in the Democratic Party to secure a county job where they won't have to exert themselves too much. Nassau County PD offered twenty years and out, with a pretty good pension. He was almost there. He had eighteen years on the job. His party ties had helped move him along, slowly but surely, making sure he was finally promoted beyond his capabilities.

"Younger, you know old man Steele. See what you can get out of him," he barked.

Ryan held his tongue. Most times, when he found himself in trouble — and that was often — the common denominator was his mouth. He couldn't stand people who used others to cover up their own inadequacies. *Dunbar wouldn't put his neck on the line—no, he's setting Peggy up as a sacrificial lamb to appease the gods at 1550 Franklin in case something goes wrong.*

"Hey, Younger," Dunbar blundered on, "don't start preaching or anything to Mr. Steele; he's too important a man to be subjected to that nonsense."

"Nonsense?" Peggy said incredulously. "Lieutenant, the Bible is the word of God!"

"Detective Younger," Dunbar snapped back, "you were warned! Don't forget the complaints against you in the Merlock case. There's no place for religion on the job! We're investigating a homicide here, not holding a tent meeting."

"Lieutenant, those charges were bogus, and they were dropped. Why don't you cut her some slack?"

Mike couldn't control himself. He knew that his very presence was like an open sore to Dunbar, and now he had rubbed salt in the wound. But he couldn't just stand by and watch Dunbar shift his own responsibility to Peggy, and then accuse her of improper practices.

Mike should have realized that Peggy didn't need any help. She looked totally at peace and didn't seem at all fazed by Dunbar's threat. But for some inexplicable reason he felt the need to protect her.

"Lieutenant, I'll try to be very sensitive to Mr. Steele," she said courteously.

Peggy Younger stood in the doorway of Edmund Steele's study. She saw the formerly august figure sitting at his broad mahogany desk with his forehead buried in his hands. His present appearance was a sharp contrast to the confident and commanding man she had encountered at those weekly prayer meetings she'd attended with her friend, Tamara.

"Sir, Miss Younger is here to speak with you," the butler informed him.

"Show her in," he answered weakly.

"Mr. S, what can I say?" Peggy said as she approached him. "I loved Tamara; she was like a sister to me." The previously stoic man strained to rise from his seat, weakly grasping onto the edge of the desk, heading towards the sympathetic detective. Finally reaching Peggy, he fiercely embraced her with what little strength he had left.

"I'm going to miss my little girl." His voice was hoarse and faint.

"Everyone will," said Peggy, her throat tightening, "especially the church community."

"Who could have done this to someone so loving and giving? Tamara was the joy of my life. . . and. . . and all those stab wounds, oh my God!" He collapsed again into his chair, his face buried in his large bony hands.

"I know, Mr. S, I know," she comforted him. "Sir, I am also here in a professional capacity. Since I'm a friend of the family, my lieutenant thought it best that I be the one to ask you some questions. Did she have any enemies that you know of?"

He looked down at his hands. "Peggy, for the life of me I really don't understand why anyone would lay a hand on her, much less butcher her until her blood covered the entire bedroom." Again the once powerful man broke down and sobbed bitterly.

Peggy waited patiently, praying silently while the grief-stricken man regained his composure: *O Father God, why couldn't Lieutenant Dunbar have waited a day, or at least a few hours, before making me question this heartbroken man? This is his only daughter. Please, O God, provide me with the words. . . Your words. . . to ease this poor man's heart."*

Peggy placed her hand in the old man's. His hand continued to tremble as she looked compassionately into his tear-filled eyes. She knew she had crossed the boundaries of professionalism. But being objective wasn't all that important right now.

"Your daughter was the most loving and giving person that I have ever known," she said. "As a police officer I have come across many evil and twisted people who have committed horrendous acts, but I can't, for the life of me imagine how anyone could take such a sweet innocent life. The violence and brutality. . . it's just beyond me." Peggy valiantly held back her own tears but could not trust herself to speak anymore for a moment.

"Mr. Steele," she said after regaining her composure, "I must ask if you know of anything or anyone who might have something to do with this?"

"Peggy, I am as bewildered as you."

She regretted having to press the issue. She continued.

"To your knowledge, had she ever been threatened?"

"What reason would anyone have to threaten Tamara?" Steele sat shaking his head.

"Could someone have been jealous of her?" asked Peggy.

"If Tamara knew someone was envious of her, she never shared it with me." Edmund Steele was emotionally spent, and he aged perceptibly before Peg's eyes.

James Steele, Tamara's brother, entered the study.

"Peg," he said speaking low, "this has been a terrible ordeal for my father, as it has been for everyone. With all due respect, he has to rest. Our doctor is going to give him a sedative."

"I am in complete agreement with you," Peggy told him. "Besides, we're finished for now."

Peggy watched as Mr. Steele's son practically carried his father up the stairway to a bedroom.

While Peggy questioned old man Steele, Mike tried in vain to get information from the guests. No one knew anything. All he got was, "Tamara was a beautiful person. Tamara was always there for everyone. Tamara gave everyone prayer and moral support. Tamara's generosity was heralded throughout the community."

Somebody didn't think Tamara Steele was that great! I guess it's up to me and Peg to find that somebody.

By now Mike had been at the Steele mansion over two hours. What had promised to be to him a night filled with endless speeches had turned out quite differently. *A beautiful woman getting whacked is always different*, he thought. *And it usually ruins the evening.*

The crime scene unit finished up. Further interrogation of the guests yielded nothing more. Mike couldn't find Peggy, so he left. They could compare notes tomorrow.

He was alone with his thoughts as he headed home through the dark streets of the North Shore, unfazed by the barrage of sports cars frantically flying past. *It doesn't make sense. I thought killing wasn't kosher for these religious types. Isn't it one of the thou-shalt-nots on their Top Ten List? Apparently someone missed that little tidbit.*

Chapter 2

Mike arrived at his Cape Cod home on Penny Lane in Levittown. It wasn't the old Tudor of Katie's dreams, overlooking the raging Atlantic on the coast of Maine, but Katie had loved the house anyway. Moonlight engulfed the front lawn as he walked up the path. Though the blooms were long gone, in his mind's eye he could still see the tulips Katie had planted, their brightly colored cups a riot of color like a rainbow gone mad.

Mike dismissed the vision as he shoved the key in the hole. From the hall he could see the light from the TV reflected on the opposite wall.

The sixty-six-year-old woman sprawled comfortably on a worn, well-seasoned couch was asleep. A mother's instinct opened her eyes, and she struggled to get up.

"Michael, are you home already?" She yawned.

"Ma, it's 11:30 at night."

"Oh, my, I must have fallen asleep. I was watching the news and they said Tamara Steele was stabbed to death. Wasn't she the one you were going to see tonight?"

"Yeah, Ma, it wasn't a pretty picture, typical drive-by media, selling their souls for a sensational story. The tabloids will probably run this story for six months. Of course these leftists wouldn't ever think of reporting on sanctuary cities harboring illegal aliens. They wait until an illegal earns a rap sheet as long as his arm. Then, *maybe* they put the story on page fourteen! And our wonderful justice system will likely sentence them to two weeks behind bars and then make them pick up Baby Ruth wrappers at a work program on Sunrise Highway."

"Son, sometimes you confuse me when you make these little speeches. I don't know what to make of them," sighed his mother, shaking her head as she headed for the kitchen. "Do you want some coffee? It's already made."

"Yeah, Ma, why not," he answered, and followed her through the doorway.

On the kitchen table, he noticed the mail placed neatly in a pile. He sat down and casually went through the stack, moaning each time he saw a bill—and there were lots of them. *Katie always took care of these things. She really kept up on the finances. Now that she's gone, I have to pick up the slack.* Mike knew that he wasn't as proficient as his late wife when it came to these things. Mundane tasks like running the household bored him to death. He threw the mail on the table and turned to his mother.

"How's Jamie?"

She heaved a resigned sigh.

"He gave me a hard time about going to bed. He wanted to watch that darn cop show. I told him it wouldn't be over till 11:00 p.m. and him having a cold, he needs his rest. But you know I can't resist the little dickens. Besides I think his leg brace is really hurting him. So I told him he that he didn't have to wear it tonight."

Mike felt his anger and frustration rising. "Mom, why the h—l did you tell him that? You know his therapist told us the brace helps his leg to straighten so it won't get atrophied."

"But he's in a lot of pain."

"If you want him to function in this world you can't coddle him."

"But son. . ."

"Mom, I appreciate all you do around here but don't fight me on this. Did he go to bed after the show?"

Mrs. Ryan took a sip of her coffee. "Not without a whole lot of fussing."

"I'll have to talk to him."

"Michael, please, it wasn't any big deal."

"No big deal? You're too easy on him! When I'm not here, you're the boss. He knows that."

"But when you talk to him, it always ends up with him crying. You're too hard on him." Her heart beat with a double ache for both son and grandson.

"I have to be hard on him," said Mike. "He has two strikes against him before he even starts — he's cerebral palsied and he has no mother. The world isn't going to mollycoddle him. I'm not going to always be around to protect him, especially with my chosen profession."

The elderly woman looked down at her coffee mug. "I wish Katie was still here; the boy needs his mother."

At the mention of her name Mike's heart felt like a bolt of lightning had struck him. "Ma, I wish for a lot of things. But wishing doesn't make it so."

"Michael, maybe you should think about getting married again."

"Oh, Ma, not this again. I don't need any more grief in my life. Anyway, you and Katie are the only two women who could ever put up with me."

"But Jamie needs a mother!"

"Mom, he had a mother — and she was the greatest mother in the world — but she's gone. *If I could get my hands on the punk that killed her, I'd strangle him. He destroyed all our lives*," His grief suddenly turned to anger.

Mike's mother took his hand and pressed it to her cheek. "Son, the time for grieving is over. You must get on with your life — find yourself a wife and a mother for Jamie."

Mike felt an uncontrollable storm of rage, hurt and annoyance sweeping over him. "Will you *please* get off my back? Jamie and I are doing just fine without anyone coming into our lives and messing everything up."

He hated himself for yelling at her. All she wanted was her son's and grandson's happiness. However, every marriageable woman that he came into contact with was a distant second to Katie — no one could ever match the wife now five years in her grave.

The next morning Mike was awakened by his alarm clock. Actually, he was already half awake. He got up, showered, shaved and after dressing, he peeked in on Jamie.

As usual, Jamie had kicked the covers off the bed. *Terrific for his cold,* Mike thought with a sigh. He was grateful it was Saturday. That gave Jamie two more days to recuperate before returning to school on Monday. Mike fixed the covers over the sleeping boy, and tried to secure them by tucking them under the mattress.

Downstairs, Mike found his mother leaning over the kitchen sink, washing a few dishes. He placed his hand on her back, an Irishman's futile attempt at an apology. Her shoulders relaxed a little.

They heard uneven clumps on the stairway. Jamie appeared in his bare feet, holding a short-legged brace in his hand.

"Hey, pal," said his father, "go back upstairs and put on shoes and socks. You're gonna get a worse cold than you have now."

"Okay, but help me with the brace, I can't put it on." As usual, Jamie's face grimaced uncontrollably as he attempted to express himself. Mike knelt to put the brace on him.

"Dad," Jamie started excitedly, "take me to Eisenhower Park today. We could play a game of touch football," he pleaded, jumping on Mike's back as he fastened the last strap on the brace.

Rising to his feet with his teenage son riding piggy-back, Mike said, "Jamie, you're just getting over a cold, and if it gets any worse, we'll have to keep you home for another three days."

"I don't mind."

"I bet you don't," Mike laughed, setting Jamie down and giving him a love punch in the arm. When Jamie laughed in response, his whole body shook. Naturally, Mike gave in to him; it was difficult to keep playing the hard guy. Jamie had been through a lot.

"We'll go to the park after I rake the leaves out front and pick up my suit from the cleaners. Okay?" promised Mike. Jamie clumped away to find his shoes and socks.

It was a fun day. It always was when the two of them were together. However, Mike felt pain watching his son's scissor-like legs trying to run and catch the football. Jamie showed a lot of courage despite his grandmother's over protectiveness.

Jamie slept well that night. So did Mike.

Easter Sunday came and Mike drove his mother and Jamie to church. He didn't see any reason to join them in the service; it might be Easter, but to him all Sundays were the same, so he spent the hour in Jilly's Coffee Shoppe, poring over *The Daily News* and *Newsday.*

After church Jamie wanted Mike to sit with him and watch a sports channel re-run of the Giants playing the Eagles. . . but Mike told him that he had to go to the squad room to finish some paperwork. He hated lying to his son, but he couldn't stand to watch football games. Not anymore, he felt his obsession for sports was the reason Katie was killed.

Monday's sunshine invaded Mike's room at 6:30 a.m. Rolling out of bed, he staggered to the shower. The biting cold water whipped him into shape.

He got in his car and headed for Garden City, making a pit stop at the local Dunkin' Donuts on Seventh Street. Even at this ungodly hour of 6:45, he saw young ladies dressed in tailored suits, carrying their laptops, their feet covered with worn-out Nikes, sprinting for the 6:50 train that would carry them to plush Wall Street offices.

He drove to Mineola and pulled into the precinct parking lot at 6:55 a.m. He walked into the squad room, hearing the same daily chatter he had been exposed to for the last fifteen years; cops herding perpetrators to holding pens as the perps sang the same old chorus: "I'm innocent; I demand to see my lawyer; you've got the wrong guy."

When Mike reached his desk he saw Peggy seated and poring over some files laid out beside her computer. He watched her for a moment, noting her neatly tailored grey pants and blue silk blouse with matching ascot. There was a certain quality to her look; he searched for the word. . . . *Spotless! Yeah, that's it, perfect and spotless.* Only her shoulder holster looked out of place. Everything else was perfect and spotless.

"My, aren't we early!" he exclaimed.

"Oh!" He had startled her, but her right cheek dimpled as her eyes traveled between the file folders and her computer monitor. "Hi, Michael." She was one of the few people to call him by his first name, other than Katie and his mother.

"You seem intense," said Mike. "What are you working on?"

She looked up from her PC. "You forgot to shave," she smiled — her typical peaceful smile — the very smile that could intimidate phonies yet brings a sense of warmth to those with an axe to grind. How's Jamie's cold?" she asked.

"Getting better, though he gives my mother a hard time."

"Oh?" She leaned back in her chair.

"Yeah, he won't take care of himself."

Peggy shrugged a little. "He's just an energetic boy and life is an adventure."

"My mother doesn't want to confront him on anything," frowned Mike.

"Well, Jamie's a good boy. He has a heavy load to carry, so *somebody's* got to be a little understanding," she said.

Mike smiled and asked, "What's that you're looking at?"

"Tamara's autopsy report. This is going to be a tough case to crack. Forensic hasn't come up with fingerprints or anything that can be learned from DNA."

Mike went over to Peggy's desk and he could smell her perfume. It was an understated scent that didn't shout at him.

"Dunbar really bothers me," she said. "I couldn't wait to get out of Tamara's bedroom. I ran out so fast that I didn't hear the time of death."

"I know what you mean about Dunbar," he replied. "She was found at 9:15 p.m. Since the party was in her honor, wasn't anyone the least bit curious as to why she was gone from the crowd so long?"

"Michael, it was really crowded, and most of the guests at the party knew one another. I guess they were engrossed in their conversations and didn't notice her absence."

Mike nodded, not very satisfied. "Did Josie or Kenny get a list of all the servants, cooks and caterers working this bash?"

"Yes, they did, but Julian Giles gave them a hard time."

"Julian who?"

"Julian Giles is, I mean was. . ." A tear fell and Peggy cleared her throat. The weekend had done little to numb the loss of her friend Tamara.

She started again. "Julian Giles was Tamara's manager. He took care of all her bookings, handled all the funds from her various healing and speaking tours plus the sale of her books."

"Maybe this Giles guy was mesmerized by the sight of all that dough. That could be a motive — maybe *he* offed her."

"I don't believe Julian has the constitution to commit a murder. Besides, I believe he was in love with Tamara."

Mike raised his eyebrows. "Was she interested in him?

"Don't be ridiculous. Julian is married, as was Tamara, and Tamara would never lead him on."

"What does being married have to do with it?"

"Michael," Peggy sighed, "you're incorrigible. How can you be so callous?"

"Easy. I've spent fifteen years as a cop, watching thieves, killers and swindlers get off with a slap on the wrist by some liberal judge."

Mike stared at his partner in sheer disbelief. He couldn't understand how a cop, especially in a Special Victims Unit, could be so naïve. *Amazing — she's been on the job for ten years and she still doesn't see that life is made up of people stepping on each other, trying to grab the brass ring.*

"Just looking at all the angles," he said. "You're involved in Tamara's church, aren't you?"

"Yes, that's how I first met Tamara. She was one of the associate pastors in The Good Shepherd Church."

"So you know all the folks that were close to her." Mike sat on the edge of his desk and folded his arms.

"Yes," said Peggy, "but you're not suggesting that one of her close friends or one of the staff had something to do with her death."

"Look, they can't be ruled out," insisted Mike. "All I know is that from what you've said, a lot of the people in your church have severe problems — they're poor, they're ignorant, some are addicts or alcoholics — maybe your evangelist friend did something that teed one of them off, and they decided to stick a shiv in her. Rattle off some names for me of people that were close to her."

"Most of the people closest to her don't fall into any of those categories," protested Peggy.

"Give me names."

"Well, there's her father, Mr. Steele. . . her brother, James. . . her husband, Billy Kensey. . ."

"Billy Kensey — why is that name so familiar?"

"He's a famous rock star –he plays *terrible* music."

"Oh, that guy. Jamie thinks he's cool. All the kids have his CDs."

"That's the one."

Mike rolled his eyes. "Well, I guess there's no accounting for taste."

Peggy continued, "For the life of me I don't know what possessed Tamara to marry him. They didn't have anything in common. He didn't have any interest at all in her ministry, and that was the most important thing in her life. Even so, there are lots of people with strange marriages — or who, as we Christians say, are *unequally yoked* — but they don't usually kill each other. Besides, I don't think Billy has it in him to kill anyone."

"Why not?" Mike refused to exclude any suspects. "I heard that Kensey's career recently made a left onto the road to nowhere, and it looks like Tamara Steele is leaving a wad of dough behind. Seems to me like plenty of motive for him to remove his wife from the scene."

"But Tamara always gave him all the money he wanted."

"Even to pay for drugs and sex?"

She gave Mike a curious look. "You may have a point; he *is* very immature."

Mike waggled his brows at her. "Don't you know by now that I'm a super sleuth?"

"Oh yes, I forgot myself," she chuckled.

Mike's expression flattened as something occurred to him, and he said, "I still can't understand why forensics hasn't come up with any prints."

"Maybe the murderer was meticulous in making sure that there weren't any."

"No one could be that *meticulous*," Mike said. "There has to be *something* we can work with; hairs, prints, saliva, *something*. We have to talk with Howard."

Peggy's lip curled a little. "I need a lot of prayer for that."

"Don't tell me you dislike our illustrious Medical Examiner — and I thought you were called to love *everyone*. Could there be a dent in Margaret Younger's holy armor?"

Peggy gave him a gentle smile.

"Michael, it's not a case of my liking Mr. Carey or not. It's just that every time I ask him a question, he acts like I'm putting him down."

"That's paranoid Howard for you, a perfect example of the civil servant mind. Don't worry about it. . . . Hey, want to grab lunch?" Mike was very obedient whenever his stomach growled; it was the only authority to which he readily submitted. "Let's go to Herb's on Mineola Boulevard. Love their corned beef."

"You're not serious, Michael, it's only 10:30 in the morning."

"It's lunchtime somewhere on this planet, Peg. C'mon, walk on the wild side."

She laughed, picked up her jacket and followed him.

Chapter 3

Howard Carey was a little man in every way: small in stature and petty. . . and a loner. Throughout his school years other students had usually teased and mocked him. Though their meanness made him seethe inside, he never showed his feelings. He just kept to himself.

The Medical Examiner's lab had been his own little world, but the weight and importance of this case now pushed his private little domain into the limelight. All eyes were on him — or at least *he* thought so. *Well*, he thought, *I'm up to the challenge. This is the chance of a lifetime.* He would have to employ his best scientific skills; this case demanded it. If his expertise aided in identifying the killer, the department, and everyone else, would finally *have to* give him the recognition and praise that he had always known he deserved.

At the crime scene on Friday night, Carey had gathered important clues pointing to the murderer, but he couldn't bring the evidence back to the NCPD medical examiner's lab. Oh no, he couldn't risk that; he couldn't trust anybody there — they would steal the credit that should be his alone. So, ignoring all the rules of his office regarding the chain of custody, he brought the evidence home.

Howard Carey lived with his wife in an old two-story house in the poor section of Westbury. The house had been left to him by his widowed mother. When Howard arrived home late Friday evening, his wife asked casually, "What's in the envelope?"

"Oh, just some stuff from the office," he said. Then he climbed the two flights of stairs to the attic and tucked the large manila envelope under a loose floorboard.

Mike had already finished his corned beef sandwich at Herb's Diner, and Peggy was still savoring the chicken salad from what she referred to as their "brunch," when Mike's cell phone rang.

"Ryan," crackled Dunbar's voice, "we just got a call from Howard Carey's wife, Angela. She found him dead, lying on the carpet covered with blood. You and Younger get your butts over there."

Mike and Peggy were already working on the Tamara Steele case. Why couldn't Dunbar send someone else to cover this one? Fortunately, Mike remembered he had a son to support; otherwise he would have told his lieutenant where to go. "Okay," was his only reply.

"That was the lieutenant," he told Peggy, pushing his plate and cup together and rising from the table. "Howard Carey was found dead at his home this morning and Dunbar wants us at the crime scene."

The two detectives jumped into Peggy's Toyota, and she put the pedal to the metal. They headed towards the Meadowbrook Parkway. Turning on the siren, Peggy wove in and out of the noonday traffic. The speedometer read eighty-five miles per hour.

Man, this woman sure can drive! thought Mike. In ten minutes they were at Carey's door. Squad cars were all over the sunburned lawn. Peggy and Mike went through the open front door into a small living room crowded with police blues. One of the patrolmen showed them to the little room off to the side that Carey had used as a home office.

His body lay on an olive-green shag rug.

"Oh, my Lord," Peggy reacted.

Detective Brian Hannity was bent over the body. He'd caught the call on his car radio and arrived about five minutes before Mike and Peggy. When they entered he stood upright and began to quickly jot down notes on his pad.

"Some mess! Someone really wanted to make sure Carey'd never make another autopsy report," Mike said as he put on his surgical gloves. Then he bent over the fallen Medical Examiner and saw the two gigantic bullet holes in the back of his head.

"Man," muttered Mike, "you could drive an SUV through these cavities. Did anyone find the weapon?"

"Not yet," replied Hannity.

"Any clue on the type of cannon used?"

"We'll have to wait for the ballistics report to be sure, but I'd wager a paycheck that the shooter used a single-action Ruger."

"Is there anything missing?

"Nothing was stolen. I'd say, from the way he was killed, someone didn't care for him very much. This wasn't random," Hannity concluded.

"It doesn't compute. Why Howard? Anyone talk to the wife?" Ryan asked.

"Mrs. Carey is obviously very shaken up. She maintains that no one she knows of had a grudge against him."

While Mike and Hannity continued, Peggy walked over to the roll top desk at the other side of the room. She reached for the plastic gloves in her pocket.

"Mike, come over here a second."

She handed him a things-to-do calendar. Written in bold letters was "CALL RYAN." Mike's phone number had been written in the note paper's margin. He scanned Carey's note:

- *Traced where the weapon came from*
- *Found fingerprints & hairs of the killer*
- *Matched them to someone at the party*
- *Can identify who murdered Tamara Steele.*

"Obviously, Tamara's murderer also did Carey in," Mike exclaimed. "Instruct the crime scene unit to go over this place with a fine-tooth comb. There has to be a file around here somewhere with the evidence and his report."

The crime scene unit searched the house for two hours. They came up empty.

"Let's talk to Mrs. Carey," Mike said. He and Peggy left the dead man's office and headed to the living room where the widow sat hunched on the old blue couch, fidgeting with the wrinkled handkerchief in her hands. Peggy sat down next to her.

"Mrs. Carey, are you up to answering a few questions?" Peggy asked softly.

"I don't know. I guess so. You know Howard and I were going to celebrate our twenty-fifth wedding anniversary next Tuesday." Mrs. Carey began to weep.

Peggy looked at the woman with compassion; meanwhile Mike's demeanor was one of obvious impatience.

"Is anything missing from your house?" Peggy began.

"No, I don't think so."

"Mrs. Carey, do you have any reason to believe that someone wanted Howard dead?" Mike chimed in.

"No, of course not!" Mrs. Carey sat up indignantly. "Why in the world would you ask that?"

Peggy gently patted her hand. "It's routine, Mrs. Carey. Just routine."

Mike toned it down. "What time did you find Mr. Carey?"

"About 8:30 this morning."

"You always wake up at that hour?"

"No, gosh, I'm usually up at 5:00 a.m."

Mike's gentleness was fleeting. "Why'd it take you three and a half hours to report him dead? Didn't you notice him when you got up?"

"No," protested Mrs. Carey. "He'd worked long and hard on something all weekend. Last night he told me he would sleep in his study, and didn't want to be disturbed until 8:00 a.m." She grabbed a Kleenex from the box on the end table.

"Had your husband ever discussed the Tamara Steele case with you?" Mike continued.

"Howard always kept his work private," said Mrs. Carey, trying not to sob. "As a matter of fact he would lose his temper whenever I asked him what he was working on. My husband never felt I was intelligent enough to understand his work. He never felt

I was intelligent enough to understand anything. It was always a sore spot between us."

"Sounds like a great marriage," Mike said sarcastically.

"I was happy enough." The woman raised wet angry eyes to Mike.

"Thank you, Mrs. Carey. We'll leave you alone now," Peggy said. As she stood up to leave, she placed a reassuring hand on the weeping woman's shoulder. Mrs. Carey gave her a pathetic little nod and sank back onto the couch.

As they left the Carey home, Mike said to Peggy, "We have to get our hands on Howard's file. It has all the answers." *Then and only then could the Steele case be solved*, he mused.

The next several hours at the precinct were fruitless, nothing but paperwork and incessant interruptions. The two detectives couldn't concentrate. Finally Mike said, "Peg, let's go to my house and review what we've got over a cup of coffee."

"Michael, I'd love to go to your house, and I would love to see Jamie and your Mother, but it's getting late," yawned his partner. "Let's start fresh tomorrow."

"No, Peg, we haven't been able to think here all afternoon with the constant activity and interruptions. I want to go over our information while it's still relatively fresh. Please, let's just give it another hour or so over coffee at my house. There's more to this case than meets the eye — something really sinister. Call me nuts, but I have a hunch there's much more to this."

Chapter 4

It was after 10:00 p.m. when the two detectives finally arrived at Mike's house. Mike checked on his mother and Jamie, and found them both fast asleep in their beds. He brought Peggy to the kitchen and reheated the pot of coffee his mother had left on the stove. Then he put his notepad and various print-outs on the table. He went to the cupboard.

"Mom made these, you want some?" he asked, pointing to the plate in his hand.

"Oh yes, I love your Mother's chocolate chip cookies."

He laid the plate on thc table and poured coffee into the mugs he had put out.

"Trust me, Peg, there's something weird going on with this case. Let's start with Tamara Steele's murder. Where's that list you made of the people who were close to her? We have to figure out who has the strongest motive for killing her; who would benefit the most?" Mike grabbed one of the chairs and sat down.

"I don't really know what to tell you, Michael. The people who were close to Tamara all seem to be such *good* people," Peggy said as she took out her notebook.

"I still think, from what you've told me, that the husband — what's his name — oh yeah, Kensey, the rocker — has a strong motive for killing her. Do you know whether or not Tamara had a will or whether our boy, Billy, has a life insurance policy on her with a heavy payout?"

"No, I wouldn't know that. Tamara and I never spoke about those things. She wasn't particularly interested in financial matters."

"Too bad; we'll have to check that out." Mike loosened his tie and, taking a deep breath, looked over at the next name on Peggy's list. He read it upside-down: Edmund Steele.

"Her old man is loaded, isn't he?"

"He owns Steele Industries, a Fortune 500 company, if that gives you any idea of his wealth."

Mike snorted. "No one will be moved to pass the collection plate for him, so it doesn't look like he would have any motive, does it? Who's next?"

"Julian Giles."

"Right, the money man."

"Yes, he handled all of the ministry's money from the book sales, healing tours and speaking engagements — you know what I mean — Tamara's sermons."

Curious, Mike asked, "What kind of turnout did she get for her speaking engagements?"

Peggy raised her eyebrows. "Tamara would receive invitations to preach at mega churches — extremely large churches all around the country. She would preach or give a teaching, and then conduct healing services."

"Yeah," said Mike skeptically, "but how many people would come to these services?"

"Thousands."

"Man, that translates into a lot of coin."

"Michael," bristled Peggy, "you have to remember that there's a lot involved in running a ministry. Evangelists just don't grab the proceeds and deposit all the receipts in their personal accounts. There are administrative costs and travel expenses; frequently sets have to be designed and built; there are publicity costs for radio and TV spots, and print ads — lots of things — and they all cost money. Tamara also donated a portion of the money back to each church that sponsored a service or event. And after all of that was taken care of — because she had her own personal wealth and didn't need the money — she would have all of the remainder of the proceeds distributed among the poor."

"Impressive," shrugged Mike. "Did Tamara keep close tabs on the cash flow?"

"No, Tamara left all that to Julian. As I said before, she really wasn't interested in the financial matters. As long as she could do what God called her to do, she was happy."

"What would have happened if Tamara had caught her financial manager dipping into the till?"

"That would never happen," asserted Peggy with a lift of her chin.

"What makes you so sure?" Mike kept his face carefully blank.

"Michael, Julian Giles was a minister of the Gospel; his morals and character are above reproach."

Mike smiled at Peggy's innocence. Though he thought that she was dangerously naïve, something in him admired her trusting nature.

"Okay, Peg, let's put this Giles guy aside for the moment. Who's next?

"Cora Smothers."

"Who the heck is that?"

"Cora was Tamara's special assistant."

"So, what's her story?"

Peggy paused, looking for the right words. "Cora had some. . . heated discussions with Tamara."

"At last, it looks like this is finally going to get interesting." Mike rubbed his hands together.

"Don't get me wrong; Cora is a beautiful daughter of God, and I can't imagine her stabbing Tamara. But. . ."

"But Tamara and Cora didn't quite see eye to eye?"

"Well, there was a rumor among the circle of people closest to Tamara that Cora may have been jealous of her."

"Jealousy is as good a motive as any to commit murder—it certainly ranks in the all-time Top Ten. What made everyone think she was jealous? What did she do?"

"As you're probably aware by the pictures you saw around the mansion," said Peggy, "Tamara was a very beautiful woman, plus the fact that she was a very kind and gregarious person. Everyone always clamored for her attention. People loved her."

"But what about this Cora Smothers, was she a dog-face or something?"

"Leave it to you to focus on looks. She's absolutely beautiful."

"What do you mean, leave it to me? I'm trying to solve a murder, and you make it sound like I'm ogling the contestants in a beauty pageant." Still, he flushed with embarrassment as Peggy's eyes teased him with an impish glint. *She knows me better than I thought*. "C'mon, Peg. Really, what's her story?"

Peggy's smile faded as she took a bite from her cookie.

"Michael, I'm not sure what to make of Cora at this point. I thought she was devoted to Tamara, but Tamara's body was barely cold when I heard that she took over the ministry. I was surprised, to say the least. I didn't expect it."

"Well, how did she treat Tamara when she worked for her?"

"On the surface," said Peggy, "Cora acted lovingly and showed her respect, but there were signs of resentment, like nasty little criticisms of Tamara that Cora would blurt out, then laugh and say she was just joking. I think she was intimidated by Tamara. It was easy for Tamara to outshine almost anyone without trying or even knowing she was doing it. Everyone loved her, attracted like moths to a flame. Cora lived in Tamara's shadow. Although she worked hard for the ministry, Cora didn't feel that she got enough credit or respect from the church."

"So, Cora wasn't popular with the congregation?"

"Not really, and I'm not sure why. Maybe it's because she has a tendency to snap at people. But I'm sure you'll be able to get past that, Mike. Beautiful as she is, I bet she'll be a hit with you." That glint was back in Peggy's eyes.

"Give me a break," he said, laughing little. Then he frowned. "Seriously, do you think Cora was intimidated and jealous enough to get Tamara out of the way? Maybe she arranged a coup and removed the competition?"

"Michael! What a notion — Cora stabbing another Christian woman — stabbing her multiple times — watching while Tamara's blood poured all over. I can't, I *won't* believe it. It's not possible!"

"Peg," Mike broke in, "you gotta cut me some slack here. Every time I mention that a friend is a possible suspect, you claim that they're too holy to do Tamara in. Just because they go to church doesn't mean they're all saints."

"Michael, I'm sorry, it's just that when you share Jesus and His Spirit with people for a long period of time, there's a special bond that develops between you. You get to know them in a very intimate way."

Mike softened. "Peg, I read a bumper sticker the other day. It says *Christians aren't perfect, just forgiven.* That makes sense to me; doesn't it make sense to you?"

"Yes, it does; thanks for reminding me." Peggy looked at the wall clock. "I can't believe it's almost 11:00 p.m. I have to prepare for a Bible study for tomorrow. I better get moving"

"You're going to church on a Tuesday?"

"Evening prayer meeting. We're studying the book of John. How about joining me?" She was angling. *Why not? Peter was a fisherman. Jesus calls us all to be fishers of men.* She doubted it would work with Mike, but she had to try — not for her sake but for his.

"Don't you know anything about the Irish?" smiled Mike. "Our tradition says that religion is the private domain of women. They are the Irishman's representatives to God." He was forced to smile at his own pitiful attempt at evasion.

"Michael, can you be a little serious?"

"I think I've had my fill of *serious* for tonight."

"Coming to the meeting would be good for Jamie." *Cast the net wide.*

"What has this *God* done for Jamie? Gave him his disability and took his mother. Religion and church — please, my son and I will pass. We're doing fine without them."

"If you refuse to go to church, then let me take him."

"Peg, we're doing just fine; please back off."

She bowed her head in resignation.

"Michael, I've got to prepare for the Bible study, so I have to go. But, don't think this discussion is over, because it's not."

Mike nodded. "I'll see you in the morning, okay?" he conceded. "We'll pay a visit to Mr. Kensey. I'm looking forward to sparring with him." He figured by getting back to the case it would ease the tension caused by the discussion on church.

"Remember that Lieutenant Dunbar wants us to go easy with the Steeles' friends," said Peggy.

"How are we going to solve this murder if we can't question people who were close to Tamara?" said Mike.

"I don't know. I'm just repeating what the Lieutenant told me."

"Leave Dunbar to me, Peg."

"Okay, if you say so."

Peggy touched Mike's shoulder, and taking her coat, walked toward the door. Suddenly she stopped and turned to face him. Her expression was one of remorse. He thought, *If I had guts I'd apologize.*

"Michael, God feels your pain and loves you very much." Peggy paused. Mike said nothing. "I guess I'd better get going. I'll see you tomorrow morning." She opened the door, then looked back and said, "I can't face the office first thing tomorrow. What if we meet at Kelly's for breakfast at seven?"

Mike nodded curtly and the door quietly closed.

Mike knew that Peggy meant well, telling him about how much God loved Jamie and him. How could he make her understand: there's no room at this inn either.

But it was freaky that she seemed to know exactly when his pain over Katie's terrible death was starting to surface. If by some miracle Peggy had found a way to invade his thoughts, then he resented the intrusion. *Christians are always telling people what to say and do, what not to say and do, and warning them that, if they don't make Jesus their Lord and Savior, they won't be saved. Saved from what? Saved for what?*

Still, if Mike was really honest with himself he knew he couldn't lump Peggy in with Christian hypocrites he had met. He believed that she *really did* want the best for him and his kid. He couldn't deny that his partner was sweet, gorgeous and fitted nicely in his life. Plus his son Jamie thought she was the best thing to arrive since that stupid video game, *Polo Brothers*.

Chapter 5

Earlier that same Monday, Samuel Bower thought about how he hated humidity. *Only in Nassau County would a day like this come in mid-April,* he thought. Bower was known to be meticulous in his dress and hygiene; not a hair was ever out of place. But on this unusually muggy Long Island day as he crossed the street to his Mineola office, the thick weather caused him to perspire profusely, wreaking havoc in his well-ordered universe. All this sweating was not in keeping with his image, but he couldn't control it. And when he couldn't control something, he wasn't happy.

He spent much of his time asserting control. He was constantly on his cell phone talking to party leaders and county legislators, making certain they strictly followed his instructions. How else could his perfect plans come to fruition? Frequently, his fierce temper erupted, consuming in its path the poor underlings who had dared to contradict or disobey. Many careers had fallen victim to Samuel Bower's temper.

But somehow today, control had slipped from his grasp. He felt powerless, a feeling completely foreign to him. In choosing political pawns to carry out plans and policies, you had to depend on the Nassau County political machine. And therein lay his problem. He was often forced to deal with morons who were adept at only one thing: screwing up the most elementary tasks no matter how clear the instructions or perfect the plan. And it went both up and down the ladder. Today's gripe was that he, Samuel Bower, top of his Harvard class, along with his impeccably pedigreed wife, still had to kowtow to a peasant like George Winthrop. It was an outrage.

To top it all off, the daughter of the wealthiest man in the county ended up murdered right in the heart of Bower's own little fiefdom. He tried to warn Winthrop of the consequences, but there was no talking to that man. Bower had no proof that Winthrop was involved in the murder; but even if he had, he couldn't have done anything about it.

Sam Bower knew he was no Sir Lancelot, but he couldn't let a little character defect like cowardice cause him to lose everything. Unfortunately, some people had to become casualties, victims of progress because they happened to be in its path. Someone had to take a fall, and it wasn't going to be him. He had a destiny to fulfill: he was going to lead this county into greatness unprecedented in its history — regardless of the price.

He was concerned about Dunbar. The lieutenant's handling of the Steele case was a debacle. That Detective Ryan and — what was his female partner's name? Peg. Peg something — oh yes, Younger, Peggy Younger. Putting them in charge of the case was a big mistake. That fat idiot Dunbar handled his people like he handled his sub sandwiches — sloppy. He never had any finesse.

County Executive Bower did his best to stay clear of people like Dunbar, but the Lieutenant was hard to avoid. At every Democratic function he attended, Dunbar would try to buttonhole him, seeking his influence for a never-ending list of favors — *can you get a county job for my son for the summer, can you get low income housing for my brother-in-law and his family,* and so on.

Frustrated with Bower's evasiveness, Dunbar resorted to coercion. He actually had the audacity to threaten to go to *Newsday*, the Long Island paper, if Bower didn't comply with his requests/demands.

Bower didn't respond well to threats. He couldn't risk Dunbar's going to the newspaper. He would have to take strong measures to keep him quiet.

Chapter 6

At four o'clock on Tuesday morning Mike bolted from his sleep. His shirt was soaked with sweat and his breathing was heavy. It was the same old nightmare. The nightmare consisted of a teenage punk holding a gun to his wife Katie's temple, and Mike's gun pointing at the punk. The punk was taunting Mike to shoot, but Mike's finger froze on the trigger. Then he heard a shot. He saw his wife collapse to the ground, but he didn't hear her body fall; all he heard was the hysterical laughter of the shooter. The laughter always woke him up.

He lay in bed, trying to get back to sleep. Tuesday would surely be long; he needed to rest if he could.

Still sleepless he got up, changed his shirt, threw on his robe and went downstairs. At the kitchen sink he splashed cold water on his face, then turned to grab some cold coffee from last night's pot. As he heated the coffee in the microwave, he noticed an envelope from the Wilson school on the kitchen counter.

"*Hey, the kid's report card.*" Reading the report, Mike's eyebrows converged. Automatically he stirred sugar and cream into his coffee and read the report several times more.

He heard a clunking descent on the stairs. Jamie stomped into the kitchen, slammed his books on the table, poured himself a glass of orange juice, and sat down to gulp it.

"Hey, Pop," he grinned, lifting the cover off the bowl on the table, "what's shaking?"

"You want to know *what's shaking*," Mike barked, walking to the table while waving the report card.

"You have to sign that," Jamie said, pouring milk on the cheerios his grandmother always left for him.

"You expect me to sign this?" Mike tossed the report card on the table.

"Okay, don't sign it," squawked Jamie. "I won't be bent out of shape." His face became contorted, a usual response when he was confronted. He apparently thought his best counter-challenge was shrugging his shoulders and returning to his breakfast.

"I love your attitude almost as much as I love your grades," Mike shot back, turning to the counter and spreading butter on a piece of toast. He laid down the knife. "Let me see: three Cs, one D, and for the grand finale an F in math. Kid, what a stellar performance. Something to be really proud of."

"I don't know what you're getting all bent out of shape about." Jamie kept his frown.

"*Bent out of shape,* you call it! Well, let me map it out for you. Without good grades, no college will accept you."

"Who said I want to go to any dumb college?"

"Maybe I wasn't clear." Mike bit his words in exasperation. "Having a disability, you have to get better grades than all the rest and excel in everything you do. You have to be one hundred times better than the normal guy. Otherwise your career is going to consist of mopping floors at Burger King."

"Burger King is cool with me. I can eat free cheeseburgers all day."

"Pal, it's not cool with me, and if your mom was here, it wouldn't be cool with her either."

Jamie's hands moved in irregular jerks. "Why do you have to bring her up?" he shouted.

Mike wanted to apologize, but Jamie had a knack at manipulation, and this report card issue was too important to get off point.

"I tell you what you're going to do," he told his son. "First of all, you're grounded through the weekend."

"I can still go to the movies this Saturday."

"Funny, I thought Saturday was part of the weekend. Oh, yes it is — sorry, you can't go. Second, I want to see your nose in your math book, and finally I want to hear you speak to elders in a more respectful tone, especially your grandmother, and yes, watch the way you speak to me. Your bus will be here in five minutes. If you miss it, don't think I'm driving you. Now you'd better get going."

Mike heard the back door slam as the boy left to meet the bus. He sat down at the table stirring his coffee, wondering if he had been too harsh. His mother wasn't the only one who reminded him that the life of any teenager was complicated. Teens were going through many changes both physically and emotionally. And Jamie's handicapping condition made his life three times as hard. Maybe he should have been more understanding, gentler.

But no — he wasn't going to back down. Jamie needed to be more mature and realistic. Mike felt it was his responsibility to be his son's guide through life. Life was tough. He had to be equally tough!

Chapter 7

The ringing of the phone lifted him from his son's problems and back to his Tuesday morning reality. He heard his mother answer the call.

"Mom, is that Peg?"

"Yes, son, do you want to speak with her?"

"No, tell her I'll meet her at Kelly's Diner."

He jumped into the shower, rinsing away his fatigue along with the terrible dream and his worry over Jamie.

In half an hour he was speeding down Hempstead Turnpike, heading through Garden City to the precinct. As he flew past school buses filled with their precious cargo, he slowed down; the image of his son aboard a bus flashed through his mind.

Upon arrival, he parked his car and made his way into Kelly's Diner.

"Detective Ryan, nice of you to join me. I hope I didn't ruin your beauty sleep," Peggy teased as he entered. It was past 8:00 a.m.

He didn't feel like telling her that a confrontation with Jamie was his reason for being late. She couldn't be that interested in his family problems. Even if she were telling him the truth when she claimed to be concerned for Jamie, Mike wasn't in the mood for her homespun remedies.

Yet when he looked at her, the green of her eyes seemed unusually emerald-like. Mike didn't know what was happening to him. Suddenly he felt totally immersed in Peg — the intimate teasing jests, warm, never offensive — her smile, the way the sunlight caressed her face. *You could swim in those green eyes.* Was he falling for her? Mike quickly dismissed the notion. He knew he couldn't afford to get involved. There were many reasons: her being his partner, Katie's memory, Jamie, her religious thing — all these factors would spawn complications.

"Sleepyhead," Peggy continued, "let me buy you breakfast."

"Why? Did you win the lottery or something?""

"Is it a misdemeanor to buy breakfast for your partner?"

"Yes, when it sends your partner into shock."

A heavy-set blond waitress came up to them; her disheveled hair indicated she'd had a rough morning.

"What do you want, detective?" Peggy smiled mockingly at Mike.

"Ham, eggs and a couple of strips of bacon."

"Really nourishing."

Mike grinned. "You're starting to get on my nerves."

She tried to stifle the giggle that caused his eyebrows to arch.

He reached into his attaché case and pulled out his list of suspects.

"Detective," he said, "should we see Cora Smothers or Julian Giles?"

She lowered her eyes, staring at her tomato juice. "I don't care Michael; you choose."

Passivity had never been Peggy's style. Mike said, "Hey, kiddo, what's up?"

"I guess I'm a little upset that I have to interrogate my friends, people I've prayed with. Now I have to treat them like potential killers."

Mike hated it when women got all emotional; and when they did, they expected men to get all emotional too — to be sensitive, to understand women's feelings.

"Well, what can I tell you? I guess it goes with the territory," he said.

Peggy caught his tone and sat up briskly. "We can see Cora or Julian. . . or maybe Billy, Tamara's husband."

"Good idea, let's pay a friendly visit to old Bill."

Chapter 8

The house — of which Billy Kensey was now sole proprietor, courtesy of his late wife — was a few blocks east of old man Steele's mansion. Only one-third the size of his father-in-law's place, nevertheless, it possessed a commanding presence. The Grecian columns and tall oaks — stoic sentries — gave the place a peaceful air.

Quite a shack, Mike thought, his eyes giving it a quick appraisal. *I bet the market value is over two million.* The circular driveway brought them to the front door. As they opened the car door, blaring hard rock music issuing from the house assaulted their ears and shattered the peace — a sharp contrast to the soft chamber music usually associated with the neighborhood.

Mike used the brass knocker to announce their presence. They were greeted by a giggling young blond woman wearing white shorts and a purple tank top. In her hand was a half-empty cocktail glass.

"Oh, who are you?" she asked, covering her thin mouth, stifling a laugh.

"Nassau County Police. I'm Detective Ryan; this is Detective Younger," Mike said. "Is William Kensey here?" They both flipped open their badges in unison.

"William? You mean my Billy. Nobody calls him William," she said almost hysterically in a voice somewhere between a wail and a scream. She had obviously been drinking all morning — probably never went to bed last night. She lost her balance, and would have fallen if Mike hadn't grabbed her.

"Ooh, thank you darling." She achieved a tipsy equilibrium. Mike held onto her a couple of seconds before letting go. Peggy frowned. The girlfriend — or whatever she was — led them down a hallway, through a well-equipped kitchen that would have made Julia Childs envious, onto a terrace overlooking a heated pool.

"Billy baby, these two are from Nassau County Police, or something." The blond gestured in their direction, using the glass as a pointer. Billy Kensey was lying on a chaise lounge with a drink in his hand, reading *The Enquirer*.

"Billy, let us begin by offering our sympathy over the loss of your wife," Peggy approached him.

"I told everything I know to your Lieutenant-what's-his-name."

"Dunbar, Lieutenant Dunbar," Mike said, his annoyance displayed plainly on his face.

Although they sensed that Kensey had had as much to drink as his girlfriend, he seemed to be more proficient at holding his liquor.

"Where were you at nine o'clock on Friday night?" Mike asked.

"Man, I don't know; I was stoned."

Mike looked at Peggy. "I didn't know that Tamara served booze or drugs."

"All I ever had when I visited her was a nonalcoholic punch. And there certainly were never drugs at any of Tamara's gatherings," Peggy said. "Looks like things have changed."

"Well, Kensey, how about it?"

"I have my own stuff. What are you going to bust me for? Possession?"

"Drug possession is the least of your problems."

"I didn't kill her."

"You and Tamara didn't seem to have the ideal marriage."

Kensey shot Mike a fierce stare. "Where did you get that ridiculous idea?"

Mike looked at Kensey and then at his companion.

"Well, we had our disagreements, but in my own way I loved my wife very much," Kensey continued, the fire gone from his eyes.

"How's your career going?"

"Very well."

"That's not what I'm reading in the trades."

"Billy, it's a known fact that your popularity is fading, and many of your performances have been cancelled because ticket sales are way down," Peggy added.

"I hit a little slump, that's all."

"A little slump," Mike repeated, walking to a glass coffee table and grabbing a fistful of nuts nestled in a ceramic bowl. "Haven't you been asking Tamara for money to maintain your various. . . amusements?" he grimaced as he seated himself on the chaise next to Kensey's.

"No, I didn't ask my wife for anything. Besides, I have my own money!"

"And what is the source of that money?"

"I have other resources."

Mike turned and looked at his partner.

"Last night Detective Younger and I ran a profile on a buddy of yours through our database, and we came up with something quite interesting. It seems that your pal operates an escort service in Manhattan, and got busted when one of his girls got caught trying to sell dope to an undercover cop."

"What does Travis Simpson have to do with me?"

"It's interesting that you came up with that name so quickly when we mentioned drug dealing," Peggy observed. "Maybe not surprising, since you were arrested in connection with that bust."

Kensey sneered. "The cops couldn't prove anything. The judge threw the case out because it was entrapment. I was out the next day. I'm a respectable businessman."

"Oh, yeah, you're a pillar of the community," Mike volleyed back, mocking Kensey. Mike sat back on the lounge, resisting his desire to heave Kensey through the glass partitions on the opposite side of the terrace.

"Why are you here?" blustered Kensey. "What do you want from me?"

"We came to offer you a challenge," Mike said. "Let's see if you can convince us to erase your name from our suspects list 'cause right now, you're *numero uno* — number one on our hit parade."

"Man, I could bash your face in for even *thinking* that I would harm a single hair on my wife's head."

"Make my day," Mike said and smiled. He had waited years to use that line.

Kensey put his head in his hands, and started to cry. "I told you before that I loved my wife very much; I meant it!" He lurched to his feet, wiping his eyes, headed for the portable bar, and reached for the martini pitcher. The girl staggered toward him from her seat, motioning to have her glass refilled. He complied. She kissed him in appreciation, nearly fell on her face, and just made it to the nearest chaise, managing somehow not to spill her drink in the process.

Peggy walked over to Kensey. "Billy, did you leave the party Friday night? I only saw you briefly. Where did you go?"

"Tamara wanted me to check her schedule, so I went to the office."

Peggy picked up an apple from the table and twirled it in her hand. "You claim that you loved Tamara very much."

"Yes, I swear I did."

"Funny, Tamara saw things a little differently. She told me privately that your marriage was disappointing and frustrating. Your extramarital affairs were hurtful and embarrassing to her. Even though she detested divorce, she was looking into getting an annulment."

Kensey grabbed a croquet mallet from a set strewn around the terrace and started toward Peggy. Mike moved so fast that Kensey never saw him coming. His left arm clamped around Kensey's throat. Kensey stopped in his tracks and retched. Mike slammed his right arm up behind Kensey's neck, bracing it with his left hand.

"Man, you make one move and I'll snap your neck."

Kensey dropped the mallet. "Let go of me! Let go, I can't breathe!" His voice hissed as he started to turn blue.

"Michael, stop," Peggy yelled.

"One twist, you creep, and I'll put you out of your misery for good."

"Michael, stop it! He's not worth a suspension; let go."

Reluctantly, Mike released him. "Buddy, as they say in the movies, don't leave town. And don't bother showing us out, not in your grief-stricken condition."

Mike turned to the tipsy girlfriend. Something flew past his head, grazing his left ear. Kensey had thrown a vase at him. It crashed to the ground, breaking into a million pieces.

"Hey, Kensey," he said, "what a shame — that vase looked to be worth a couple of bucks. You'd better keep your day job because I don't think the Yanks are going to sign you as their centerfielder."

Kensey's face suggested that Mike and Peggy had overstayed their welcome.

Chapter 9

They rode along Clinton Avenue, involved in their own thoughts, until Peggy broke the silence, "You really enjoyed baiting him, Mike."

"Peg, the creep was going to make mashed potatoes out of your head. I didn't provoke that," he defended himself.

"I think you're jealous of him."

"What? Are you serious? What does that sleaze have that I would want?

"Money, connections and the company of attractive women."

"I guess you don't know me very well. My idea of a good time is watching a Mets game with my kid, accompanied by a pizza and a liter of real coke to wash it down."

"I wonder."

"You know, I really don't need you to be on my back about this stuff."

She fell silent. Mike regretted telling her off, but all he was trying to do was his job. Why did everyone want to be inside his head?

"Peg, Tamara's husband has to be a prime suspect." Mike needed to redirect the discussion back to the case; he refused to give any consideration to Peggy's assessment of him.

"We haven't come up with any compelling motive yet," Peggy said. "We could probably establish opportunity, but what proof do we have? We've got nothing on him, Mike. The background check didn't show anything substantial — no large insurance policy, and Tamara's ministry didn't have a lot of money. Tamara's staff paid the bills and gave the rest away."

"His wife is murdered and her body is barely cold, and he's messing around with a teeny bopper," muttered Mike. "Then we get the weepy boo-hoo routine; I don't buy it."

"I don't think Billy possesses the brains or the courage to commit murder."

"Okay, let's go back to motive. Let's make some assumptions. Tamara's ministry is taking off and his career is tanking. Envy? Could he have been so jealous of her success that it enraged him? It's a possibility, Peg; he gets stoned, and with his warped brain he goes into a rage and kills her. How does that sound?"

"I don't know. It sounds weak to me," Peggy replied.

"How about money? I called a friend of mine who works out of Manhattan South. He told me that Kensey has a lot of markers out to guys who aren't very patient with people who don't pay their debts on time. . . Let's see," he continued, "old man Steele must have bankrolled his daughter's ministry, and I assume that Tamara made her husband the chief beneficiary of her will. . ." He was thinking out loud.

"I told you," Peggy reminded him, "the ministry didn't have any money. They gave it away."

"They gave the money away," he repeated, "*because she had her own personal wealth and didn't need it* — you said so yourself the other day. Did she have a will? Did we find a will?"

"I called her attorney's office," Peggy replied. "He's out of town. His secretary told me there is a will and they'll send us a copy when he gets back next week."

"Maybe our boy Billy was after whatever is in the will. Maybe he knew she was going to have the marriage annulled, and he had to get rid of her before that happened so that he could get whatever is in the will," he speculated.

"But we don't know yet *what's* in the will. She could have left everything to charity for all we know. Tamara would do something like that," Peggy objected. "All we have are a lot of assumptions and too little information. Besides, I still don't think he has the stomach for murder."

Since Mike and Peggy were deadlocked over Kensey, he just continued driving back to the precinct, where he parked the car and they both went into the office.

It was nearly noon. The rest of the day was spent digging through files and writing up reports. At 5:00 p.m., having had the unusual pleasure of not encountering Lieutenant Dunbar the entire afternoon, Peggy and Mike walked in silence out to the precinct parking lot. With a few nondescript words they parted, getting into their respective cars.

Mike's eyes followed Peggy as she scooted behind the wheel. She drove off. Suddenly he was flooded with mixed emotions. He was glad the day was over; he was tired and wanted to go home. He had seen Peggy drive off like that hundreds of times — but today, for the first time, it bothered him — he didn't want her to leave. He wanted. . . he didn't know what he wanted. *She's just your partner*, he told himself. But he was becoming ensnared in the warmth and gentleness that was Peg. Even when she was all business, those qualities were right below the surface. He was captivated. He tried to dismiss the feeling, but it remained with him the rest of the night, disturbing him.

Chapter 10

Mike pulled into his driveway around 5:30 p.m. His mother greeted him as he opened the front door; a map of concern was painted on her aging face.

"Ma, what's up?"

"Mike, Jamie got detention this afternoon. He's in his room. Would you speak to him, son?"

Mike was tired and hungry. He'd rather face another murder case than have to confront Jamie. But he pushed himself up the stairs.

Jamie made light of detention. "Sounds like dirt, Pop, but really, it was just for something nutty in the cafeteria. A couple of kids and me were fooling around and the principal came in to see what was shaking and we all got detention."

Okay, Jamie, I guess you've done your time. Let's have chow and then maybe we could tackle that math book."

They finished the schoolwork in time to watch a half-hour sitcom. At 10:00 p.m. Jamie went to bed.

After saying goodnight and hearing his son's thumping ascent up the stairs, Mike said, "Guess I'll look through some papers before I turn in. Gee, Mom, you look upset."

From beneath a stack of books, Mrs. Ryan drew out an envelope. She handed Mike an opened letter from Jamie's school. Despite his objections, she always opened his mail. He could have read her the riot act now, but figured it was a waste of energy. She always treated him as if he was still a kid.

Mike unfolded the letter, noting the Wilson Academy logo at the top, which depicted a distinguished man looking down at a good-looking boy in a wheelchair. His eyes scanned down to the signature of the school guidance counselor, Opal Hanover, at the bottom. Then he read the text:

Dear Detective Ryan:

I am writing to inform you of our deep concern regarding your son Jamie's behavior.

We at Wilson Academy believe that, with a concerted effort and much hard work on his part, we can help Jamie become fully integrated into society. Recently, Jamie has exhibited a very violent temper that, unless brought under control, may hinder his development and progress toward that goal.

There have been several occasions on which he was physically aggressive toward other students. In each instance, staff members had to pull him off another child. We are concerned about his behavior.

I would like to meet with you to discuss this further. Hopefully, together we will be able to develop a plan to overcome this problem and prevent future occurrences. This is critical to Jamie's future.

I am available Thursday, the sixteenth. If you cannot meet with me on that date, please call to arrange an alternate date.

Sincerely,
Opal Hanover
School Psychologist

"Mike, you're going to keep that appointment, aren't you?" His mother wrung her hands nervously.

He stood there holding the letter.

"Well?"

"Of course Ma, but I can't call now; the school is closed. And Miss Hanover probably has a hot date." He grinned. His mother didn't miss the tinge of sarcasm.

"This is serious. You're son is in trouble. Don't you care?" Mrs. Ryan stared at him.

At that moment Mike felt too weary to care.

"Ma, I promise to call Miss Hanover first thing tomorrow. You're right. Of course this is important. But right now I'm so tired I can't even think straight."

Satisfied, she patted his cheek, releasing him to go to bed.

Mike found himself feeling guilty. He had to admit to himself that tonight — and many other nights — he didn't want to have to deal with any more of Jamie's problems. His tense frame collapsed under the cool sheets. He noticed that his mother had changed them. Inhaling their freshness, he fell into a deep sleep.

Chapter 11

On Wednesday morning, Mike and Peggy met at their usual spot for breakfast. Peggy ordered half a melon, plain yogurt and a whole-wheat bagel. Mike smiled to himself.

"What's so funny?" she grinned.

"You're such a health nut."

"What do you expect me to be? Like you, clogging my arteries with greasy eggs and bacon."

"Peg, at least I'll die happy."

"That's a mature point of view."

"Hey, give me a break."

"We haven't seen Cora Smothers or Julian Giles yet. Who do you think we should see first?"

They were back to the case. She dreaded discussing the case because it always led back to where she didn't want it to go: back to her friends, her brothers and sisters at church.

"You pick this time," said Mike.

He noticed that her countenance had changed. She looked distant. She took out her copy of the suspect list and gave it a glance.

"Cora Smothers, I guess — Tamara's assistant." Peggy sighed.

"Right, she was second banana."

"Second what?" Peggy's eyebrows narrowed.

"A vaudeville term my old grandpop used to use. Second string, second in command."

"I know what it means. I just don't think it's a nice way to refer to my friend. . ."

"Okay, okaaay. Don't be so touchy," he interrupted her. "Is Cora Smothers a healer too?"

"Michael, don't you listen to anything I say? God does the healing, not. . ."

"Right, not man. I forgot." Mike ran his fingers through his sandy, bushy hair. "Then does she have this. . . *gift* too, like Tamara did?"

"She would like to think so. But no, Cora's role was answering mail, booking engagements, walking Tamara's collie and making sure the evangelist's personal life didn't interfere with her ministry. Generally, she worked with Julian Giles."

"I get it, general secretary and chief-cook-and-bottle-washer. A slave."

"I wouldn't have put it that way, but yes, you got it right."

"Let's pay a visit to Miss Smothers."

It was about 10:30 in the morning. Mike's Mustang merged easily onto the westbound side of the Northern State Parkway. In just a few minutes they were at the parkway's end, where it put them on the Long Island Expressway heading toward Manhattan. Traffic was light. A half hour later they entered the Midtown Tunnel.

Once they immerged from the tunnel onto 36th Street, the traffic was maddening. They turned north on Madison Avenue. Stop and go, stop and go. It was another half hour before they reached 63rd Street. As they approached the intersection, Mike maneuvered between an angry Hyundai and a yellow cab whose driver screamed something in a language Mike didn't recognize; the gestures, however, left no room for misinterpretation.

Mike pulled into a tight little parking lot that could hold about two dozen cars if you squeezed them in with a shoe-horn. He jumped out and went around to the passenger side. Despite the traffic, the mood between him and Peggy had lightened as they traveled.

"Michael, I'm impressed," she said as he opened the door for her. "Is this the new you? Mister Manners?"

"Don't get excited. It's just that the handle came off the door last night and you can't open it from the inside."

They walked the long block to Fifth Avenue. Cora Smothers' address was that of a tall brownstone facing Central Park. Mike followed his partner as she climbed the stone steps. Peggy pushed the bell and they were entertained by a Bach fugue. He remarked that he was more partial to David Sanborn.

A lanky woman came to the door. She had on black tights and a sweatshirt covered by an unbuttoned man's shirt that she wore like a smock. "Peggy!" the woman cried with a squeak. "What a surprise!"

Mike's appraisal was quick and discreet. Peggy was right; Cora Smothers was a very attractive woman.

"Cora, this isn't a social call. I have to inform you, we're here on police business," Peggy said, trying to sound as professional as possible under the circumstances. "My partner, Detective Ryan." She gestured toward Mike.

"This sounds ominous," said Cora, taking a step backward.

"Is there somewhere inside where we can talk?" Mike really wanted to get this over with. He found the city nerve-wracking — the traffic, the noise, the smell. Some people thrived on it, but not him. He couldn't wait to get out of there and back to Long Island.

Cora led them through a very pretentious hallway to an even more pretentious sitting room. She gestured with an open palm toward two ornate Victorian chairs. Mike and Peggy sat down. Peggy was calm. Mike was immediately uncomfortable.

"Miss Smothers," he said briskly, "we are interrogating all the guests that attended Miss Steele's reception the night she was murdered. We hope you can help us. Is there anyone you know of that would have reason to kill her?"

Her eyes widened, and she suddenly grew pale.

"I'm trying to get that tragic night out of my head."

Peggy went over and placed her arm around her friend. "I'm sorry, Cora, but we have to get to the bottom of this. I know it's hard, but think. Do you know anything that could shed some light on this?"

"Who would be *insane* enough to kill our Tamara? I can't imagine that anyone could have a rational motive," Cora said softly.

Cora removed a pill from a bottle on the end table next to her, placed it in her mouth and washed it down with some water she poured from a crystal decanter.

"Headache, Miss Smothers?" Mike felt his eye-brows arch as he said it.

"Just something prescribed by my doctor for nerves," she replied, resenting his attitude.

A dam seemed to burst within her as she turned to Peggy. "I don't understand why you're questioning the people who were close to Tamara and involved in the ministry. We were all her friends, you know that. We all loved her. I know you think one of us killed her! We're your friends too — how can you think that?" she gushed. "It had to be someone *insane!* No rational person could have done a thing like that."

Cora stood up and began pacing the room, wringing the ends of her shirt.

"There's a lunatic out there with Tamara's blood on his hands," she quavered. "What's to prevent him from coming after me next?"

"Cora, our investigation so far leads us to believe that she knew the killer. Maybe he's a lunatic as you said, but he's a lunatic that she knew. C'mon, Cora, help us. Think!" Peggy's voice was soft and soothing, yet insistent. "Did you see or hear anything suspicious that night? Did anything or anyone seem out of place?"

"Peggy," protested Cora, "you *knew* Tamara. Everyone practically worshipped her."

"Well, Miss Smothers, someone obviously didn't *worship* her," Mike interjected. "Tell me about your relationship with Miss Steele. How did you get along? Was there ever any friction between the two of you?"

Cora glared at Peggy. "Your partner seems to be intimating something. Maybe you can tell me plainly what's on his mind."

Peggy was about to answer Cora, but Mike put his hand on Peggy's arm, stopping her. "Look, Miss Smothers, I have a job to do; and my job is to find whoever murdered Tamara Steele. The only way to do my job is to ask whatever questions I think are necessary to whomever I think it's necessary. Now, if you won't cooperate, then maybe you have something to hide. Maybe you'd better get a lawyer. Looks like you can well afford it," he said, casting a glance around, acknowledging the lavish furnishings.

"Peggy, I refuse to be harassed in this manner by some. . . *detective*." Cora spat the word out. "One call to West Street and before this peon makes another sarcastic remark, he'll be back on a beat."

"Cora, take it easy," reasoned Peggy. "This is just routine questioning; you can't take it personally. Anyone who was connected with the victim in a murder is a suspect. It's a process of elimination." The soothing voice wasn't working.

"Can't take it personally? How else can I take it?"

"Sorry, Cora, it can't be helped. Maybe you know someone who was angry at or jealous of Tamara." Peggy spoke firmly yet gently as she put her arm around Cora.

"I just can't fathom anyone hating her." Cora relented; her shoulders slumped.

Mike took that as his cue to join the interrogation. "Rumor has it that you and your boss didn't exactly see eye to eye."

Cora Smothers lost all semblance of control. "That's ridiculous and a downright lie," she screamed, clenching her fists.

"*Is* it so ridiculous, Miss Smothers? People heard you and Miss Steele going at it."

"What do you mean, 'going at it'?"

"Fighting, Cora, he means fighting — arguing." Peggy rolled her eyes at Mike.

"Peggy, you better put a muzzle on that Neanderthal."

Peggy, ignoring the comment, plunged right ahead. "You do have a history of locking horns with Tamara."

"*Et tu, Brute!* For your information, Peggy, that was our way of challenging one another — our way of brainstorming," Cora sneered disdainfully.

"I understand that Miss Steele wasn't very pleased with your association with the ministry anymore," Mike chimed in once more.

"Whoever spread that rumor was jealous of our relationship. We were so in sync with one another we practically finished each other's sentences." Cora was so angry she almost choked on the words.

There was silence.

"Isn't it true that Tamara asked for your resignation?" Peggy asked quietly.

Mike thought, *That partner of mine is sooo smooth; she could charm the skin off a snake. I bet if it was me that asked the question, this dame would have gone ballistic.* They hadn't specifically planned it, but Mike liked playing Good Cop/Bad Cop — it worked.

"You're against me too, Peggy?" It was as much a statement as a question from Cora. "I thought we were friends."

Peggy continued calmly, "Cora, I'm a police officer. I have to do my job."

"Okay," said Cora, "I admit, we did have words — sometimes very heated words — but it doesn't mean I wanted to kill her." The fight was gone out of her. As tears welled, Cora's eyes wandered to the bottle of pills.

"Michael," said Peggy, "I think Cora's had enough for today. We'd better go."

Chapter 12

Mike and Peggy started their Thursday pouring over files, not sure what they were looking for.

"Ryan! Phone, pick up on line two," the desk officer shouted. Nassau County had neither the means nor the desire to enter the twenty-first-century with regards to technology; a sophisticated telecommunication system wasn't even up for discussion.

"Ryan here." His tone reflected his boredom.

"Detective Ryan, this is Opal Hanover."

"Opal who?" He felt as if he was in a fog.

"Opal Hanover. I'm the school psychologist at the Wilson Academy."

"Oh, yes, Miss Hanover. What can I do for you?" Mike still couldn't recall why her name was important to him.

"Detective, I called your home a few days ago and spoke to a woman there. . ." She paused, waiting for a reply.

"Oh, yes, that would be my mother. She watches Jamie while I'm on the job."

"On the job?"

"Oh, I'm sorry — a police expression; haven't you ever watched any cop shows on TV?"

He figured a little levity would lighten the situation. It didn't take long for him to find out he was sorely mistaken.

"I'm afraid my work doesn't permit me much time to watch television, Mr. Ryan. I really have to meet with you to talk about Jamie."

Here we go, the conversation he wanted so much to avoid. "Yes, Miss Hanover, I wanted to call you, but I'm working on a very important case — a lot of pressure from the brass — and it's been consuming all of my time. I haven't had a moment to even catch my breath."

"Detective, we all have tight schedules. Don't you think your *son* should be your top priority?"

"Lady, I love my son, and I resent your implying. . . " He didn't get a chance to finish.

"Detective Ryan, I'm not *implying* anything. You're sounding rather defensive," she said coolly.

"Miss Hanover, when do you want to see me?" he capitulated. He knew better than to start sparring with a shrink. They don't fight fair. They twist words to make them mean what you didn't say. They manipulate you into a corner — and when the smoke clears you don't even know your own name.

"I could see you on Monday, the twentieth, at 9:00 a.m."

"Okay, I'll see you then." He slammed the phone down, mumbling under his breath. He was fuming.

Peggy cocked an eye at him from her chair behind her desk. "Wow, who was that? Thank God, whoever you talked to was on the phone and not standing here, otherwise you might have emptied your .45 and they would have been toast."

Mike growled, "She's some dumb liberal, who happens to be Jamie's school psychologist."

Peggy tilted her head. "Michael, she's just trying to help."

"Please! I think Julian Giles is next on the list."

Giles owned an expansive estate in the hamlet of Glen Head, a stone's throw from Bayville. His bio showed that he was once a popular minister in a well-known church. He had a reputation as a gifted preacher, and was courted at one point by an evangelical television station. They wanted him to host a show interviewing various Christian celebrities, and each program would conclude with him preaching a Sunday sermon.

No one really knew why the project was shelved. Some reports held that Julian was helping himself to the love offerings of his church. Others said that he had become involved with the church organist. None of the accusations were ever substantiated. Still, the rumors were enough to quash the TV program. Speculation became so widespread that Giles was forced to tender his resignation from his church ministry.

Despite all of this, Edmund Steele liked Giles and believed he was innocent. He brought Giles on board to oversee his daughter's ministry and manage her affairs. It was getting too big to continue without proper management. Besides, Tamara had neither the aptitude nor the desire to manage the business end of it.

As Mike and Peggy reviewed Giles's information, Mike looked at his watch.

"It's 9:00 a.m., Peg; I have to take the first part of the afternoon off for an appointment with my mom at the bank. If we leave right now, we could make it out to Glen Head to interview Reverend Giles and be back in time for Mom's appointment."

They arrived at the Giles' residence.

Mrs. Giles came to the door, wearing a dressing gown with flowing blue patterns on it. The sweeping robe covered her slacks. She looked to be about fifty with sandy hair.

"Good morning, Rachel," said Peggy. "This is Detective Michael Ryan. We're here to speak to Julian."

"Is anything wrong? Did anything happen to Jo Ann?"

"Excuse me, Mrs. Giles, but who's Jo Ann?" Mike asked.

"My daughter, she just started attending Bryn Mawr and we're a little concerned. She's never been away from home before. Julian accuses me of being a little silly about it; I guess he's right. Julian is never wrong."

"No, Rachel," Peggy told her. "I'm sure Jo Ann is fine. We wanted to talk to you and Julian about Tamara."

Rachel Giles led Mike and Peggy into the living room. The furnishings were like props from a melodrama set in a mansion in the English countryside in the 1930s. There were two plush wing-back chairs with gold rosette upholstery. "Rachel, what a beautiful portrait of Martin Luther!" exclaimed Peggy.

"Yes," agreed Rachel as she joined Peggy in front of the painting. "He was such a commanding figure."

Mike stood by awkwardly.

"Rachel, I heard voices. Do we have guests?" said a tall, well-formed man in his late forties, entering the room.

"Yes, dear. Margaret is here to see us, and this is her partner, Detective Michael Ryan."

"I am pleased to meet you, Detective Ryan," he said, extending his hand to Mike. He kissed Peggy on the cheek in greeting.

Giles's large frame dominated the room. He sat down on the couch and put his arm around his wife, giving her a peck on the cheek. Her eyes lit up, all of her attention focused on him. Her adoration was apparent; she worshipped her husband.

"Darling," said Rachel, "they're here to discuss Tamara Steele's murder."

"Such a brutal death! And a colossal loss to the religious community. Her murder is a great personal loss to everyone who knew and loved her. How could anyone slaughter such a beautiful child of God? It is beyond my comprehension."

"Julian," said Peggy, "we thought that, since you had such a close working and spiritual relationship with Tamara, you might be able to help us. Can you think of anyone who might have wanted to harm her? Did she have any enemies?"

Giles shook his head. "Margaret, everyone that we worked with loved Tamara. Mr. Steele is a very wealthy man. Maybe she inadvertently surprised a burglar who sneaked in as a guest."

"Mr. Giles," Peggy reminded him, "the reception was by invitation. Anyone unauthorized would not have gotten past security. We don't think it was an intruder. We think the murderer was someone she knew — someone whose presence would not arouse suspicion."

Giles's eyes widened in genuine dismay. "Oh, my Lord, you have to be mistaken! Everyone associated with Tamara is a Christian. These are people with a close relationship with the Lord. None of them could possibly do such a thing."

Mike spoke up. . "Right now we can't rule out anyone."

Giles sent an incredulous look toward the detective. "Does that include me?"

"Mr. Giles, since you were close to her, then it follows that you're a suspect. I'm sorry, it comes with the territory."

"This is an *outrage*. I can't believe that you think I'm capable of murder." Giles rose from his chair.

Peggy deeply respected Mike's ability as a detective, but she frequently disagreed with his method of questioning. He could certainly use a little more tact. She decided to try a different approach.

"Julian, can you suggest anyone who had any kind of grudge against Tamara, regardless of how insignificant it may seem to you?"

Rachel reached a hand toward her husband. He took it in his, sat down again, and responded, "As I said to your partner, I don't believe anyone who really knew her would have been capable of murder. Those weren't the kind of people she associated with."

"Rachel, I'm going to have to ask Julian some very sensitive questions. You might want to leave the room," Peggy said softly.

Julian jumped from the chair. "My wife and I do not keep secrets from one another! Rachel, you can stay!" Rachel was obviously frightened, not of Julian, but of the turn in the conversation.

"Okay, Julian," said Peggy soothingly. "I have to ask: did you ever make any romantic overtures toward Tamara?"

Julian began breathing heavily; beads of perspiration began to form on his forehead.

"*How dare you, Margaret!* You, a member of our congregation, accusing an elder? How can you do such a thing?"

Mike figured it was time for him two add his two cents. "Mr. Giles, Detective Younger merely repeated a rumor that's been circulating. They say you tried to make a move on Miss Steele. No one suggested that you were successful. Rumor also has it that you don't handle rejection very well. Maybe she hurt your ego so much that you lost your cool. Maybe you decided that if you couldn't have her, no one would. How does that sound, Mr. Giles?"

Julian's face was red. A vein throbbed in his left temple. "I have never been unfaithful to my wife! And I can't believe that you could be so cruel as to say something like that in front of her!"

"It was you who insisted that she stay," Mike reminded him.

"Darling, I'm so sorry that they hurt you like this," Giles said, putting both arms protectively around his wife, hugging her. The woman must have always been mesmerized by the man. She returned his affection by caressing his face.

"Who's spreading such malicious lies?" Giles demanded, releasing his embrace and standing up with an air of wounded dignity.

"Just something we heard," Peggy told him, but her attention was on his wife. Rachel's expression never changed. Her look was pure devotion.

"Reverend Giles," Mike continued, "you still haven't answered Detective Younger's question. Did you or did you not have romantic leanings toward Tamara Steele?"

"I'm a married man," he insisted, "and I follow biblical teachings. The seventh commandment prohibits adultery. I understand *thou shalt not,* Detective Ryan. I wouldn't do such a thing!"

Mike continued to grill him. "C'mon, you know there have been other rumors of hanky-panky associated with you. It's not the first time."

"If you're referring to Deborah Pinkerton, that accusation has been dropped. That vicious lie is kept alive by certain persons in the church wishing to undermine my ministry."

"Seems like the congregation is not too thrilled with you," Mike said, unable to hide a grin.

Peggy rose from her seat. "Julian and Rachel, thank you for your time. I hope our interview hasn't upset you too much. We're just doing our job. We'll be on our way now."

The two detectives showed themselves out as Julian Giles continued to comfort his wife. Mike and Peg jumped into Mike's car and headed back to the precinct.

Chapter 13

Mike had arranged weeks ago to take early Thursday afternoon off to accommodate his mother. She insisted that he talk over her investment portfolio with her financial adviser at TRW Financial Services. For the life of him, he didn't understand why she counted on him in these matters; he was certainly no financial wizard.

Two minutes into the meeting with Vikram Dahlilal, Mike's eyes glazed over. The remainder of the thirty minutes were a blur — a hole in time. Mike didn't understand the stock market, he didn't understand mutual funds, or dividends, or annuities, but most of all he didn't understand Mr. Dahlilal. The clipped Indian accent with emphasis on the wrong syllables bounced off his inflexible Long Island ear; nothing penetrated. Mike spoke and understood

New York English. He was also fluent in "cop" and "crime," two closely related dialects of the street. Anything else required an interpreter. Mike was not a bigot. He didn't dislike Mr. Dahlilal. He just didn't understand him.

When he left the TRW office his head was in a fog. *Ma would have done better if she had checked things out for herself*, he thought. His mind didn't snap back into focus until he reached the station house and was finally back in his own element.

Mike and Peggy had drawn columns on the whiteboard on the wall next to their desks. The top of the first column bore the name of Tamara Steele. And the name of a major suspect headed each of the subsequent columns: Billy Kensey, Cora Smothers, Julian Giles. Beneath each name were whatever facts the detectives thought were relevant and possible motives. Mike was reviewing the board when the phone rang, shattering his concentration.

Mike hated the phone. It always brought bad news. If he had been a judge in Alexander Graham Bell's time, he would have sentenced the inventor to twenty-five years to life. He also would have sentenced whoever invented the answering machine to count each grain of sand on Jones Beach, a much longer sentence than Bell's.

Peggy picked up the receiver, listened, then replaced it. "Michael, the lieutenant wants to see us in two minutes," she announced.

It was just as he thought — bad news.

"I know he wants to ruin the rest of *my* day, Peg, but why does he want to see you?"

"That's a cheery attitude; now let's go and find out what he wants."

He followed his partner like a pup on a leash, resigned to the fact that if he resisted she would have to just drag him to the meeting with Dunbar.

The lieutenant sat poring over spreadsheets sprawled across his desk. After what had seemed to Mike like a century, Dunbar finally lifted his head.

"What in the world do you two think you're doing?"

"Excuse me, Lieutenant?" Peggy committed the cardinal sin of asking Dunbar to explain himself.

"Are you deaf as well as lacking any common sense, Detective?"

Peggy started to reply, but Mike squeezed her arm and she thought better of it.

"Does either of you brilliant detectives know what I'm talking about?"

Now Peggy thought silence was the best policy.

"I got a call from the County Executive. . ."

"How is his holiness?" Mike broke in.

"Ryan, you're a real smart guy. I wonder how smart you'd feel patrolling Franklin Avenue in Hempstead on the graveyard shift."

There goes my mouth again, Mike thought. "Lieutenant, what did the County Executive want?" he said apologetically. He regretted his little quip and wanted to get back to the purpose of the meeting.

"County Executive Bower wants to know why you roughed up Mr. Kensey," the lieutenant said through clenched teeth.

"The man should watch where he's going. He almost fell and I had to catch him by the throat," Mike answered, tongue-in-cheek, mouth bypassing brain.

"So, you admit choking him!" Dunbar flared.

"All I admit is that Billy Kensey happens to be clumsy." Mike's words propelled Dunbar from his chair.

"Look," he warned, thrusting his face close to Mike's, "if you embarrass this administration you'll wish you were never born."

Red-faced with anger, Mike didn't budge. "Why don't you just sweep this under the rug, Dunbar — like you did with my wife's murder?"

Dunbar turned redder than Mike and sat back in his chair.

"Mike, you know we didn't have any evidence against Carter." Now Dunbar's voice was milder.

As Dunbar calmed down, Mike flew into a rage. He felt his two hands on Dunbar's throat. Peggy tried to pull him off the Lieutenant. The desk sergeant and two patrolmen, who happened to be outside, charged in when they heard the commotion.

"Keep that maniac off me," Dunbar shouted, taking a series of halting breaths. "He almost killed me."

"Killing is too good for you," Mike shouted as the three men wrestled him to the floor. One of them tightly twisted Mike's arm behind his back.

"I ought to suspend you indefinitely," Dunbar screamed, still out of breath.

"Take your best shot," Mike answered, struggling to free himself from the cops who restrained him.

Peggy bent down and cupped her two hands on his beet-red face, "Michael, calm down, this isn't going to accomplish anything."

One of the blues looked at the Lieutenant. "Sir, what do you want us to do, book him?"

Dunbar straightened his tie and shouted, "No, you idiot, let him go."

They loosened their hold on him. Mike shrugged them off and got up slowly, his eyes continuing to shoot daggers at Dunbar.

The lieutenant couldn't mask the fear that paraded across his face.

"You two had better be careful," he said. "This investigation is ruffling a lot of feathers." He nervously shuffled some papers on his desk. "Don't you all have work to do?" he barked after a brief pause.

Everyone but Mike stared at the floor, offering no reply. Mike continued to glare at Dunbar.

"Well, then, get out of here," Dunbar said, regaining his composure.

Mike stalked out of the room; Peggy followed.

Mike's feet made a beeline for the parking lot as Peg continued after him.

"Michael! Michael, for the love of God, wait. . . wait for me!"

He maintained his pace, but Peggy ran, overtaking him before they reached the car. Grabbing him by the shoulder, she spun him around, her eyes penetrating into his.

"Tell me, what in all creation went on in there? Are you crazy?"

"Leave it alone."

"Michael, you were like a madman in there. Please talk to me."

"Forget it!"

She stared at him, her eyes pleading.

"I've never seen that much anger in your eyes. You were ready to kill him. What's between you two that triggers such anger?"

Mike's sweaty palms ran through his hair.

"Peg, I don't want you to get involved in this."

She let go of him, placing her hands on her hips.

"Michael, I am already involved, if for no other reason than by virtue of being your partner. You and I are responsible for each other."

Looking at her, Mike remembered the bond between them. It was more than just the bond between partners on the job. He took her arm and they walked to his car.

Chapter 14

Mike got into his Mustang and threw the newspaper and empty coffee cup from the front passenger seat onto the floor in the back so Peggy could get in. He slid his seat all the way back and turned toward her, slouching against the door with his head back, resting against the glass. As she got in, she slid her seat back too and faced him.

They sat in silence as visions of Katie ran through Mike's head. Even now he could see her pretty face with her blonde curls cascading to her shoulders, her soft brown eyes ever smiling. He could hear her soft voice, soft as a May breeze. He didn't know what to do with all the emotions that filled him — his love for Katie and her absence that caused him to ache — his hatred for her murderer — his seething anger at Dunbar, whom he blamed for the county's failure to prosecute the kid. And there was Peg, sweet Peg, his partner, his friend. . . Peg, who was woven into the fabric of his life in a way he didn't understand and couldn't admit. He decided he had to trust her. He had kept all his emotion over Katie's tragic death bottled up inside for so long, he was ready to explode. He popped the cork.

"Katie was the gentlest, most loving person in the world. People used to feel privileged just to be near her. She never had a negative thought or word about anyone — except herself.

"When Jamie was born with cerebral palsy, she blamed herself for his disability. If only she had been more careful, if only she had eaten the right foods, if only she had exercised more, if only she had quit smoking, if only. . . if only he hadn't been born disabled. Whatever caused Jamie's problem, she believed that it was her fault.

"She always treated me like I was the bright spot in her life." Mike gave a sardonic little laugh. "Me — Mr. Sunshine. She always made me feel like I was king of the universe. I couldn't do anything wrong in her eyes. Boy, did she have it backwards!

"And you know me, typical Irish cop, big-mouthed and cynical. God forbid that I should show my wife — my sweet, adoring wife — how much I really loved and adored *her*. Instead, I made Katie the brunt of all my wisecracks. I would make fun of her manner of speech, her laugh — anything was fair game at her expense. I did everything I could to hide the fact that I was crazy about her. It was all standard procedure for the Irish male, so no one ever dared accuse me of being sensitive. And Katie went along with my charade, taking everything in stride because she loved me so much. Yet, despite all my macho bravado and feigned indifference, Katie made my knees quiver.

"God, how I loved her. And now she's gone and it's just me and Jamie. No matter where I start I always wind up thinking about Jamie." Mike allowed a brief smile to soften his tense features for a moment.

"I think about the kind of life Jamie has. It's so hard for him. Everything he's gone through, the cerebral palsy, seeing Katie murdered, he's going to live with that the rest of his life. No kid should go through that. I worry that it has robbed him of his childhood. I shudder every time I think about it. For him, these are supposed to be the good old days. What kind of a childhood could you call it? . . . Some kind of normal. Worrying about Jamie makes me think back to when I was a kid.

"What I remember most when I was growing up was Sunday mornings. Ma would try to drag me and Pop out of bed to go to eight o'clock Mass with her. We knew that, if we pleaded and objected loud enough and long enough, she would eventually throw her hands up and walk to St. Brigit's over on Twelfth Street by herself; I guess she had her prayers for company. After Mass she'd stop at Fava's bakery for seeded rolls, assorted doughnuts and a coffee ring.

"She'd come home and find us exactly where she'd left us, still snoring. I would be hung over from lack of sleep after watching Saturday Night Live. Pop would just be hung over," he said matter-of-factly.

Mike was silent. Peggy waited. After a long minute, he continued, "Ma would take off her hat, and head straight to the kitchen. We could hear her as we slowly awakened. She would fill one iron skillet with sausages and bacon; and in another, she'd fry potatoes and scrambled eggs.

"It was always the smell of the bacon that aroused us. We would jump out of bed, scramble for our slippers and grab whatever clothes that didn't make it into the hamper the night before. She would always hear us as we bounded down the stairs. She said we sounded like cattle on the run, headed for the feed trough. We would sit there and savor every bite. Man, it was good! I can almost taste it.

"Sundays Pop was off duty, so after breakfast he would hold court in his undershirt at the kitchen table. He'd read *The New York Post* as he sipped his third cup of coffee, and he would have a smelly cigar clenched in the corner of his mouth.

"As he read the paper, each story would wind him up and we'd all get a tirade of commentary on the week's collection of family disputes, burglaries, gangland wars, on and on. When he finally got around to berating the justice system, complaining about perps he caught thumbing their noses at him because some liberal judge released them within hours of being booked, we knew he was winding down and it was time for court to be adjourned.

"Then would come my favorite part of the day; me and Pop would settle in for the fall classic – namely watching New York Giants football. It was a passion we shared. Pop loved the Giants as much as I did, but he always used to tease me about them.

"'Mikey,' he used to say, 'how can you root for such bunglers? They can't even hold on to the ball.

Why do you let them break your heart year after year?'

"But I was always an optimist. Deep down in my soul, I knew Pop was wrong about the Giants."

"Sounds like great memories," Peggy smiled, her comment interrupting the longest personal discourse she had ever heard from Mike. Realizing how special it was, she was sorry she had stopped him, but he continued.

"I guess I never gave it much thought before. The memories were always just. . . there. But yeah, those were good times. It always seems good when you're a kid.

"Even after Katie and I got married, my love for the Giants didn't change. I guess I was still a kid — a stupid, stupid kid! In 2004, when they played their archrivals, the Philadelphia Eagles, which eventually led them to the NFC Eastern Division playoffs, I was oblivious to everything else. I *had* to watch that game. It was all I could think about.

"Some of the guys from the precinct came over to our house to watch it with me. Katie knew how important it was to me, but still she asked me to take her, Jamie and my mother to the eleven-thirty mass. Why, did they decide to go so late *that* day? I was furious. The game was going to start at one o'clock, and mass wouldn't let out until twelve-thirty. We would have to battle our way through the parish parking lot, and if we were lucky we *might* make it home just in time for the kickoff — *maybe.*

"By the time we got to the church I was fuming. I was about to blast her for ruining my plans, but Katie was Katie. She just smiled. She placed her hand through my arm and kissed me. How could I yell at her after that? Then she turned around, joined Jamie and my mother, and they all walked up the marble steps into the church.

"After depositing them at church, I drove over to Neil's Deli to pick up the six-foot hero, salads, and the case of Coors I had ordered. Neil's, like every other deli and take-out place in the Metropolitan area that day, was a madhouse. The whole area caught the same sickness — Giant fever. It was an epidemic. I stood on line like all the other men, gathering provisions for the game. Funny now that I think about it, there were only men on the line. I think, like me, they must have all taken their women to church and given them orders to pray for the Giants.

"The deli was buzzing. Everyone was comparing statistics. Could Collins deliver like Eli Manning?

Would the Giants' defense stop the elusive McMahon, and the Eagles' back, Moats? I remember one guy boasting about the Giants beating the Eagles twice during the regular season.

"Twelve-thirty came and I had to pick up the church contingent. As usual my wife had to talk to what seemed like every single parishioner before she could leave. There she was, busy chatting away and laughing, and completely ignoring me and the time. When they finally climbed into the car, Katie planted a friendly peck on my cheek and smiled. How could she miss the steam coming out of my ears?

"I said, 'You know, Katie, the guys are arriving at twelve forty-five and there's a one o'clock kickoff.'

"I remember her answer: 'Yes, Mike, I know; everything will be ready for kickoff; I know how important this game is to you.' She lovingly squeezed my jaw, called me a sourpuss, and told me, 'Don't be so grouchy.' Then she said, 'It's such a beautiful day. Look at those red and gold leaves. God can really paint a picture.'

"I snarled, 'Yeah, and when they die and fall to the ground, guess who has to rake them up?'

"'Oh, honey, what am I going to do with you?' She moved closer to me, and placed her head on my shoulder. Katie always made it difficult for me to stay mad at her. She didn't play fair." He allowed himself a small chuckle.

"The guys from the precinct got to the house a few minutes *after* the kick-off. All my fussing and fuming was for nothing. And, of course, marvelous Katie prevailed. She managed, in spite of my frantic rushing around, to have everything ready when they arrived. All the snacks were strategically placed, so everyone had a clear view of the TV while they stuffed their faces.

"It's funny how I remember every detail of that day. The Giants had beaten the Eagles twice before, but that didn't mean this game would end the same way. Any time there was the Blue Men versus the Birds, it was always a nail biter.

"Ever since 1982 when they acquired Lawrence Taylor, the defense had been the key factor in the Giant's success. In this game too, the defense held the Eagles. "The Giant's offense was impressive; it spelled doom for Philadelphia's chance of winning the NFC. The game was tied at 23 points apiece. McMahon appeared to be disoriented, so he didn't pose his usual threat, and Osi Umemyiona sacking McMahon eroded the Eagle quarterback's confidence. In the fourth quarter the Giants were still leading by a touchdown.

"Everyone except me was in a state of euphoria, despite the lackluster play by the Eagles. *True* Giants fans, by nature, aren't very optimistic. I didn't want to be overconfident, only to be let down by stupid mistakes. Given the history of these two teams, I knew if you allowed the Eagles to hang around and didn't put them away, they could come back to bite you in the behind. It felt like someone was banging bongo drums in my stomach.

"The Eagles got another field goal, cutting the Giant's lead to three points. Then the Eagles' David Akers threatened to tie the game

"All of sudden, Katie was standing in front of me blocking the TV set, and I squirmed in my chair, trying to see past her. She said, 'Honey, we're running out of beer. Go and pick up a case at the Seven-Eleven over at Jameson." What a time for a conversation about beer!

"I said, 'Can't you go? This game is crucial; I really can't miss it.'"

"'But Mike, the store is by Edwards Avenue and there's a lot going on there. Gangs hang out at the Grant's shopping Center. I'm a bit frightened.'

"I told her, 'Come on, Katie, you're letting your imagination run away with you. There's nothing to worry about.'

"She said, 'Okay, I guess I can't expect you to leave now, anyway. You're probably right; I'm overreacting.'

"As she was about to leave, I said, 'Why don't you take Jamie with you?' She kissed me, took him by the hand, and left. That was the last time I ever heard her sweet gentle voice," he said sadly, pausing a second between each of the last few words.

The deep breath he took gave him a second to regain his composure, and he resumed at his previous pace. "Akers' kick hit the crossbar and the Giants maintained their lead. The guys were yelling with joy, giving each other high fives, and bragging about our marvelous team — and then the phone rang.

"The voice at the other end of the receiver said he was the desk sergeant from the East Meadow Precinct. For the life of me I couldn't understand why anyone at the forty-fifth would call me.

"'Detective Ryan?'

"Speaking."

"'You had better come to the Seven-Eleven over at Edwards Avenue. There's been a shooting."

"'But I work out of Mineola; besides, I'm off duty. Why are you calling *me*?"

"'Detective, you need to come.'

"I told Hank, my partner at the time, and, like me, he thought the call was weird. He said, 'C'mon, I'll ride with you; we'll straighten this thing out.'

"We drove to the Seven-Eleven. There was the usual garbage strewn about the parking lot, and four squad cars. We entered the store and saw an officer holding a seventeen-year-old kid with tattoos up and down his arms in custody. The kid's hands were cuffed behind his back. They all stood a few feet from the victim, who was shrouded in a body bag. A sergeant on the scene approached Hank and me.

"He asked if I was Detective Ryan. After he checked me out, he turned his attention to the body of the victim. It was all very impersonal.

"I said, 'Yeah, what's this all about?' My impatience was obvious. I can't believe I never put two and two together. My brain still had a total disconnect.

"The sergeant didn't say anything, only squatted down, lifting the corner of the body bag.

"There she was, my beautiful Katie, lying cold and motionless like a broken flower. It was like someone shut the air off from my lungs. I stood in suspended animation. And I knew I had lost her smile, her sweet, sweet smile, along with every good thing in her that had neutralized all of the negatives in my life — all the negatives in *me*. She was gone. . . gone forever. The Giants failed to make the Super Bowl that year."

He told Peggy about his recurring dream.

"Michael, how heart-wrenching for you," Peggy said soothingly, her hand caressing his forearm.

"At first I was unable to think or feel anything; my mind and body were numb. A thousand-pound weight lay on my chest. Breath left me. Suddenly a hundred thoughts ran through my head, all at the same time. What's the meaning of anything without my Katie? Who's going to diffuse my temper, this bomb in my stupid brain, when I'm about to explode? Who's going to ruffle my hair like she did when she passed by me? Who's going to put the light on in my darkened world?"

"You must have been devastated," Peggy said with tears in her eyes.

"And Jamie, I thought, what's to become of Jamie? And then I remembered. . .

"I started screaming, 'Jamie — where's Jamie? Where's my son? Where's my son?!"

"The sergeant said, 'You mean the crippled boy? Is he your son? We have him outside in a squad car. He's okay. He's very shaken up, but he's not hurt. He's okay."

"I rushed outside and spotted the car where Jamie sat with a police woman. He wasn't okay!

"Jamie sat there, dead silent. He was shaking and quivering, his eyes glazed over. He must have been in shock. The minute he saw me he just started to scream. I will hear that scream until the day I die. I tried to hold him and calm him down. He just kept screaming and went spastic in my arms. I didn't know what to do.

"Katie would have known. She knew how to handle him; she *always* knew how to handle him. She cuddled him when his world fell apart, something I couldn't do. You've got to be sensitive to take care of a disabled kid. They need special treatment. You have to know how to be strict and gentle at the same time. You have to know how to deal with the doctors and the therapists.

"And I'm such a clod. My education was a couple of courses in criminal justice. That doesn't help much in caring for a cerebral palsied kid. How do you prepare for that? You can't prepare. It has to be part of you. It takes a mother's love."

"Jamie had so many strikes against him already — and now this. Katie wasn't there for him. She would never be there for him again."

Mike stopped. He was emotionally spent. Peggy leaned toward him and clasped his hand. Her grip was so intense, it seemed she would never let go. The warmth of her presence engulfed him, and he allowed himself to start to drift. He felt safe for the first time in a very long time, like everything was going to be all right. He wanted to remain in this moment for the rest of his life.

Soothingly yet piercingly, Peggy spoke. "Michael, you and Jamie are very special to me. This devastating loss is too much for you to bear alone. You need God's help and His comfort. I know you are sick and tired of hearing about being born again. I know we Christians have our share of hypocrites and crazies, but please don't judge the Master by some of the messengers. *He* is faithful and true. If you would only open your heart and invite God into your life, you would find an unbelievable peace, a peace that passes all understanding, peace in the midst of the storm. I know you would. I know it sounds impossible, but you would. He will hold you in the palm of His hand. He will wipe away your tears."

As Peggy shared her faith, she continued to caress Mike's hand. He suddenly trusted her with a kind of trust he had never given anyone. Peggy spoke of a God he didn't know; one you could talk to as a friend, and trust with the deepest, darkest secrets of your soul. He wanted to trust God. Peggy said God knew all about him and He loved him anyway. How he needed that love! And he needed forgiveness: forgiveness from God, forgiveness from Katie. . . and Jamie.

Mike wrestled with his thoughts; Peggy took both of his hands in hers. A calm he couldn't explain enveloped him. He started to relax.

But there was something nagging at him, a tugging at the back of his mind. He started thinking about lost opportunities — the times when he had made himself unavailable to Katie because of his need to feel macho; refusing her tenderness because to do otherwise would show his vulnerability. He wanted to fall on his knees and beg her to forgive him. He wanted one more chance, but it was too late. He had traded the love of his life, and the safe harbor for his son, for what? For an afternoon football game. It was all his fault. He could never forgive himself.

He suddenly grew angry. No, it wasn't only *his* fault; it was that kid, that punk kid with a gun, who was high on crack. That kid was the one who had prevented Katie from giving Mike that last chance — that chance he would never have — a last chance to obtain her forgiveness. Hatred burned within him.

Peggy felt the tension return to his hands. She interrupted his thoughts. "Mike, God loves you so much that He sent his one and only Son to this earth to be amongst us, and to be one of us, to experience our pain and anguish, and know firsthand the devastation of our sin, yet never knowing sin Himself. He came to show us righteousness, and lead us and guide us away from sin and back to the right way, and in the end, to pay the price to free us. He allowed Himself to be crucified on a cross so that we could be free to come back into relationship with God the Father. That's how much He loves us, Mike. That's how much He loves *you*."

Mike shut her out. It was as if he heard the sounds of battle around him, and he wanted to join that battle — join the battle and kill that kid. And if he could, he would kill the God that had allowed that kid to kill his Katie. As Peggy rambled on about love, all he felt was rage and a lust for blood and vengeance.

Mike removed his hands from Peggy's grasp. *What was I thinking? I knew I should never have revealed so much. I know that I have to keep my thoughts and feelings close to the chest — can't show the chinks in the armor, can't expose the weak spots.*

She's getting too close. Somehow I have to rebound, batten down the hatches and cover up. I have to protect myself, Mike thought as he crawled back inside himself where the pain, though intense, was familiar; almost comforting. Mike put the mask back in place.

"C'mon, Peg," he said, "born-again Christians are just like everyone else — phonies, liars and hypocrites. Look at Jim Bakker. He became a millionaire with the nickels and dimes of poor unsuspecting souls searching for any glimmer of hope to rise up from their miserable lives."

As Peggy looked at him, she smiled sadly, sensing that the enemy had won the day. She tried oncc more.

"We are all sinners, Mike. The Bakkers, like the rest of us, are the weak who fall short of the glory of God. But that's not important, Michael. A more important question for you to ask is whether you want peace, 'the peace that passes all understanding,' the peace that only God can give. You can go around exploding like you did in the Lieutenant's office, or you can allow Jesus to put out the fire so you don't have to explode any more. He knows your suffering and wants to take your pain away. He already did it on the cross; you just have to receive and accept the peace he offers. You have to let go of all the pain and the things that are eating you up inside. Give them to Him. Give *yourself* to him."

Mike felt caged, and he didn't enjoy it. "Look, kid, I'm not into this God stuff."

She knew that Mike wasn't ready to surrender. Katie's murder was too fresh in his heart. He was still too angry and bitter. She sensed that he needed to forgive God for allowing Katie to be taken away from him and Jamie so suddenly.

"Michael, I'm through sharing Jesus with you. . . for now," she said and got out of the car. The battle was over, but not the war.

As Mike pulled out of the parking lot, he could see her in his rearview mirror re-entering the station house.

Chapter 15

It was Saturday morning; two weeks had gone by since Tamara Steele's murder. Even though it was the weekend and just 7:30 a.m., Mike's eyes were wide open. He had been lying in bed, sleepless for the last three hours. Peggy and Katie. . . Katie and Peggy. . . they kept going around and around in his head. The conversation with Peggy was haunting him and he had no peace. That's what was keeping him awake. . . or maybe it was just the endless tapping of the rain on the roof. Where was that peace that Peggy talked about? It eluded him.

Mike could hear the TV clearly, even though his mother had the sound turned low. She was watching the *Today Show*, just as she did every morning. The perky anchorwoman's voice changed pitch and her demeanor turned somber.

"This just in to the NBC news desk: Cora Smothers, assistant to the recently murdered evangelist, Tamara Steele, was found dead in her Fifth Avenue brownstone early this morning. Police say the maid discovered her lifeless body hanging from the chandelier in her bedroom — an apparent suicide. Details are spotty. However, it appears that Ms. Smothers left a note confessing to the murder of Tamara Steele, and also to the murder of Nassau County Medical Examiner Howard Carey. Repeating that last bulletin. . ."

Mike had bolted from his bed and was already dialing Peggy's number.

"Put on Channel 4".

"Michael, what is it?"

"Just put on Channel 4," he repeated, and hung up.

She called back seconds later.

"Michael, my God, that's horrible! What in heaven's name could have possessed Cora to take her own life?" Peggy had been too distraught to hear the rest of the piece.

"Peg, didn't you hear about the note?"

"Note? What note?"

"Cora left a suicide note admitting she murdered Tamara Steele *and* Howard Carey."

"What??? Oh Lord, I can't believe it. There has to be some mistake. There has to be some other. . ."

"Peg, hold on a minute. I've got another call."

It was Dunbar. For the first time since Mike had known him, he sounded cordial, almost congenial — totally out of character. Mike was suspicious. The lieutenant was off the phone in ten seconds and Mike got back to Peggy.

"Peg, that was the Lieutenant; he wants us at the precinct. I'll pick you up at your place in fifteen minutes."

Mike hung up and jumped in the shower. He groaned as the freezing water attacked his body while his mind raced. He couldn't help thinking that it wasn't possible that Cora Smothers committed suicide, much less committed the two murders.

His nose began to itch as he rushed to get dressed, a sure sign that something wasn't quite kosher. His nose was rarely wrong. Maybe their investigation was making someone nervous. Were he and Peggy getting too close to something? Ruffling some feathers, maybe?

He pulled up to Peggy's place. Grey clouds gathered quickly, and it seemed there would be a deluge any moment. Mike thought *when Jamie gets caught in a storm he tries to make a run for it, but always trips and falls. He winds up wetter than if he had just walked to get out of the rain.*

Peggy opened the car door. “You must be sick of hearing this, but Cora didn’t kill herself and she certainly didn’t kill Tamara. She just couldn’t do such things,” she blurted as she slid into the passenger seat next to him. She was out of breath from sprinting to beat the rain.

“Detective, I have to agree with you,” he said. She blinked in surprise.

When they arrived at the precinct they went right to Dunbar’s office.

“Mornin’, Ryan, I appreciate your getting here so fast, especially on a Saturday.”

“No problem, Lieutenant,” said Mike.

“The NYPD Fifty-Ninth Precinct has extended full cooperation to us, and we have a meeting with them at eleven at Miss Smothers’ brownstone. So, let’s get on our horses and ride.”

Mike was glad Peggy had come with him in his car instead of taking separate cars. She was understandably upset. Someone was knocking off her friends like ducks in an arcade. He didn’t think she should drive. They remained silent as he guided the car, weaving and bobbing through the Saturday traffic running to the Midtown Tunnel.

They arrived at Cora's apartment. Wooden horses cordoned off the small group of bystanders that had gathered, leaving their curiosity unsatisfied. Blue uniforms stood guard while the suits interviewed people from the neighboring apartments. Mike and Peggy climbed the large stone steps, passing through the opened doors.

Mike walked over to the corpse on the floor where it had been placed when the police cut it down from the chandelier. He put on plastic gloves and unzipped the body bag. Cora Smothers' once lovely face was swollen and contorted; her complexion was now blue and ashen. Marks from the rope were visible on her neck. Peggy looked over Mike's shoulder and suppressed tears. Dunbar walked over.

"Well, detectives, this sure simplifies things for us. Now we can wrap up two cases that were going nowhere fast." Dunbar had a knack for saying exactly the wrong thing at exactly the wrong time, and he wasn't stopping with that one statement.

"I guess it's a wrap, folks," he announced, "There's nothing more for us to do here." He seemed to smack his lips. Everyone on the team nodded their agreement in unison. . . everyone accept Mike and Peggy. They remained silent.

Something had prompted Mike to bring his own camera. Although the crime scene unit had taken a whole lot of photographs, and they were usually very thorough, Mike also began snapping pictures. Dunbar spotted him.

"Ryan, what the h—l are you doing? Are you moonlighting now, working as a crime scene photographer?"

Mike looked the lieutenant straight in the eye and said, "Evidence sometimes has a tendency to disappear. I'll keep my own photos."

Nothing could have surprised him more at that moment than what he saw on Dunbar's face: *fear*.

Chapter 16

The remainder of Mike's weekend was tense. He kept an eye on Jamie, making sure that he was working on his math. Though Jamie was quiet for most of the two days, he conveyed to his father how miserable he felt about being grounded.

Mike arrived at his desk at 9:15 a.m. on the following Monday. He glanced at his appointment calendar and gasped. In bold letters were written: *Opal Hanover — 9:00 a.m.* He sprinted to the parking lot and jumped into his car. "C'mon baby, rev those 360 horses and move," he ordered. When he reached the school it was 9:45. He prepared himself for a lecture by this Hanover woman. She didn't disappoint him.

Opal Hanover was not what Mike had expected. He didn't know what he had expected, but she wasn't it. He slowly and deliberately gave her a thorough appraisal. She wasn't exactly Britney Spears, but she couldn't be mistaken for Rosie O'Donnell either. She had a nice face with a slender nose upon which were balanced narrow, gold-rimmed reading glasses. Her auburn hair was pulled back from her face and swept up in a bun. She wore a well-tailored gray herring-bone suit with a burgundy blouse, and an old-fashioned cameo pin at her throat. In all, he thought she was attractive in a schoolmarmish way.

"You're late, Detective", she snapped, looking up from the open folder on her desk, which was probably Jamie's. It was not a good way to start a conversation with Mike Ryan.

"Couldn't be helped," he responded acidly. "You want me to write *I am a bad father and I promise never to be late again* on the blackboard five hundred times? Oh! I can't do that. You don't have a blackboard!"

"I don't find you amusing."

"You don't? Miss Hanover, I find that surprising, because my friends think I should moonlight in comedy clubs. In fact, my lieutenant would like to see me devote all of my energy to comedy and stay out of his hair."

"Detective, if the entertainment is over, may we turn our attention to your son, Jamie? That *is* why you're here, isn't it?"

He heaved a huge sigh and said, "Okay, Miss Hanover, let's talk about Jamie."

She turned back to the file on her desk, searching methodically for the information she wanted. She was tapping the desk with a pen as she scanned the documents. It made him uneasy.

"Jamie has been displaying a very aggressive personality trait," Miss Hanover began. "He is acting out, and has become a behavior problem — for example that time he gave Benjamin Safer a black eye."

Mike stood up and went in back of her chair to look over her shoulder at Jamie's file. She turned rigid.

"Anything else in your report about this Safer kid?" Mike demanded. "Something to the effect that he's a wise guy, and is always in my kid's face? Or are you satisfied having only half of the story?"

"Where did you get that information?" Miss Hanover swung her chair around to face him, forcing a little more distance between them.

Mike thought he had her on the ropes. “My kid tells me everything — the good, the bad and the ugly.”

He couldn’t bear to tell her that his relationship with Jamie was strained lately. That would open up a can of worms and he didn’t want to be analyzed.

“Benjamin isn’t really relevant here,” said Miss Hanover. “There are many instances where Jamie has lost his temper. This is just one of them, and I’m afraid that one of these days he’s going to injure some poor child.”

Mike’s blood began to boil and he felt a sudden uprising of his Irish ancestry. “You make my son sound like Jack the Ripper!”

The psychologist stared at him, studying him intently. “Now I see where Jamie gets his bad temper.”

Mike retreated to neutral territory. He began pacing back and forth on the thick plush carpet in front of her desk. He felt like he was being swallowed up by quicksand, sinking deeper and deeper. He was losing control, and he couldn’t let that happen. He knew he had to maintain his composure.

“Miss Hanover, do you have any idea what Jamie’s been through?”

"We realize that Jamie has special needs because of his disability. All the children here do. The type and degree of help they need depends on their particular disability and the extent to which it inhibits them. But like every other student, Jamie has to adjust to his limitations." She scanned the file. "I believe there's mention of an incident somewhere in here. . ."

"Well, Freud I'm not," said Mike. "But I believe the little tidbit I just shared with you about the Safer kid *is* somewhat relevant, and may explain some of my son's 'behavior problems.'"

Hanover frowned and shuffled some papers in the folder. "I guess that would present Jamie with some difficulty."

"Well, don't get too excited about it," he said, "otherwise you might break a blood vessel." He began to wonder what planet Hanover was from.

She removed her glasses and leaned back in the chair. "You know. Detective Ryan, sarcasm won't help Jamie. I think he may need the services of a therapist; may I recommend one?"

"You certainly may not." Mike's temper hadn't settled down yet. "That's all he needs, some empty-headed liberal whacko who believes every traditional thought is a by-product of the Spanish Inquisition."

"Detective, I don't know where you get your ideas."

"From the streets, lady, from the streets. Your colleagues have done a real bang-up job. They've convinced everyone that it's okay for boys to play with dolls and girls to be truck drivers. They think the goal of all education is to teach kids how to express themselves. They teach the kids about all the different freaky lifestyles, and meanwhile they neglect the important stuff, the practical stuff, like history and civics and English grammar. Well, their enlightened education system certainly leaves something to be desired. Maybe if history was stressed more, the kids might be able to name the first president, or know what country we fought in the American Revolution. Here's a novel idea — instead of pounding nonsense into their little heads about alternative lifestyles, maybe the schools could show them how to construct a readable sentence. Wouldn't *that* be nice?"

The psychologist had tuned out halfway through Mike's impromptu speech. "Mr. Ryan, none of that is relevant to Jamie's problems."

"Tell you what, *Mizz* Hanover," he said, making the *Z*'s sound like a fly, "I'll make a deal with you. I'll leave it to the Wilson Academy to teach my son the three *R*'s, and you leave his behavior problems to me."

Mike turned on his heels, marched out the door, slamming it behind him, and strode to his car.

"This is not over," Miss Hanover shouted after him. "We haven't resolved anything." But there was a very odd look on her face as she watched him leave.

Chapter 17

Mike felt like the walking dead. He arrived back at the precinct at 10:30 a.m. after his round with Hanover. He was surprised to find Peggy already at her desk. He *wasn't* surprised to see her head buried in a file from the Steele murder case.

As he sat down at his desk, she looked up. "Good morning, Michael."

He failed to return her greeting. He just rubbed his face with his hands. Jamie, his problems at school and Hanover consumed his thoughts.

"I said 'Good morning,' Michael."

"Sorry, guess I'm not awake."

"You look terrible. Is there anything wrong?"

"Nah, I just didn't sleep well."

The day's delights weren't over. Mike's telephone rang. Dunbar's voice on the other end was tense and his message was short. He told Mike that Peggy and he were off the Steele case and reassigned to robbery. As Mike started to protest, Dunbar said, "Stuff it," and hung up.

So there Mike sat. . . with Peggy, both of them feeling frustrated and suspicious — very suspicious. *Why the change to robbery?* There was something going on, but neither of them could put a finger on it. Mike had a hunch that someone at county was behind this ridiculous reassignment, but he couldn't figure out who or why. He kept this speculation to himself. A moment later the departmental mail carrier deposited a pile of folders on Mike's desk.

"That was fast," he said, as Mike fingered through the pile of folders. There was a series of break-ins in the very posh and wealthy village of East Hills. "So much for expensive security systems," he said, handing Peggy some folders from the top of the stack. "Let's take a look at these."

A few minutes after 11:30 a.m., his phone rang. It was Opal Hanover. W*hat the aitch ee double ell does she want now? I only left her a few minutes ago*. He had to hand it to her. If nothing else, Hanover was persistent.

"Yes, Miss Hanover," he said tiredly into the receiver. "Did I leave something in your office?"

"No, Detective Ryan." Miss Hanover's voice was prim. "I just thought our meeting was counter-productive at best. Let's try this again. We have to take some constructive action to resolve Jamie's social issues. His future hangs in the balance. I would like you to meet with me again, as soon as possible. Could you meet me tomorrow evening at 6:30 in my office?"

Mike knew she was right. "Let's see, tomorrow is Tuesday. Okay, we'll take another run at it. Six-thirty — see you then."

"Did I hear you say 'Hanover'?" Peggy asked. "What does *she* want?"

"She wants me to meet with her tomorrow night."

"Didn't you just meet with her this morning? She must be a glutton for punishment!" Peggy paused. "Are you going?"

"I have to for Jamie's sake. If I don't maybe she'll take it out on him."

"Aren't you being a little paranoid?"

"I don't think so. . ."

Tuesday dragged on, but Mike didn't mind. He was in no hurry to lock horns with Opal Hanover again.

He thought 6:30 p.m. was an odd hour for a meeting with a school psychologist. Being a cop makes you suspicious of everyone and everything. It's COP 101, mandatory indoctrination. *Katie hated that trait in me; she said I was too cynical. I told her it was genetic. Funny, how we were such opposites. She loved the world and everybody in it — trusted everyone too — didn't believe anyone would ever intentionally harm her. I trusted no one, so I became her favorite project — make Mike more human! Make me love and trust like she did. Well, the bullet that killed her put an end to that. I guess it proves who was right.*

Of course, he didn't arrive at the school until 7:05. There was only one other car in the parking lot. He assumed it was hers.

He knocked on her office door. She opened it and was taken aback when she smiled and said pleasantly, "Please come in."

She looked different. *No bun!* Her hair hung down to her shoulders.

As she walked to her desk he followed her. So did his eyes. He noticed the way she walked. *I don't remember her moving like that yesterday!* A faint alarm sounded somewhere in the back of his head.

"Miss Hanover, I'm sorry I'm late. Let me explain before you get all *Dog Day Afternoon* on me. My lieutenant wouldn't let me leave until I finished all the paperwork for a case I've been working on." As he spoke, his excuse sounded ridiculous in his ears, like a kid telling his math teacher why he didn't have his homework — *the dog ate it.*

"Detective, relax. Not to minimize the importance of this meeting, but I realize that this is not your *only* priority. I recognize that you have other obligations." Her eyes seemed larger than he remembered. *Ah. No glasses.*

"Come, let's sit over here. It's more comfortable." She motioned to the leather couch in front of the bookcase. Mike noticed the rich furnishings for the first time, and was a little ticked off that his tuition money was used to provide Hanover with all the comforts of a home far more sophisticated than his own.

"Come," she said, "sit." She patted the couch next to where she now sat. She had positioned herself in the center. Obediently, Mike sat down next to her. He could smell her perfume. *C'mon let's get this over with.*

She shifted her body, and he found himself just inches from her. He shifted round to face her, causing his leg to nudge hers. His hands began to sweat. She kept staring into his eyes. Another faint alarm went off in his head. He withdrew an inch or two until the padded leather arm of the couch stopped him. Seeing him back away, she allowed a little distance between them.

"I'm really sorry, but I have to inform you that Jamie was caught fighting again today," she said softly.

Getting up from the couch, he began to pace.

"I guess it didn't impress him very much when I spoke to him about this last night. When I go to work his grandmother watches him. She tries her best to keep him on the straight and narrow. It's hard for me keep more control because of my hours. I guess we'll have to take stronger measures with him."

She stood up, blocking the course of his pacing. She looked up at him and raised her hand to his lapel as if to remove a feigned piece of lint. Like the *tilt* light on a pinball machine, warning lights started flashing in his brain. *My God, she really is coming on to me.*

"No, no, Mike, don't be so hard on yourself. May I call you Mike?" she asked coyly. "I find informality works best in these situations."

He wondered what she meant by *these situations.*

"Please sit down. You're so tall that I'm straining my neck just to look at you."

Reluctantly he accommodated her and sat down again, as far into the corner of the couch as he could get. Again, she sat herself right next to him.

"I realize how difficult things must be for you. I don't know how you handle it."

"Well, I have Jamie and my work. That's a pretty full plate, but if I do find a little time on my hands, there are some guys on the force that I hang out with."

"Yes, but how do you fulfill your personal needs?" she said, placing her arm on the back of the couch.

"Excuse me, Miss Hanover, I. . ."

"Opal, call me Opal."

"I don't know where you're going with this. . ."

She began sliding her hand up and down his lapel, and it freaked him out. *This is nuts!* He grabbed her wrist, forcing her to stop. She frowned a pouty frown. He had to put an end to this craziness.

Opal crooned, "I was thinking that — I know your wife has been dead some time now — I was thinking you might be in need of some *feminine* companionship."

This was getting too weird. He stood up to leave. "Miss Hanover, I really appreciate your concern, but I've had a long day and I want to spend some time with my son before he goes to sleep. He really needs me."

He was about to turn to go when from her seat on the couch she grabbed him around the waist, holding him tightly.

Her voice was now filled with desperation. "Mike, what about our needs? We're always doing for others. "

She quickly rose from the couch, encircling his neck with her arms. He pushed her away.

"Hanover, this is nuts," he said as he backed away from her. "Get hold of yourself! This is crazy!"

She flew at him screaming, her fists flailing. "What? Am I *crazy* now? Crazy like your son?"

He felt his hand rise, ready to strike. Suddenly they both froze.

With her face two inches away from Mike's, Opal gasped, "You were going to hit me, weren't you?"

He unclenched his fist and dropped his hands to his sides.

"Then do it," she taunted, not moving away. "Go ahead, hit me. I dare you."

He gently pushed her aside and walked fast out of the office, through the double doors to his parked car. He sucked the cool night air into his lungs. He stood for a moment, incredulous. Then he got in the car.

How, he wondered, could anyone in their right mind, much less a prestigious educational institution, give someone as unstable as this whacko such a sensitive position as a school psychologist? He could only guess how many kids she must have screwed up.

He vowed she would never be allowed to even glance at his son again.

Chapter 18

A few days later, Mike and Peggy were sitting at their desks, immersed in a sea of petty larceny cases. Peggy's phone rang and she answered it. After a few moments Mike heard her say, "I'm sorry, but my partner and I are on another detail." After a long pause she started to protest whatever she was hearing from the other end of the phone. "But. . ."

There was another pause, and again Peggy's voice: "But. . ."

After three or four more "buts" Mike heard her say, "Okay, Reggie's Diner — Nassau Road — 11:30 tonight. Yes, got it. I'll see you then." She was quickly scribbling notes as she spoke. Mike's nose was still in the file he had been reading, but his eyes were on his partner.

"What was that all about?" he asked, lifting his head.

"A man who worked for Tamara claims he has proof that Cora didn't kill herself or Tamara."

"Did I hear you say you're going to meet him at 11:30 p.m. at Reggie's diner? That dive? You know that it's in the north end of Roosevelt, right? You don't seriously intend to keep that appointment, do you? It's a battleground over there! A lot of street punks and a couple of gangs in the middle of a turf war. It's not the place for an evening stroll."

"I know. I'm touched by your concern, but I think I can take care of myself," she said, a hint of resentment in her tone.

"Peg, we've got to let this go. I know Dunbar is a moron with no backbone, but he's still the boss. I think he has us chasing punks stealing from dime stores because someone over at West Street ordered him to pull us off the Steele case. We have to leave it alone. What you're doing has trouble written all over it with a capital T."

Peggy's chin was lifted and her lips drawn thin as she said, "I thought you and I were on the same page. Neither of us believes that Cora killed herself, and we both know that she wasn't responsible for

Tamara's murder. But someone's trying very hard to pin it on her. I think they forged that note to make her death look like a suicide — a pretty bow to tie everything into a nice, neat package. So tell me, Michael, what *do* you make of all this?"

It pained him to think that she was losing respect for him. *But I can't risk my shield over this. I can't afford to tick off Dunbar and the County Executive anymore than I already have. It's not about me. Jamie's future is at stake.*

"I think we have to play out the hand that's been dealt to us," he said.

"You mean wasting our time rounding up juvenile delinquents; a job any uniform can handle?"

"Yes, I mean exactly that." Mike's voice was even, but emphatic. "Why not?"

"Don't you care about justice, Michael?"

"What justice, Peg? The only justice I'm interested in is the county paycheck I get at the end of the month for chasing lightweight punks, and putting up with the phonics who send us after them instead of letting us do our jobs and solve these murders."

"I can't believe you're that cynical." Tears began to form in Peggy's searching eyes.

"Well, maybe I've come by my *cynicism* since I lost Katie to a no-good punk with a gun. And to boot, Nassau County wants to sweep her murder under the rug because the perp's daddy is a high-level official — gotta protect the families of the privileged few. What about *my* family? What about *my* son, growing up with no mother?"

"You have no proof that the perp is getting special treatment."

"I know the kid's name, and I know that his old man is none other than Commissioner Adams of General Services."

"Michael, you have to be objective. Isn't the boy seventeen and still a minor?"

"What difference does that make, Peg? Jamie is still minus a mother."

"You've been on the force for fifteen years. You know that the system protects minors — and that's how it should be!"

The conversation was going far off track, but Mike's tender spot had been jabbed and his mouth spewed his pain.

"Okay, Peg, we'll try it your way. Why don't we sit down, sing Kum Ba Yah, hold hands and pray for justice?" Mike was sneering. "Maybe some liberal county judge will give him a slap on the wrist and sentence him to five in Attica. Then he can become 'born again' and be paroled after eighteen months, followed by six months of picking crabgrass on the Southern Parkway. And maybe, just maybe, a car will jump the divider and splatter his worthless butt all over the roadway. That's *my* kind of justice!"

Mike knew his anger was getting him nowhere, and he hadn't intended to take it out on Peggy. He took a deep breath to calm down, and remembered what got him so worked up in the first place was her phone conversation.

"So," he said, not realizing how harsh his voice still sounded, "you're going to meet this joker at Reggie's — a perp hangout — at 11:30 p.m.?"

"Why do you care?" she snapped. He had never heard her speak so sharply to anyone, and his mouth snapped right back before his brain could shift gears.

"You forget, Detective Younger, you're still under my supervision. I'm still responsible for you."

He knew he had made a huge blunder. He saw daggers with double serrated edges coming from her eyes.

"After all these years you're going to pull rank on me? You're really too much, Michael."

Mike's tone softened. "C'mon, Peg, that neighborhood is a war zone."

"Yeah, right." Peggy's voice dripped with sarcasm. "As I said before, your concern is very touching, and I wouldn't want you to jeopardize your *illustrious career* with the Nassau Police Department *just to catch a murderer.*" She paused for a split second, then said in a more ordinary tone, "You don't have to worry about it. My shift is over at 4:45, and what I do on my own time is neither your concern nor the department's." She stood up and stuffed the papers on her desk back into their folders. "I'm going down to records now, if it's alright with you," she added bitterly.

"Peg, come on; give me a break," he said, grabbing her arm. She jerked her arm from his grasp and angrily stalked off down the hall.

There was little use running after her. Mike figured he had done enough damage for the day. But he was determined to be there at the meeting that night. If anything happened to Peggy, he would never forgive himself.

Chapter 19

Mike guessed Peggy wanted to avoid him because she'd been down in records for the last three hours. Questions began to ping-pong around in his mind. *Why did I paint myself as such a jerk? Was I really afraid of being thrown off the force and not being able to support Mom and Jamie? Or did I have a deeper reason? Could it be that I have feelings for Peg, so I made myself appear like a loser to scare her off? How complicated would it be to have her in my life? Am I afraid of commitment?*

He was making out a report on some kid who broke into a mom-and-pop candy store over on West Main Street in Oyster Bay. He wondered how the little jerk managed to travel all the way from Greenwich Street in Hempstead to the affluent hamlet on the North Shore without a car.

He looked up from his laptop and smiled at the two familiar faces he saw. “Hey, Carl and Jelly! How’s the world treating you guys? Sorry I didn’t make Frankie’s bachelor party, but I’m up to my eyeballs with stuff regarding my kid. He’s been driving me so crazy I can’t even remember my name.”

They called the heavy-set one Jelly because, when he laughed, his whole body shook. He wasn’t laughing now. Mike realized that their expressions were somber and didn’t change when he greeted them.

“Mike, I have to book you,” Jelly said. He looked tense.

“Jelly, don’t you think we should do this by the books? Read him his rights! We can’t let him walk just because we didn’t follow procedure,” Carl said. “The brass will be all over us. Besides, he is accused of a serious crime, you know.”

“Hey, Carl, what’s wrong with you?” defended Jelly. “Are your shorts too tight? This is Mike we’re about to arrest!”

“Arrest? Jelly, what are you talking about?” Mike said in disbelief. It didn’t register.

Jelly's round face looked confused but resolute. "Mike, I'm very sorry. Please, come with us, we have to ask you some questions."

"Jelly, have you guys been smoking funny cigarettes? What the h—l is this all about?" Mike didn't budge from his seat.

"Ryan, do you know a Miss Opal Hanover?" Carl asked, leaning his hands on Mike's desk.

"Sure, she's my son's school psychologist. What's it to you?" Mike knew even as he said the words that his temper was getting ahead of him once more.

"You know, Ryan," said Carl, straightening, "you were always quick with that smart mouth. I wonder if you'll be able to talk yourself out of this one."

Mike was about to lose his temper completely, and he knew it. He decided to give his demand for an explanation one more try before he plastered Carl all over the office wall.

"Jelly. Please. Tell me what this is all about."

Jelly was a terrific guy to hang with. He never let anything ruffle him. Carl Luba, his partner, often derided him, saying he was too soft on perps. Carl would even call Jelly "unprofessional" because he didn't always go by the book.

But it was always Jelly who diffused the tense situations. He didn't take things too seriously; he would just tell everyone to relax. He knew that everything would work itself out, and if it didn't, well, then he would take care of it. Jelly was very capable.

But this time was different. Jelly was dead serious.

"Man," he said to Mike, "I hate to tell you, but you're being charged with *sexual assault.*"

Mike felt suspended in mid air — like he was having an out-of-body experience. He seemed to be floating near the ceiling, observing the three men at his desk, of which he was one. Then realization brought him crashing down, back to reality.

"You mean Hanover? She's charging me with sexual assault?"

Jelly nodded.

"This is nuts. For the record, that psycho was coming on to me. I had to push her away." As soon as he said it, he wished he hadn't.

"C'mon, Jelly," Carl said, "We're wasting time. Let's take him downstairs and hand him over to the guys from the Twenty-Fourth."

"Hey!" Jelly snapped at Carl. "Mike is one of our own. What's your hurry?"

"Look, the guy is accused of a crime, and the Sarge ordered us to bring him downstairs. That's all there is to it!" Carl didn't look at Mike.

Mike suspected that Carl Luba had resented him ever since Mike was awarded the citation for talking a woman out of jumping off the Robert Moses Bridge. Luba had spotted the woman first and called it in, so he thought he should have shared in the commendation. The police commissioner saw it differently. Now Luba's buried feelings were complicating the scenario. Mike decided to simplify things.

"Look, Jelly," said Mike, "I know you have no choice in the matter. I'm going to have to answer their stupid questions anyway. I know the drill, so let's go."

Downstairs was really the basement of the building. Tubes and pipes with asbestos covering ran the length of the ceiling in all directions. The three cops passed a cage containing stolen articles that remained unclaimed. Voices echoed off the plaster walls.

Jelly and Carl escorted Mike past the bullpen and into the interrogation room. There they left him. Within twenty seconds, Mike was joined by two suits he didn't know.

There were the usual four chairs around the table: one for the perp, two for the detectives on the case, and the fourth one in case the perp lawyered-up. Mike didn't even think about a mouthpiece. Why should he? He was innocent, and he was a cop. He was confident that, when they heard the details, these guys would know that the charges were bogus. They would all have a good laugh, and then be on their way.

"Detective Ryan, you want something to drink? Coke? Coffee?" One of his interrogators reached into his breast pocket and offered Mike a cigarette.

"No thanks, fellas; let's just get this over with. I have to see my kid, and then I'm meeting my partner at 11:30 tonight. We have to check some leads."

"Listen, Ryan," said Charlie, the detective who had offered the cigarette, "Don and I don't think you have to worry about any cases right now. Do we, Don?" Don looked blankly at Mike and didn't answer.

"You won't be doing any police work for awhile after the court and the disciplinary board get through with you." He was so close that Mike could smell the coffee and cigarettes on his foul breath. The odor made Mike queasy.

"Hey, man," said Mike, "this is crazy. Like I told Jelly and his partner, Luba, this lady Hanover is really off the wall."

Don, a stout detective with a receding hairline, walked over and put his arm around Mike's shoulder. He said, "Mike — can I call you Mike? We're all family here." He paused. "Mike, we know how it is. A woman dresses in a particular way, and begins to come on to you. . . then when you pick up her signal and give her what you think she wants. . . before you know it, she's screaming bloody murder."

Good Cop. He couldn't believe they were trying to pull this routine on him. He and Peggy used it more times than he could remember.

"Look, Ryan, Opal Hanover is a respected professional in the community. Why would she risk her job and reputation for a romp in the hay with you?" said Charlie. He was playing the Bad Cop. His face was so close that his bushy mustache almost touched Mike's lips.

"Charlie, back off. He's one of us," Good Cop Don said softly. He took his arm off Mike's shoulder.

"C'mon, man, this is a hatchet job. We're brothers, cops, and you guys are ready to hang me out to dry," Mike said as he stood up and straightened his tie.

"Sit down!" shouted Charlie. For the next several hours, Mike responded to their litany of questions. They kept on pounding him, asking the same questions over and over, nine different ways. When they ran out of questions, they started from the beginning again. It was an endurance test.

Mike didn't like sitting on this side of the conversation; he preferred it the other way around. He struggled to control his temper, but he could feel the heat rising under his collar. Same questions, same answers — it was getting old; and it was getting late. He glanced at the clock on the wall. Eight o'clock. He started getting anxious.

"Oh, Don, do you have any tissues?" Charlie said mockingly. "I think Nassau County's prize cop, Detective Ryan, is going to cry."

Mike's muscles tensed. He leaned on the balls of his feet with his fists clenched. As he sprang from his chair, Don anticipated his move and grabbed him from behind, stopping him in his tracks. The interrogating partners smiled. They were getting to him.

"Now, Mike, you're not going to slam my partner, are you? If you have him laid up in the hospital, what am I going to do for backup?" This last comment came from Don; he apparently forgot which role he was playing today. His attempt at humor wasn't funny. *Sounds like something I would say,* Mike thought. It annoyed him to admit it. He forced himself to relax, and Don let go of him. He sat down again.

"Look, he said reasonably, "I know you guys have a job to do, but I have to go to an important meeting with my partner. I have to cover her back. Please, let me go. We can continue this game tomorrow, okay?"

But, it wasn't okay.

Chapter 20

Mike couldn't believe two fellow detectives would keep hammering him with questions until 11:30 p.m. He felt sure he was being set up. In the end, though, there was no way the department could nail one of their own on a trumped-up charge like sexual harassment without evidence. The department informed Mike, that they didn't have enough to hold or suspend him, so he would be restricted to desk duty while their investigation continued. The department couldn't leave a cop on the street with charges pending against him. Detectives Charlie and Don finally let him go.

Mike flew out the door to his car. He couldn't give any more thought to the Hanover incident for the moment. Right now, he had to focus all his attention on Peggy. Roosevelt was a hotspot of street crime in Nassau County. Especially at night, that section belonged to the thugs from the "'hood." The only other people on the streets were drug buyers from surrounding areas. *Some progressives might label me a bigot for even entertaining such notions,* thought Mike, *but statistics don't lie.*

He was so worried about Peggy; his car seemed to be moving in slow motion. *She has to be out of her mind. That area is dangerous at this time of night! She's walking into a lion's den. Her personal involvement with Tamara and Cora is clouding her judgment. Looks like she threw her street smarts out the window along with every precautionary police measure she ever learned. Ten years on the job and she goes into a situation like this on her own with no backup. I can't believe it!*

He arrived at his destination. Reggie's Diner had seen better days. The once-polished aluminum panels below the glass were now rusted and pitted. The half-lit neon sign cast a dull pink glow on the sheet of plywood covering a plate glass window that had been broken when someone threw a chair through it two years ago. When Mike pulled into the parking lot he spotted Peggy's car among the half-dozen others in the lot. It was parked on the right, near the alley that went behind the bodega next door. He parked his car and went in.

His eyes scanned the room quickly in the glare of the fluorescent lights. There were only ten people in the place. Two booths were occupied. Four men talked loudly at one while two men sat eating at the other. A lone man sat at a table sipping coffee. The counterman was having an animated conversation with the single customer seated there. The short-order cook behind the counter was turning a hamburger on the grill. *No sign of Peg.*

Conversation ceased as all eyes turned to Mike. Street people were as attuned to cops as cops were to them. They didn't need a uniform or a badge to identify *the man* – they could smell him. There was silence.

Mike walked over to the now quiet counterman. "Has a white woman been in here in the last hour or so? Five foot six, reddish hair?

"No white woman been in here lately, except Annie. She came in a while ago with her pimp for a hamburger."

Mike walked past the counter and through the door at the far end. A pay phone hung on the wall between the doors to the two restrooms, its wire dangling where the handset used to be. He checked the restrooms. The stench of the ladies' room was as nauseating as the one emanating from the men's room. Still no sign of Peggy.

He went back to the parking lot to check Peggy's car. As he moved to the driver's window, he heard a rustling sound in the alley just beyond the car. Then he heard a moan.

Mike removed his pistol from his holster and a small flashlight from his pocket, which he didn't turn on. *Makes too good a target.* He squinted as he stepped cautiously from the bright light of the parking lot into the darkness of the alley, trying to force his eyes to adjust to the darkness. His senses were heightened, ready to react to the slightest sign of danger.

A single bare bulb over the back door of the bodega made a small circle of dim light. The rest was shrouded in shadows. A few feet beyond the lit area he could discern someone's foot extending from between two overflowing garbage cans. He approached slowly. He turned the flashlight on. The beam fell on Peggy's bruised and bleeding face – all other color drained from it – only the red of the blood and the purple of the bruises remained. She lay there on the cold concrete among the discarded food containers, beer cans and candy wrappers. His heart jumped into his throat. He quickly ran the light down the length of her body. Her legs were full of blood, and her bloody right hand clutched her stomach as she groaned again with pain. He holstered his gun and knelt next to her. He cradled her head in his hands.

"Peg! Peg, can you hear me?"

Another groan.

"Peg, talk to me. Can you speak? What happened? Who did this to you?" Mike was frantic. His mind flashed back to Katie. All he could see was red.

"When I get my hands on whoever did this, I'll. . ."

"Michael, my legs, I can't move them," Peggy groaned, cutting him off mid-sentence.

He sat down next to her and placed her head in his lap. His police sense and training switched to autopilot. "Baby, hang in there." He reached into his right breast pocket and pulled out his cell phone. "Call dispatcher," he said, using the voice call feature, which connected him directly to the police dispatcher.

"Dispatcher," crackled a voice.

"10-13 — I've got a 10-13 here — officer down! Need an ambulance *stat* at Nassau Boulevard and. . . oh, c'mon, what's the cross street here? Morgan! Nassau Boulevard at Morgan Avenue in Roosevelt. Got that? Nassau and Morgan in Roosevelt. We're in the alley next to the parking lot of Reggie's Diner."

The dispatcher repeated the location back to Mike.

"Yes, that's it," he replied, "the alley next to the parking lot." He turned his attention back to Peggy.

"Everything will be all right. His eyes scanned her, trying to discern if there were wounds other than the obvious ones.

"I feel like someone is kicking me in the stomach. . . continuously. . . he won't stop. Michael, make him stop," she said weakly.

"Okay, sweetheart, just be still. The ambulance is coming. It will be here in a couple of minutes — only a couple of minutes more," he said as he removed his jacket and placed it over her trembling body.

Mike was grateful when Peggy passed out. He knew she needed relief from the excruciating pain. He felt a knot in his gut. Questions ran rampant in his mind as he held her in his arms and waited.

Who was the guy on the phone telling her to meet him in this God-forsaken place? Who did this to her? How many were there? Was the attack on Peg linked to the guy on the phone, or was this a random attack?

This Tamara Steele case had more twists and turns than a running back. Something gnawed at Mike as his mind struggled to put the pieces in place. *That's it! Pieces! All the suspects are merely pawns, and the murders are part of a much larger scheme! But what? What's the motive? What are they trying to accomplish?* Something told him the answers could be found at 1550 Franklin Avenue, the County Seat. That's where he would find the prime movers in this mystery.

Mike couldn't wait to get his hands on the elected perps at 1550 Franklin Avenue, but he knew he had to be careful. They were not to be toyed with like street punks. He would have to walk a tightrope. If he slipped up, it would mean the end for him. The higher-ups would discard him in a trash heap — like they had just tried to do to Peggy.

Meanwhile, help was not arriving.

What's taking so long? When there's a 10-13 we pull out all the stops! It means one of our own is in trouble, and the cavalry comes running. In the academy the instructors told us, "On a 10-13 you remove any and all obstacles there may be that would prevent or delay you from coming to the aid of a fellow officer. You go over, under, around or through whatever is in the way. "just get there!" That's the code of the brotherhood.

While Mike waited, he made another call and arranged for a couple of blues to pick up their cars. He would ride in the ambulance with Peggy to the Nassau County Medical Center.

Then he called the hospital, hoping it was Tim's shift. Mike's cousin, Tim, had been working in the ER at the County Medical Center ever since he graduated nursing school eighteen years ago. Sure enough, Tim was on duty. Mike gave him a heads-up on Peggy's condition.

"Mikey, don't worry, we'll take good care of her," said his cousin. "I'll be waiting for you." Like everyone else in the law enforcement family, Tim thought Peggy was terrific. And like everyone else, he teased Mike about taking the stroll down the aisle with her. Mike would just smile and say, "Nah — too skinny." Then he and Tim would laugh.

After an eight-minute eternity the ambulance arrived. The medics were careful but wasted no time. When the vehicle arrived at the NCMC Emergency Department, Tim was waiting for them. The resident in charge was at Tim's side.

"Okay, people," barked the resident, "let's get this lady into surgery; she's losing a lot of blood."

Mike started walking along side the gurney, but Tim stopped him.

"Mikey, we called in the best team we have for her. Let them do their job," he said. "If you want to do something useful, pray."

Mike felt helpless, but he knew Tim was right, and he found a seat in the waiting room. He gave no thought at all to Tim's suggestion to pray; to him, prayer was another word for thinking hard about Peggy while he couldn't be at her side.

Five hours passed as Mike paced the waiting room floor. It was nearly 6:00 a.m. He'd been up for 24 hours straight and felt exhausted. He decided he needed to find a very large cup of very strong black coffee to see him through. The cool morning air braced him, pushing back some of the fatigue as he walked outside the Emergency Room and around the curved sidewalk to the main building, which housed the hospital's cafeteria. He knew Tim would call him the minute there was any news.

It was very warm in the cafeteria, enough to put a person to sleep. The coffee Mike sipped as he sat at an empty table was weak and tasted like dishwater — not exactly what he needed. Two nurses with food trays sat down at the next table. Within ten minutes he'd finished the coffee and was headed back to the Emergency Room.

Mike's cell phone rang as he entered the sliding doors. It was Tim calling to let him know that Peggy was going to be okay. The surgeons had done a good job; she was now in the recovery room and would be put in a private room as soon as she woke up. He would be able to speak to her then for a few minutes.

He got off the elevator on the fifth floor, where Tim said he could wait. As he turned the corner from the elevator, he saw Henry and Tina Younger, Peggy's parents. They had come on the red-eye from Kansas City as soon as they received the "next-of-kin notification call" from the precinct. Mike met them on several previous occasions when they'd come to visit Peggy.

The Youngers were the kind of people everyone gravitated to, kind and friendly to everyone. You could tell where Peg inherited her gentle spirit. Tina made a beeline for Mike, wrapped her arms around his neck, and began to sob.

"Mrs. Younger, have you been brought up to date on Peg's condition?" he asked. Feeling awkward, he discreetly extricated himself from her embrace. She turned and hid her face in her husband's shoulder.

"They let us peek in on her in the recovery room, and we talked to Dr. Harris before they sent us up here to wait," Henry Younger said, holding his wife with one hand while shaking Mike's hand with the other. His firm grip conveyed his customary sincerity. "Our little girl is in a lot of pain. She's all cut up. The doctor said there are two major lacerations on her legs, and a wound to her abdomen."

Mr. Younger added, "Dr. Harris said it appears that she's out of danger. I hope he's right."

Mike couldn't believe the old man's thoughtful, calm reaction, you'd think he was taking about a stranger, not his own daughter.

If this happened to my kid, thought Mike, *I don't think they would have restraints strong enough to hold me. I'd bomb the whole stupid' town to get whoever did it!*

Peg once told Mike that her father had retired from the police department. She said he'd been hardened by the experience but after becoming a born-again Christian seemed gentler and more understanding. Mike remembered how he scoffed at that.

Chapter 21

The doctors said Peggy would be in recovery for a couple of hours. Mike decided to go home and take a shower. Fortunately, when he got to his house, no one was home. Jamie was at school, and his mother must have gone shopping. *Thank God!* He wasn't ready to tell either of them about Peggy yet; he wanted to wait for the dust to settle a little. The shower and change of clothes refreshed him.

He returned to the hospital. As he walked past the reception desk, his cell phone rang. He flipped it open and saw the name Kennedy on the screen. David Kennedy was his lawyer. He was about to answer it, when an old man in a rent-a-cop uniform with a shiny tin badge marched doggedly up to him. He looked about ninety years old if he was a day.

"Sir, I have to ask you to turn your cell phone off. Hospital policy."

The old man delayed him just long enough for the call to be kicked to his voice mail.

"Okay, old timer," said Mike, "I just have to check my messages."

"Sir, I told you, you can't use your cell phone in the hospital!" repeated the elderly guard. "If you're not going to listen to me, I'll have to escort you from the premises."

Mike looked down at him, his blood began to boil. With the day that he had, Peggy's condition, and no sleep, it took all the restraint he could muster not to put the old geezer over his shoulder and dump him in some senior home.

"Look, sir," said Mike, "I know you have a job to do, but I think you take it too seriously. Perhaps you'd better back off." He reached into his breast pocket and flipped his shield.

It took about a second for the poor old man to transition from Mr. Voice-of-Authority to looking like a patient headed for the cardiac unit.

"I'm sorry, officer, I didn't mean. . ."

"It's Detective Ryan, and don't worry about it. I'll go *outside* and check my messages, okay?"

"Yes, I'm sorry, Detective. Please excuse me. If you need anything, just ask."

Peggy would have blown a gasket if she'd seen how he intimidated the old man. And she would be even angrier if she saw how much it amused me. Mike justified his actions by telling himself he needed a little levity to lighten the mood after the last couple of days.

He went outside so the old man wouldn't have a stroke. He took out his cell phone and punched in his lawyer's number.

Besides being his lawyer, David Kennedy was also Katie's brother, and an all-around good guy. He handled all legal matters for both sides of the family, and he was good at his profession.

After two rings, his receptionist answered.

"David Kennedy, please."

"Who's calling?"

"Tell him it's Mike Ryan."

"May I ask what this is in reference to?"

"First of all I'm his brother-in-law and second, he's handling a case for me. Put him on." Mike felt himself losing patience. He wondered why everyone seemed to have a problem with him lately.

"You don't have to get *testy*, sir; I'm just doing what Mr. Kennedy pays me to do. It's my job."

He took a deep breath. "*Please*, just get him for me."

"Okay, *sir*. Please hold. I'll see if he's available."

Mike waited for a few minutes.

"David Kennedy," came the familiar voice.

"Hey, man," blurted Mike, "what's with your receptionist? What's keeping you from showing her the door? She got great legs, or what?"

"Whaddya say, Mike? It's good you returned my call."

"What's up?"

"Well, it looks like Miss Hanover's crew has a genuine case against you."

Mike was shocked; his jaw dropped.

"You have got to be kidding. I was doing everything I could to shake that woman off *me*! What case could they have?"

"There's a witness."

"What? What witness? There was no one in the school except that whacko Hanover and me."

"Apparently there was a janitor who says he heard screams coming from Hanover's office. When he went to check, he says he saw you groping her."

"Groping her? Listen! In the first place, therc was no one else there. And second, I never touched her. I hate to sound paranoid, but I'm being framed."

"Mike, do you know how ridiculously lame that sounds?"

"C'mon, there's no other explanation. I don't know why, but someone is out to get me. It's more than this Hanover thing. Ever since my partner Peg and I got involved with the Steele murder case, we've been running into snags. Did I tell you? Peg's in the hospital — someone tried to kill her. Thank God, she's going to be okay. But the last three days have been too much. First Peg and I get reassigned, then I get suspended, then Peg gets cut up after being lured to Roosevelt by someone who said they had information about the case. . . and now this Hanover thing! I tell you, it's more than coincidence."

"Okay," David broke in, "Let me look into this janitor character and see what I come up with. By the way, Mike, we have to appear in court next Wednesday, the twenty-ninth."

"God! So soon?"

"Yeah, I know that's quick. Somehow, Judge Roth's docket was suddenly clear, so we're on."

"Yeah, right. One more *coincidence*."

I can't believe the timing! What else could go wrong?

Chapter 22

Mike went up to the fifth floor to Peggy's room. When he exited the elevator, her parents were in the same spot where he'd encountered them earlier that morning. They explained that Peg threw up her lunch. They were waiting there while two aides changed the bed and cleaned her up.

"Not surprising," Mike quipped. "Have you ever eaten the food in one of these places?" His meek attempt at levity fell on deaf ears.

"Michael," said Mrs. Younger, "You go in, and see Margaret. She's anxious to talk to you."

Margaret? His brain froze for a moment. "Margaret" didn't process. Then he realized. "Oh — you mean Peg! Sorry — too little sleep." He'd forgotten that her parents called her by her given name.

When he walked into Peggy's room the sight of her really shook him up. She was lying on the bed, her lovely face covered with bandages.

"Hey, kiddo, how ya feeling?" he finally managed to whisper, after a long pause.

"I'm glad you're here." She tried to smile, but winced in pain instead.

Mike was surprised that, in spite of her pain and discomfort, her usual calm demeanor hadn't changed. She still had that inner peace that shone through no matter what. But something wasn't right. Her greeting was so casual; it was as if she were speaking to a stranger. He was suddenly afraid that the wounds to her head might be affecting her thought processes. He hadn't considered that possibility before. He didn't know what to expect from her. He didn't know what to expect of himself either.

During those hours that he spent pacing in the emergency room, not knowing if she would live or die, he thought about what his life would be like without her. He found that prospect impossible to consider. She was a light in his darkness. His heart had turned a corner. This crisis had forced him to a decision point that he had been avoiding for God knows how long. He was finally able to admit to himself that he loved her. He didn't want to go on without her.

How could he tell her that? This was uncharted territory for him. Surely now was *not* the time. But what had she just said as she lay there before him on the hospital bed? She was glad he was there.

"Where else would I be?" he said at last in response to her comment. "You're my partner, aren't you?" He spotted a grin through the exposed space around her mouth. "Really, how're you feeling?"

"Good, everyone has been especially kind to me."

He looked at the bandages on her legs. The sight of them threw a switch in his gut. He was back in anger mode. He thought about gathering a bunch of cops, especially those who were close to him and tearing Roosevelt apart until they found whoever did this to her. He was back to being Detective Mike Ryan.

"Peg, could you identify whoever did this to you?"

"It was dark and it all happened so fast, I can't give you a description."

"But you had to have seen something. Take your time and concentrate. You know the drill."

She took a few moments to think, and then said, "I remember that I was supposed to meet Juan at 11:30 p.m." He then realized that her thinking processes were unaffected.

"Yeah, I remember," Mike burst out, "and I remember I told you not to go."

The visible parts of Peggy's face tensed up. "Michael, do you want me to recall the facts? Or are you more interested in convincing me how right you were? And by the way, I still disagree!"

"Sorry, Peg." He realized he was badgering her. *As usual, I have to be right, even if it means disregarding Peggy's emotional state. What's wrong with me?*

"Michael, they were wearing ski masks."

"How many were there?"

"Three. . . I think. . . maybe four."

"What else?" Mike thought his head would split, his desire for more details was so huge. "What else do you remember that could help us identify them?"

"Well, I remember they spoke with Hispanic accents. One. . . he was young. . . a teenager, I think. He had tattoos up and down his arms. I remember a skull and crossbones on his left arm. . . I think." Peggy's brows knit above the bandages. "Michael,

I sound like every distraught victim I've ever interviewed. I just can't remember!"

Carefully, he placed his hand over hers. "Yes, you can. Concentrate! What did they say?"

"I don't know."

"C'mon, Peg, what did they say to you?"

"I don't know what they said. They weren't talking to me. I don't know!"

Mike released her hand. "Okay, Peg, you did fine. Just relax."

She started to cough uncontrollably. Mike's heart began to pound. He grabbed the cup of water next to the yellow pitcher on the food tray. He lifted her, tilting her head forward and touching her lips to the rim.

The last time Mike held a woman in his arms was the day he'd picked Katie up in the body bag from the hard tile floor of the convenience store.

When Peggy finally stopped coughing, she managed a sweet smile and thanked him. He carefully laid her head back on the pillow and she closed her eyes. She looked peaceful. She possessed a purity he had never encountered in anyone else. He had seen it in her before, but it never moved him like this. Suddenly, he found himself kissing her dry lips. She opened her eyes.

"Michael? What was that all about?" She didn't seem angry or disturbed by what he had done, merely surprised.

"Peg, I don't what came over me. I'm sorry, please forgive me." He lost control. As if he had been an impartial observer, he watched himself kiss her. He wanted to stop himself, but the other self had a mind of its own.

"Michael, maybe this is the wrong question to ask, but under the circumstances, there has never been a better time. What do you feel toward me?"

There, she has me backed into a corner. Do I fight, flee, or surrender? Before, I saw her wounded and hurt I had no need to keep my guard up, no fear of rejection. But now. . . I want to hold her in my arms, to love her and be loved in return. And I'm scared. Mike knew now that he was ready for her love: a pure love with no strings attached and no hidden agenda. It was time to lay it all on the line. Okay, dealer, all in!

He gulped and said, "Peg, all I know now is that I want you to be at my side forever. If you're willing, I want you to marry me. I also want you to be a mother to Jamie, and maybe have a kid of our own."

He saw a tear falling from her eye. She reached out her hand and softly ran her finger down his face.

"Michael, I have always loved you. I never said anything because I know how committed you are to Katie's memory, and I would never interfere with that."

He could do nothing less than speak the whole truth. "Peg, I will always have a tender spot in my heart for Katie. I'd be lying if I said otherwise. She was like you, loving, giving and beautiful, but she's been gone for five years now, and. . ."

"You think it's time for you to let her go," she finished.

"Yes, I guess that's it. You are so much sharper than I am," he laughed.

For some reason Mike didn't understand, her mood changed. She looked away, and he became uneasy. Maybe I said too much, maybe I went too far — exposed my feelings too much. Oh God, will I ever get it right?

He took her hand again. "What's the matter, sweetheart?" he said. "Did I lay too much on you all at once? I know — I came on too strong. I'm sorry, but. . ."

"No, Michael, no! I love you! I've prayed for this for the longest time. I've wanted to be with you. I've wanted to be a mother to Jamie." She began to sob bitterly.

"Michael," she wept, "it won't work. . . it can't. We wouldn't be equally yoked."

"Whoa, girl, you lost me there!" Mike's face reflected his bewilderment. "What the h—l are you talking about?" It wasn't anger, just pure confusion in his voice.

"Michael, what I just said — 'equally yoked' — is a quote from the Bible. Have you ever read the Bible?"

"Some passages are familiar to me. I guess I heard parts of the Bible at Mass when I used to go with Ma." He felt himself frowning. He really didn't know what point she was trying to make. Whatever it was, it eluded him, and it disturbed him very much.

Twisting with an effort, she picked up the leather-bound book that was beside her on the night table. "Well, that's the problem. The Bible, the Word of God, has been part of my life — part of me — ever since I was eight years old, when I invited Jesus to be the Lord of my life. And that's the point: He is the Lord — my Lord.

"The Bible isn't just a book," she continued. "These pages are a love letter from God. In it He has revealed himself, and the limitless love He has for us. He shows that love in the gift of His Son. In our own right, we are not worthy to stand in His presence, but through the sacrifice of Jesus, God's only Son, He has opened the way for us to be adopted into His household. We can now approach Him as a loving Father. It's His plan for redemption of all mankind."

Peggy stopped, plainly tired. Mike took the opportunity to say, "That's very nice, but what's that got to do with you and me?"

She drew fresh energy from somewhere. "Michael, my commitment to the Lord isn't merely a belief system. God has a plan and purpose for each of us. The Bible shows us how to live to fulfill that purpose. It tells us how we are to live, to think, and how to love. In it God teaches us, not just a way of life, but *the* way to *the* life. Following my Lord is just like breathing for me. It's not optional."

"So believe it if you want to." Mike felt as though he were falling from a height into a pit of disappointment. "I won't stop you."

Carefully, Peggy shook her head and said, "Being 'equally yoked' is when a man and a woman share the same love and dedication to God — Father, Son and Holy Spirit. He has to be central to both their lives; otherwise the relationship is doomed from the outset. If you don't have that relationship with Him, you can't have the proper relationship with me. Don't you see? We're just not on the same page, Michael."

Michael felt almost as if he were in competition with some other guy. "But Peg, you can do your thing any way you want — I won't stand in your way! Religion just isn't for me. That doesn't mean I love you any less. Obviously church has helped make you the wonderful person that you are — that's why I love you. But I can't be you. Please don't ask me to be who I'm not. It's been great for you, but I've seen too many people that have used God to extort pennies from old ladies."

"The majority of pastors, priests and ministers are holy men living spiritual lives, whose goal is to bring people to God," she said resentfully.

"Come on, Peg, give me a break! They're all con men!"

Again her bitter tears flowed.

"Michael, we're worlds apart about the most important thing in my life: God! You don't know how I've yearned for you to tell me that you love me, but I've seen too many marriages fall part because one partner has a relationship with Jesus, while the other loves the things of this world. It just won't work! Michael, you're asking me to allow you to just tolerate the most important thing in my life, the core of my being. I'd have to be crazy."

"But Peg, Jamie and I both love you, and we both need you."

Peggy grasped his hand.

"Michael, loving and caring about you and Jamie is very tempting. I want to with every fiber of my being. But I couldn't bear being married to you, knowing that you're not ready to make Jesus the Lord of your life too. We'd always be pulling in opposite directions."

Mike wasn't ready to give up. "Come on, Peg, don't tell me you're going to throw away what we've found because of a philosophy. We have been with each other far too long for that."

"Michael, you just don't get it. But it's really not your fault," she said, shaking her head slowly. "You haven't found God's Spirit — or, more accurately, you haven't allowed Him to find you — because you obviously haven't suffered enough. You're not ready yet to give up your pain," she said mournfully. "As soon as I get on my feet I'm going to ask for a transfer."

Ask for a transfer! Mike's reaction was knee-jerk. "Peg, if you don't want to marry me, it's all right. I'll have to live with it. It may be tough for a while because I love you so much. But you can't break up this team. We work so well together. I can't work with another partner."

"Michael, it has to be this way."

"But baby, you can't give up on us so easily." Mike felt his heart torn in two.

"Michael, I can't take anymore of this. It hurts too much. Please. . . go."

He knew she had made up her mind. He didn't have anything else to say. He kissed her forehead and left the room. He heard her sobbing as he closed the door.

Chapter 23

The next few days were intolerable for Mike. Every day he tried, without success, to see or call Peggy. She insisted that she didn't want anything further to do with him. Her parents and the hospital staff complied with her wishes: he never got past the gatekeepers.

He wished he could divert his attention from her by burying himself in his work, but the administrative drudgery of being restricted to desk duty bored him to death. It was no diversion at all, if anything, it made things worse. No matter how much he tried to keep busy and occupy his mind, he couldn't erase the constant image of Peggy from his thoughts.

Some of the other cops from the precinct visited her and gave him updates regarding her condition. She was recovering well; the doctors were amazed at her progress. She was in rehab. Her abdominal wound was healing. Physical therapy was restoring the use of her legs, she's already walking with a cane and they didn't think she would have any permanent disability from the leg wounds. Her facial wounds were expected to all but disappear with no discernible scars.

On Tuesday night he sat in front of his television, supposedly watching a baseball game with Jamie. Both the boy and the grandmother could tell Mike's mind wasn't on the game. Neither said anything when Mike went to bed at 8:45 p.m.

Chapter 24

Mike arrived at the precinct Wednesday morning, six days after the attack on Peggy, and parked himself at his desk. He sat staring blankly at the framed picture of Jamie that stood beside his computer when he suddenly remembered the hearing about Opal Hanover. He had been so obsessed trying to cope with Peggy's absence that he had completely forgotten about Hanover's charges against him.

He was supposed to be at the Supreme Court building on Old Country Road in five minutes. Mike knew if he hurried he could it make to court without a moment to spare.

David Kennedy, his lawyer, saw Mike jogging down the hallway and walked briskly toward the approaching figure. The lawyer gazed at his watch.

"Man, you really cut it close."

"I'm sorry; I forgot this da—ed thing was today."

"Mike, you like to tick off judges. You have to take these proceedings seriously. This judge could break you or set you free; you don't want him upset with you."

Mike heaved a huge sigh. "Man, I'm sorry. What can I tell you?"

He stared at Mike and shook his head, unable to believe Mike's indifference.

Both men headed down the long hallway towards the courtroom. They walked through the doors and took their seats at one of the two tables facing the judge's bench. Opal Hanover and her lawyer, Sam Benedict, were seated at the other table across from them.

Mike took note of Hanover's attire. He didn't know whether she was coached or if Opal Hanover just instinctively knew how to impress the court. Her well-fitted tailored black skirt hung just below her knees. Her plain white blouse was topped by a burgundy cardigan and a matching scarf demurely adorning her neck, a sharp contrast to the outfit she wore at their last meeting.

She looked at Mike and held onto her attorney's arm as if for dear life. Apparently, she was trying to convince her lawyer that Mike was a dangerous individual from whom she needed protection.

Everyone stood as Judge Abraham Roth climbed the steps leading to the bench. He looked tired and bored, and Mike knew he was in for a rough time. The judge glanced at the plaintiff and the defendant.

"Okay, counselors," he mumbled, "bring me up to speed. Preliminary reading of these briefs warns me that this case is going to be a messy and an annoying experience."

"Your Honor," began Sam Benedict, "Detective Michael Ryan of the Nassau County Police Department, a man who has sworn to protect and defend the citizens of this county, has committed an egregious and disgraceful act: sexually molesting my client.

"Miss Hanover is a well-known and respected member of the psychology profession. As a result of her dedication and concern for Mr. Ryan's son, she arranged to meet the detective at an unusual hour in order to accommodate his schedule. In the course of that meeting Detective Ryan, thinking they were alone in the building, attempted to sexually assault

Miss Hanover. We hold the Nassau County Police Department fully responsible for his actions, and we demand a full apology. In addition, we expect the department to pay my client compensatory and punitive damages in the amount of ten million dollars."

Mike couldn't control himself. "You've got to be kidding. Why don't you ask for a billion dollars? It's just as ridiculous."

Judge Roth heaved a heavy sigh and said to David Kennedy, "Counselor, I'm in no mood for client outbursts. I have an ingrown toenail jabbing my big toe. I have no need for further pain in other parts of my anatomy. Instruct your client that further outbursts will not be tolerated. If he persists with this behavior he will be held in contempt. Am I understood?"

"Yes, Your Honor," replied David with a hard look at Mike, "we apologize, and I promise that my client will restrain himself in the future." He whispered in Mike's ear, "Mike, will you cool it? Judge Roth is not crazy about cops. It's going to be enough of a challenge for us to exonerate you without you alienating him even more."

Mike was fuming, but he kept his volume low. "What do you mean, a challenge? When he read the brief it should have taken him five seconds to throw this stupid case out."

"I wish I was as certain as you," murmured David.

Mike talked through his teeth. "Man, I did not touch that woman. In fact, she came after me. I did everything in my power to break out of her grasp."

David shook his head. "What about their witness? They say he saw you."

"How can there be a witness when we were the only ones left in the building?"

"Mike, are you sure you didn't see anyone walk past Hanover's office?"

Mike rolled his eyes. "How many ways do you want me to say it? There was no one else there."

"Mr. Kennedy," groaned the judge, "if you're through having a reunion with your client, we eagerly await a demonstration of your legal skills. Please, present your case."

"Forgive me, Your Honor," said David. "We contend that the plaintiff is wasting the court's time in even hearing this case. It is a travesty of justice to suggest that Detective Ryan would entertain the notion of forcing sexual attention on the plaintiff, or anyone else for that matter. This is a man of exemplary service for fifteen years as a member of the Nassau County Police Department. During his tenure serving the public he has received numerous commendations and awards for bravery and excellence in police work."

Unimpressed, Judge Roth said, "Okay, okay, counselors, the court acknowledges each of your attempts to paint your respective clients as marvelous and virtuous citizens, but the court also recognizes that one of the parties is engaging in falsehood or, at the very least, distorting the truth. So let us get to the truth through testimonies. That's how it's usually accomplished, isn't it counselors?"

"And I thought *I* was sarcastic," whispered Mike.

"Now," the judge continued, "since the defense is on the defensive, start earning your fee, Mr. Kennedy."

"Your Honor, I call Detective Michael Ryan." Inured, Michael complied and took the stand. "Detective, state your complete name, please."

"Michael Sean Ryan."

"Tell the court the circumstances that brought you and Miss Hanover together."

Mike tried getting comfortable in the seat, straightening his tie and adjusting his sport jacket. Remembering the whole scene later, he realized his fidgeting must have made him look guilty. Finally Mike said, "Ms. Hanover is a psychologist at Wilson's Academy, the school my son, Jamie, attends."

"Michael," asked Kennedy, "does Jamie have a physical disability?"

"Yes, Jamie was born with cerebral palsy."

"Could you explain his condition to the court?"

He cleared his throat and spoke firmly. "Your Honor, cerebral palsy is a condition affecting the motor parts of the brain. In my son's case he has a speech impediment and has difficulty walking. As such, we thought the academy could help him with his speech problem and prepare him for the difficulties he would encounter in the outside world."

David said, "I read in Miss Hanover's file on Jamie that he has had trouble in school. The file contains reports that he is frequently fighting with his classmates."

"Yes," said Mike, "and I guess that's why Miss Hanover contacted me — to discuss Jamie's behavior."

"Did you meet with Miss Hanover?"

"Of course! I love my son, and I want to know about any problems that could put roadblocks in his path to becoming a mature and responsible adult. I met twice with Miss Hanover."

"How did your first meeting go?"

"Well, after the initial niceties I thought it became very strained." Mike did not look directly at Opal Hanover, but he sensed her shifting in her chair.

"Can you be a little more specific?" asked David.

"Well, as I previously stated, I love my son very much. I believe that, other than his physical disability, Jamie is a very normal child. He sees how the other boys are. He believes that with much effort, and by de-emphasizing his disability using the sheer force of his will, he can perform as well as they do. Sometimes, despite his best efforts, his condition prevents him from achieving the goals he sets for himself. It frustrates him and makes him angry."

"Obviously, you are very close to Jamie," said. David "We can imagine how much he loves and respects you. How does he feel about his mother?"

Mike trusted that David knew what he was doing, but he couldn't understand the rationale for bringing up Katie.

"Jamie loved his mother very much. Unfortunately, she's no longer with us."

"Why is that, Detective Ryan? What do you mean 'no longer with us'?"

Mike inhaled deeply. "Five years ago, my wife was gunned down by a teenager holding up a convenience store."

"Your son must have been devastated."

"Of course! he adored his mother." Mike made himself speak at a normal pace, ignoring his bristling emotions.

"Katie was your wife's name?"

"Yes. So at our first meeting, I was trying to convey to Miss Hanover that some of Jamie's anger stems from the fact that Jamie saw his mother murdered. Of course Jamie is angry, and very hurt."

Mike looked at Hanover. Her face suddenly turned crimson. To his amazement, she sprang to her feet and cried out, "I was acting as a professional trying to help you and your son, Detective Michael Ryan, and you acted like an animal." Mike saw the same rage and the same crazed look on her face that she had the night of the alleged attack.

"*Mis*-ter Benedict," said Judge Roth with open disgust, "you must control your client. Since she claims she's a professional, tell her to act like one and show some restraint in this court."

Hanover's lawyer bent down and whispered something in her ear. She started nervously arranging her blouse and sweater; then she began twisting a pen in her hands.

David resumed his questioning. "Okay, Michael, where were we? Oh — we were talking about your first meeting with Miss Hanover, and you had stated that Jamie was going through a difficult time since his mother's murder."

"Yes, and I was also saying that it seemed that Miss Hanover was acting a little hostile towards my son. And, she put me on the defensive, questioning whether or not Jamie was receiving good care."

"Who takes care of him while you're at work?"

"My mother has been watching him ever since Katie was killed."

"Okay, Detective, moving on to the day in question, the day you are accused of attacking Miss Hanover: Tell the court what transpired during that second meeting."

"I have to admit that I was confused and angry," said Mike, frowning. "Miss Hanover almost insisted that I meet her a second time. You see, my partner and I are working on a complex case and I was annoyed that I had to waste my time meeting with Miss Hanover again.

"When I arrived, Miss Hanover looked rather strange to me. She was wearing an outfit that was very revealing, but I just assumed she had a date or an affair to attend after our meeting."

"Detective, I hesitate in asking you this question, but I feel it may have some bearing on your state of mind when you met with Miss Hanover."

Mike shrugged. "Go ahead. I have nothing to hide. I didn't do anything."

Mike didn't know what David was up to. He became aware that he had absolutely no control over what was happening, and he didn't care for the feeling.

"How long has your wife been deceased?"

"Five years," said Mike.

"And have you been with other women since she passed away?"

"You mean sexually? No. I guess I really didn't think about it. I don't have time for women, what with my job and my kid."

"Okay, Detective, let's go back to your meeting with Opal Hanover. What exactly happened?"

"Well," sighed Mike, "I was late for the appointment with her. And I thought she would be annoyed, like she was when I was late for our first meeting, but surprisingly she was not. I found the questions she asked very strange. She wanted to know if I was lonely and missed the companionship of a woman. It made me uncomfortable. Here I thought the purpose for the meeting was to find ways to help my son, and now we were talking about my private life. She moved closer to me on the sofa. I shot up off the couch and asked her what in the world she was doing; I headed for the door.

"But she grabbed me around the waist; I told her she was crazy. Then she really lost control, running right at me and hitting me with her fists, shouting, 'Crazy like your son?"

"When she said that, I almost lost it. I remember that I raised my hand to slap her, but the thought of Jamie stopped me. I knew she would bring me up on charges if I struck her. I dropped my arm. Then I just ran out of the room as fast as I could."

"Detective, did you in any way encourage Miss Hanover's advances?" queried David.

"I most certainly did not," Mike said. "I was there for one reason and one reason only: to discuss my son."

"Did you flirt with Miss Hanover at any time, or convey to her in any other manner the idea that you were physically attracted to her?"

"I assure you and the court that I couldn't be, because I was so turned off when she opened her mouth at our first meeting." Mike knew he was laying it on thick, but it was all he could do to maintain a steady tone. "She was so antagonistic and demeaning I couldn't stand her."

"Detective, is there anything else that you wish to tell the court regarding this incident?"

"No, I think we covered it all."

"Okay, Detective, thank you." Dave said turning toward his chair. As he passed the plaintiff's table where Opal Hanover and her lawyer sat, he said, "Your witness," inviting Benedict to cross-examine.

Benedict stood up and approached the defendant's table. His smile reminded Mike of an animal stalking its prey.

"Detective Ryan," he began, "you're telling this court that you don't find my client in the least bit attractive?"

Mike answered straightforwardly. "I guess other men might find her not bad to look at, but she doesn't do anything for me."

"So you're telling the court that she doesn't appeal to you at all?"

"Yes, you heard me." Mike resisted asking Benedict if he was hard of hearing.

Benedict leaned forward, suddenly aggressive. "Aren't you in fact lying to this court? That you not only found her attractive, but you asked her out at your initial meeting? And when she turned you down, you became hostile and obstinate? Didn't you, in fact, barge into her office demanding that she go out with you? And when she refused you grabbed her, ripped her blouse off, and wrestled her to the floor!"

"What?" roared Mike. "That's a lie! I never touched her — she was coming on to me, and wouldn't take 'no' for an answer!"

"Your Honor," barked Dave, on his feet and striding toward the judge's bench, "Mr. Benedict is harassing my client. Maybe you could remind him that there is no jury present, so he need not act like he's Clarence Darrow."

"Thank you, Mr. Kennedy," responded the judge. "The court appreciates your procedural instructions.

But if you don't mind the court will try — without your assistance — to maintain order on its own."

Dave Kennedy turned on his heel and sat down again. Judge Roth turned to Benedict and cautioned, "Come on, Mr. Benedict, stop performing." Benedict, having taken a few unruffled steps backward, strolled again toward the witness box.

"Detective Ryan," he said, "accept my apologies. Maybe you can explain why Miss Hanover's blouse was torn that night."

"It wasn't torn when I left," said Michael.

"Oh," responded Benedict, "you claim that the blouse wasn't torn when you left. Detective Ryan, have you forgotten the eyewitness who saw you force yourself on my client? And when you saw him you ran?" Benedict again unleashed his sinister grin. He looked like a greedy fat guy eyeing a juicy porterhouse steak. Mike took a deep breath, hoping it would help him keep his temper and not pop this joker.

"Look, I don't know what you're talking about. There was never anyone else in the room, or anywhere else in the building that I know of. The only time I touched her was when I was trying to restrain her. I told you, she wouldn't take 'no' for an answer."

"You're still sticking to that story, Detective Ryan?" smiled Benedict.

"I am," asserted Mike, "because it's the truth. Maybe Miss Hanover could be desirable on some level, but I did not then, and do not now, have any interest in her at all."

Mike looked at Hanover. He was glad the court officer searched everyone coming into the courtroom for concealed weapons because, from the look on her face, if she had access to a gun she would have blown him away. His blood began to boil.

"And the guy who claims that he saw me" — Mike was starting to shout as Dave motioned to him to hold his tongue — "that guy must be a phantom because Ms. Hanover and I were the only ones left at the school. It was after seven o'clock at night, and no one else was there!" Mike's face was turning red.

"You have an explosive temper, Detective Ryan, haven't you?" asked Benedict.

"*Mis*-ter Benedict," said Judge Roth again, "before you start another line of questioning, we're going to adjourn. We'll resume these proceedings in two weeks; I need a vacation."

"But, Your Honor," protested Benedict, "this is a crucial part of our argument. You can't leave us hanging like this. My client needs closure. She has been through a terrible ordeal."

"So have I, Mr. Benedict, so have I." The judge reached for his gavel. "Case adjourned till May sixteenth at two o'clock. And, Mr. Benedict, I expect to hear testimony from your witness — the one so conspicuously absent today — at that time."

Hanover's reaction was something to see. The veins in her neck looked as though they were about to explode.

They all stood up as Judge Roth headed for his chambers. Mike tried to avoid Hanover as they both turned to leave.

"I'm going to get you, you despicable degenerate," she hissed through clenched teeth. Mike ignored her and turned away. She grabbed him and spun him around as she screamed, "You're not going to get away with violating me, Detective!" She was seething with anger.

Dave stepped between Hanover and Mike. "Hey, Sam, how about controlling your client?" he said.

"I'm sorry," intoned Benedict, "but this case really has Miss Hanover overwrought."

"If she's interested in some peace then why doesn't she just drop this ridiculous suit? Everyone, including Roth, believes her charges are bogus," said Kennedy.

Hanover stuck her face in Dave's. "That sex fiend has to be punished. If I had my way, I'd put that monster behind bars and throw away the key."

"Sam, this woman needs help," Dave said as he grabbed Mike by the arm and pulled him toward the courthouse steps. They took Kennedy's car and drove to a coffee shop on Mineola Boulevard. After they sat down and placed their order, Dave said: "Brother-in-law, don't get peeved, but are you sure no one else was in the building besides Hanover and you?"

Mike was as calm as can be. "Not unless you're counting mice and rats."

"Mike, be serious."

"Hey, man, joking around is the only way I can keep my sanity, otherwise I'd go Dog Day Afternoon. Then you'll really have a case to defend, not this phony case, this total waste of time. In answer to your question, to the best of my knowledge, Hanover and I were the only two people at the school."

Dave heaved a sigh and continued. "We have to see if anyone else was scheduled to be at the building at that time of night."

"If indeed there was — and I'm not changing my story — then it could only be a janitor or some cleaning crew."

"Well, we have to find out for sure. Though Hanover appears to be a nut case, she's too shrewd to just manufacture a witness. Anyway, we've got two weeks to find out."

Dave paid the check and Mike walked him to his car. They agreed to keep in touch.

Chapter 25

Mike was back at the precinct the next morning. He wanted to forget about Opal Hanover and allow that mess to take its course. He couldn't do anything about it, anyway, so why should he obsess over something over which he had no control?

He wished he could apply that philosophy across the board. He couldn't help obsessing over Peggy, and no matter how hard he tried he couldn't erase her from his thoughts. His desk faced hers. Each time he looked up from his paperwork, he would envision her there. In his mind's eye he could still see the peculiar way she would tilt her head when she was deep in thought about a case. But, she wasn't there anymore. Only the pain remained with the memory.

There was one good thing about the Hanover mess; it did distract him for a few hours. But that was only temporary. Every time he pulled into the precinct parking lot Peggy's face and smile would flood his mind anew.

The spring flowers blooming in the next two weeks might as well have been dead leaves for all Mike noticed. As Peggy healed, Mike's pain grew worse. The time at the precinct, shackled to his desk, was pure torture; the sight of her empty desk seemed to suck the life out of him. At mealtimes he would stop at their favorite breakfast and lunch places, but he wouldn't go in; a hollow knot seemed permanently lodged in his stomach and he had no appetite. His interest in other things was practically nil. He didn't even watch baseball anymore.

He spent less time with Jamie and more time sitting in his room staring at the wall. His ebbing interest in life had his mother worried sick. She had never seen him like this before. Even after Katie's death he wasn't this bad.

No matter what assignments he was given, his performance was sub par. There were only two cases he had any interest in, the ones relating to the only two women he ever loved. He made a decision. He marched into Dunbar's office.

"Lieutenant," said Mike, "this desk detail is making me nuts. You have to put me back on the street. Let me start working on cases again. I can't stand this."

"You've got some nerve, Ryan," Dunbar smirked. "You're the one who decided to play footsy with the woman from your kid's school. You're lucky you still have a job. If it was up to me you'd be gone, but because you're still in the preliminary stages of your hearing I can only take you off the street for now. I can't wait for them to formally indict you so I'll be rid of you. Now get out of my office and get back to work."

Mike's anger flared, but as he opened his mouth to blast Dunbar, his cell phone rang. He stormed out of Dunbar's office. "Ryan," he growled into the phone.

"Mike." it was David Kennedy's voice. "I'm glad I could reach you."

"Yeah, what's up?" Mike answered. Tomorrow was the date for the next hearing.

"Mike, you sound down. Well, this should cheer you up. I have some good news.

"I could use some good news," Mike interrupted. "What's going on?"

"Opal Hanover dropped the charges!"

"She did? Why?"

"All I know is that Sam Benedict called me and told me they were dropping the charges. He didn't say why. Don't look a gift horse in the mouth, man, just be glad."

"Well, thanks, that is good news. Thanks for letting me know. I have to get back to work. I'll talk to you." Mike hung up. He felt relieved, but his emotions fell far short of elation. He still felt uneasy. He had to save what energy he had for Dunbar.

He marched back into Dunbar's office.

"What do you want, Ryan? I thought I made myself perfectly clear. Get back to work!"

"Lieutenant," said Mike," I just got word that Opal Hanover's charges against me have been dropped."

"Well, that's news to me. I haven't heard anything," shrugged Dunbar.

"My lawyer just called and told me. You should be getting official notification shortly."

"I don't believe it. And even if it is true, so what?"

Mike clenched his jaw. "So, I want you to take me off desk duty and put me back on the street, like

I said before. You have no reason to keep me inside now."

Dunbar didn't look happy. "When I get a clearance from Internal Affairs I'll let you know. Until then, get back to what you were assigned to: desk duty."

Mike knew that arguing would just make matters worse. He would just have to wait for Internal Affairs to process the matter.

It didn't take long. An hour later, Dunbar was at Mike's desk. "I just got the call from Internal Affairs. You're officially reinstated," Dunbar said, and turned to leave.

"Wait a minute, Lieutenant, what about my assignment?"

"What about it?" Dunbar said. "What do you want?"

"Anything but this! C'mon, Lieutenant, put me back on the Steele case. It's getting cold, and nobody knows it better than me and Peggy. Since she's still out, I'm your best bet to solve it, and that will take the heat off you."

"I'll check what cases are open and I'll let you know," Dunbar said over his shoulder as he walked away.

Mike really didn't care whether the Steele case got solved or not. What he really wanted to find out was who had engineered the attempt on Peggy's life, and — since he was convinced the two were somehow related — who halted the investigation of Katie's murder. The key to both, he thought, was somehow intertwined with the Steele case, so that's what he had to go back to.

He wanted to find out more about Billy Kensey. Peggy knew the various suspects very well, and she had taken meticulous notes of all their interviews. Mike walked over to her desk and sat down.

Partners, who trust each other have no secrets between them, not even their computer passwords. Mike logged in, clicked onto Peggy's documents and opened the case folder marked "Steele." He opened Billy Kensey's file containing Peggy's detailed notes. Though Mike only knew Tamara Steele through Peggy, he had to agree with her assessment — a class act like Tamara marrying a low-life like Kensey was completely out of character. It didn't make sense. What did she see in him? As he continued to study the file he felt someone standing behind him. He looked up.

Dunbar was there with a young man in his early to mid-twenties. He held what appeared to be a personnel file in his hand. "Detective Ryan," he said, "meet Carl Banning, your new partner."

Mike stood up and shook the guy's hand, an automatic reflex. Then the lieutenant's words sank in.

"Lieutenant," he protested, "Peg will be back on the job in the matter of days."

"Yeah, well, I'm putting you back on the Steele case. Carl is going to assist you."

Mike sat very still and said, "No offense, Carl, but I'd rather work alone. I don't need or want another partner."

It was like a steam pipe had burst in Dunbar's head. "Ryan, when are you going to realize that I'm the lieutenant? When I tell you something, it's not a suggestion! Nassau County PD doesn't really care about your opinions or thoughts on how things should be done. What they care about is that you obey the orders you receive from the chain of command. Since you are a member of this squad, you are to obey your lieutenant. And since I'm the lieutenant, you have to conform to and obey my orders! *Do I make myself clear?"*

Mike didn't feel like sparring with Dunbar. There wasn't any payoff in butting heads with him. He just let the dead silence linger.

"Nothing to say, Ryan?"

Mike decided to just ignore Dunbar. He said to Banning, "Okay, Carl, you might as well sit at Detective Younger's desk until she comes back from sick leave."

Dunbar flashed an exaggerated grin. "Oh, and Ryan, I neglected to tell you, Younger isn't coming back; she put in for a transfer. I guess she got tired of your Irish charm."

Mike couldn't have been more shocked if Dunbar had sucker-punched him. He remembered Peggy telling him she was going to ask for a transfer, but he didn't think she would actually do it. He couldn't believe she would completely remove him from her life.

Satisfied that he had finally managed to ruin Mike's day, Dunbar left him with his new partner.

"Okay, Mike," said Banning congenially, "what are we working on?"

Mike immediately resented Banning. *Some nerve — he's not here two minutes and it's already "we"! Not so fast, Buddy!*

Mike calmed himself and said, "You've heard about the Tamara Steele murder?"

"I think I read something about it in *Newsday* a while back."

Boy, this guy is gonna be a great help, thought Mike.

Mike went over to the file cabinet and threw the Tamara Steele case file on the desk.

"Here read this," he ordered coolly, and went back to reading Peggy's notes on Kensey. From its contents, he guessed love was blind. After the honeymoon was over and reality set in, Kensey must have been an embarrassment to Tamara at the few religious functions he attended with her.

"Man, what was with your ex-partner?" asked Banning casually.

"You mean Peggy, my partner? Why, what's wrong?"

"Yeah, whatever," said Banning. "Her desk is full of all these religious pictures and Bibles and things. They give me the creeps. There's no room for any of my stuff." He tossed one of Peggy's books from a drawer onto her desk.

"Look, give me Peg's things. If they bug you that much, I'll take care of them."

Mike didn't bother to wipe the scowl off his face as Carl wearily handed him the rest of Peggy's belongings.

"I'm going to visit Billy Kensey. That'll give you plenty of time to organize your stuff," Mike said briskly, turning away.

"Hey, Ryan, cut me some slack, I was just assigned to this unit."

Mike thought about it. "You're right, I'm sorry. Why don't you stay here and get acquainted with the case. I'll see you later."

Banning grumbled, "Yeah, whatever."

Mike was glad Banning didn't press it further; he wanted to be alone. He was getting into his car when he remembered he wanted to check something about Kensey on the Internet. He was grateful that he didn't have to go back to his desk; his laptop was in the trunk. As he got out of the driver's seat to retrieve it, he saw her — Peggy.

A lump rose up in his throat, and he tried to duck into his car, but it was too late. Their eyes met and he knew it would be impossible to avoid her. He didn't know if he could take the pain.

He hadn't seen her in two and a half weeks. Although she limped a little, you would never know she had lain swathed in bandages such a short time before. She really looked pretty. But while she brought joy to his eyes, his heart and mind were racing in different directions.

"Michael!" Forgetting her injuries, she started to run towards him and almost stumbled. She slowed down. When she reached Mike she gave him a soft kiss on the check. His stomach became hollow. He remembered feeling that way when he received a harmless kiss from the first girl he ever had a crush on when he was a kid. How could something so innocent elicit such a response?

"Hey, kid, you look great. It's as if you were never down," he said.

"The Lord is so good, Michael. He really placed His healing hand on me."

Here she goes again — "the Lord" in every thought and every sentence. I guess, since she shared her feelings and her faith with me the last time we talked, she thinks it's all out on the table, so she doesn't need to restrain herself any more. Or maybe it's the transfer — no longer any need for restraint, nothing left to lose.

"How are Jamie and your mother?"

"Mom is okay. . . and you know Jamie."

"And you, Michael, how are you doing?"

"Things are moving along. You know, busy; same ol' same ol'."

"Michael, I've been thinking about you and praying for you constantly." Peggy lowered her eyes, then raised them to meet his. "Michael, I miss you."

"I thought you were relieved, not having to see this ugly face," he said, the mask of humor ever ready to hide the pain.

She smiled sadly. "Michael, can't you be serious for one moment?"

Seeing her expression change, he said slowly: "Peggy, I was serious the last time we spoke. Remember what it got me?"

She looked down at the asphalt. "Michael, I can't help it. Though I'm in love with you, we can't have a relationship until we're on the same page about God. It would always be a wedge between us."

"I want you in my life so bad I can taste it. But if I say that this Jesus is the most important thing in my life just to convince you to be my wife, it would be a lie. It would be a mockery of you, and of our love — and even of Him. I can't do that to you — to us."

She looked up at him. "Michael, can't we go somewhere and talk? I have to explain more about what Jesus has been doing in my life and what he means to me. Maybe it will help you understand."

"No, Peg, what would be the point? We did that already and. . . and. . ." Openness and honesty about his emotions were not his strong suit. Time to change the subject. "Besides, I'm on my way to take another crack at Kensey."

"Couldn't you see him another time? This is important."

"Peg, I'm surprised that you expect me to shirk my responsibilities just to have a cup of coffee with you," he grinned.

"Michael, please. I love you!"

"But Peg, there's a condition on your love. No, Peg, I can't see it. I'd better get going now."

Mike felt her eyes follow him as he left her in the parking lot. He wished he could accept this Jesus she kept harping about, but he couldn't just say he did and not mean it. He couldn't understand or define it, but there was a certain integrity in his character that he could not violate, even for her.

He thought he was gradually getting over her, that Jamie and the Hanover mess had all but erased her from his mind. But seeing her just now revealed how much he had been lying to himself. The image of her was etched in the forefront of his mind just as it had always been. She was asking too much. What she demanded was faith, and he couldn't give what he didn't have.

Chapter 26

When Mike rang Billy Kensey's doorbell a woman answered. She was just as flamboyant as Kensey's former love interest. Although she didn't appear to be high, she was just as giddy as her predecessor.

"Detective Ryan here to see Billy Kensey."

"Billy," she shouted over her shoulder, "a Detective Ryan to see you." She led him inside.

"Hey, Ryan, give me a break. What do you want?"

Though it was only two in the afternoon, Billy was already in pajamas — or maybe still in pajamas — and he looked as if he had every intention of frittering away the rest of the day with his plaything. Again, he was high on something.

"I missed you," Mike said. "I don't see you on MTV anymore, and I haven't heard your latest CD on the radio lately. Looks like your career is still in the dumper. I don't know if I can survive the culture deprivation."

Kensey sneered. "Man, I don't know what you're talking about; the kids are buying my music, and I get bags and bags of letters and tons of e-mails from my fans."

"That's not what I hear."

"Detective, tell me, why are you harassing me? You know I can make your life a living

h—l if you don't stop bugging me."

"Gee, pal, am I harassing you? I thought we were having a nice chat. I'm your most loyal fan. But I just want to know something. I think I read somewhere that you'd asked your wife for a loan, and she turned you down. In fact, wasn't Tamara always refusing to give you money for — what did she call it. . . your many hare-brained schemes?"

"I don't know what you're talking about. Tamara and I had an ideal marriage."

Kensey called to his new "friend" and clicked the ice cubes in his glass as if signaling a barmaid for another drink. She understood.

"Kensey," said Mike impatiently, "you're either lying to me or whatever you're drinking has made you oblivious to reality. Isn't it a fact that Tamara was threatening to divorce you if you didn't stop your extracurricular activities?"

"That's a bald-faced lie. Where did you get that garbage?"

"It's all over the trade papers and some of your friends have been telling reporters about your downward spiral."

"And you call yourself a cop," laughed Kensey. "If you depend on the media and the Internet to solve cases, you're in deep trouble."

"Who said anything about the Internet? I got my information from more reliable sources — your friends."

Kensey bit his lower lip. "They're all just jealous of me. They always were."

"Oh, yeah, you are the envy of the entertainment world. A lot of people say you argued with your wife all the time."

Kensey shook his head dismissively. "Ryan, be serious, every couple argues at some point in their marriage. It wouldn't be a normal relationship without some spirited differences of opinion."

"But I hear that they were so spirited they stopped just short of coming to blows."

"That is preposterous; where is your proof?"

"We don't have much right now, but we do have plenty of motive," warned Mike.

"You're grasping at straws. You have nothing and you're wasting my time." Kensey turned away to stare out the window.

Mike went on the attack. "Well, for starters, Mr. Kensey, you're broke. During your marriage to Tamara, you acquired some pretty expensive habits. I hear you like to play the ponies and poker, but you're not very good at either. In fact, I heard you lost $1.5 million that you didn't have, and the people holding your markers are not very patient. And when you asked Tamara to cover your debt, she refused, didn't she? Maybe it was because of all the ladies that occupied your spare time. Was that it? She didn't like your girlfriends?"

"Ryan, are you going to arrest me for something? If so, I'll call my lawyer. If not, then get the h—l out of here, I'm busy."

"Oh, yeah, I see how engrossed you are in your work," Mike said, looking at the blond turning the page of a Victoria's Secret catalog. "If I were you I wouldn't be taking any long trips. Okay Billy, we'll keep in touch."

Chapter 27

Michael and Katie had fostered a tremendous self-esteem in Jamie. Katie was sure everyone would ignore his deficiencies because of his wonderful personality.

On the rare occasions when the neighborhood gang allowed him to hang around with them, it was only for their amusement. Jamie didn't care; he wanted so much to belong that he chose to interpret their derision as some form of acceptance.

Mike tried to talk to Jamie about this method of choosing friends. His approach only resulted in conflict. Again, he had to impose a week's curfew on Jamie because of his low grades.

"Jamie," he said that Friday afternoon, "why don't you invite some of your friends from school to come over tomorrow? Maybe we can have a little party or something."

Hope lit Jamie's eyes. "Can we invite the guys?"

"You mean those neighborhood punks? They're the reason for your lousy grades and stinking attitude. No, I don't think so."

The boy started to sulk.

"Well, kid, how about your friends in school?"

"I don't hang with cripples."

Mike's eyebrows rose. "Jamie, that's a little hard."

"If you were real, you would agree with me," retorted Jamie. "Forget the stupid party idea. I'm going upstairs."

After school on Monday, Jamie sneaked out to meet the gang, hoping they would let him hang out with them.

"Hey, Jamie," said a boy named Bobby, "all the guys want to go to Roger's. You wanna come?"

Jamie couldn't believe Bobby was inviting him. Bobby was always so cool and so funny; and he was the leader of the gang. Until then Bobby was a major cause of Jamie's depression, because he always called Jamie a dork and made fun of the way he *talked.*

Jamie was so excited that his mind reeled and his heart soared. He was accepted! That meant he was now normal — like them! He believed nothing in his life could go wrong again. He was elated.

He knew his father would be really mad.

Heartsick, Jamie said, "Guys, I can't go. Roger's is two miles away. If my father finds out I went there I'll be grounded for a week." He wasn't about to tell anyone he had already been grounded, and he certainly wasn't going to tell them they were the reason.

"Come on, buddy, how is he going to find out?" Bobby asked.

"Believe me, he'll find out. He has his men all over."

"Come on." Bobby's voice was mildly derisive. "Are you chicken?"

"I just don't want to get in trouble."

Bobby shrugged. "I guess the guys were right. You're too much of a baby to join the Spiders."

"You mean you want me to be in the Spiders?"

"We did before you went all girly on us. Go ahead, do whatever some dumb cop tells you to do, just because he's your father." Bobby taunted.

Jamie resented Bobby calling his father dumb, but he wasn't going to risk alienating himself just to defend his father. Not now. Too much was at stake.

"I'll go with you, but let me tell my grandmother."

"There you go again, being chicken. By the time you go home and come back it'll be too late. Either you want to be a Spider or you don't. Make up your mind."

"Okay, count me in."

It took an hour for the boys to amble over to Roger's Sporting Goods. Once inside the store the gang went wild, knocking items off the shelves, toppling over displays and screaming throughout the store. Jamie was frightened, so he headed for the baseball department.

Bobby ran by and ducked behind the rack of jackets next to Jamie. "What are you doing?" he snarled.

"Hey, Bobby, isn't this a cool mitt?" Jamie replied.

"Take it."

"Nah, I don't have any money. Anyway, I have a glove already."

Bobby's lip curled. "Who said anything about money? Just put it under your jacket and walk out of here."

"That would be stealing!"

"What? Did your cop daddy tell you that? Look, if you really want to be a Spider, you have to steal; we all steal."

Jamie thought, *I'm so close.* He could be a member of the Spiders. How could he back out now? He saw the other members of the gang running for the exit, each clutching an unbagged item. A red-faced manager pursued them, shouting for them to stop.

Jamie picked up the glove and also headed for the exit, trying to stay on the carpeted areas so his braces wouldn't thump too loudly. By the time he got out the door his partners in crime were already a block away. Suddenly he felt a strong hand on his shoulder.

"You're in deep trouble, son."

After spending the day perusing files in various Nassau County departments, Mike arrived back at his desk a little after five. His new partner was still organizing his desk. Mike sighed as he flopped into his chair.

"What's shakin' bacon," Carl said, looking up and taking a break from arranging his various knickknacks.

What's with this guy? Probably spends his evenings watching Nick at Nite.

"Nothing much," Mike replied, "just trying to solve a couple of murders to earn my paycheck."

"How'd it go with what's his name?"

"You mean *Kensey, William Kensey*," Mike rolled his eyes.

Mike's phone rang. "Eighth Precinct, Detective Ryan."

"Michael? Michael, it's Mom. I don't know what to do, I'm so upset. I didn't watch him."

"Mom, calm down, take a deep breath. Tell me what happened. Take your time."

"It's Jamie. He's in serious trouble."

Mike wasn't ready to panic. He'd had this conversation before. His mother always exaggerated when it came to Jamie.

"Mom, is he hurt?"

"No, he isn't hurt."

"Was he in a fight at school again?"

"No, but. . ."

"But what? Tell me what happened!" He felt himself losing his patience with her.

"He was in Roger's Sporting Goods Store."

"Mom, that's 2 miles from the house. What the h—l was he doing all the way over there? You not supposed to let him out of your sight."

"Michael, I try to watch him but he gets away from me." She started to cry.

He felt a little sorry for his mother. Maybe he gave her too much responsibility. She always took everything so seriously; she always felt everything was a matter of life and death.

"Mom, stop crying and please tell me, what happened to Jamie?"

"He got caught shoplifting." She started crying again.

"Mom, it's okay. Stop crying, you'll get sick. Why don't you take a couple of aspirins, make yourself a cup of tea? Put your feet up and relax, watch the TV or something." She finally composed herself and hung up.

Mike figured that Jamie was at the Thirteenth Precinct in Bellmore. It took him twenty minutes to get to the station. He went to the desk officer.

"Excuse me, you have a Jamie Ryan. I believe he's charged with shoplifting."

The officer chuckled. "The kid is too young to lawyer-up. Besides, I wouldn't quite call him a hardened criminal. I don't think his picture's going to make the post office."

Mike smiled and took out his shield.

"Oh, excuse me, Detective; I didn't know you were family. I think the owner of the store is a real creep to press charges on a cripple."

If Mike was there for any other reason than to pick up Jamie, he would have taught the officer the politically correct way to describe a person with a disability. Though he didn't buy most of the liberal nonsense spread by the media, he did resent how society still looked down on the disabled. But Mike was too tired to get on a soapbox. *Once he gets beyond his problems, Jamie will become a person to be reckoned with in his own right. He won't need me to run interference for him.*

"Is the arresting officer available?" he sighed.

"Yes, Officer McShane is in the squad room; I'll get him."

Five minutes went by and Mike saw Jamie coming through the double doors of the detention room. He looked even more handicapped than usual. Any tense situation caused him to be more spastic. The patrolman held his arm, making him more off balance.

Though Mike was disappointed that Jamie would do such a stupid thing as shoplift, he didn't want this experience to be so traumatic that it would crush his spirit.

"Hey, kid," he said without anger, "this is the last place I thought I'd see you."

Jamie only looked down at the floor, continuing to hang his head, ashamed to look at his father.

The patrolman brought Mike and Jamie to an empty desk.

"Detective Ryan, where do you turn out?"

"I work out of the Eighth in Mineola."

"Oh, I heard that you people have a pretty heavy caseload right now."

"Yeah, we're keeping busy." Mike appreciated that Patrolman McShane wanted to sugar-coat an embarrassing situation, but all Mike wanted was to speak to Jamie and find out the details from the boy's own lips.

Mike stared at his son. Jamie still hung his head and his eyes remained downcast. Mike knelt on one knee and lifted his son's head. He looked sadly into Jamie's face, not understanding what he saw.

"Jamie, could you tell me what happened?"

Jamie looked away. Something was strange about him. Mike expected his son to be embarrassed. Instead the youth seemed defiant, almost hostile. His head was cocked to one side and he seemed to be looking for a fight — and his opponent was Mike.

"Come on, Jamie, look at me. I want to hear your story. What happened?"

"Nothing happened."

"What do you mean nothing happened? Did you or did you not steal a baseball glove?"

"So I took a baseball glove. What's the big deal?"

"What's the big deal? The big deal is that you broke the law and took something that didn't belong to you. I bought you a first baseman's glove only three weeks ago. Jamie, this is crazy. I don't get it, son. You know that stealing is wrong — and you have a glove. But you had to steal another one?"

"All you care about is your stupid law."

Mike sat stunned. The patrolman looked awkwardly away, not sure what to say. He finally broke the silence.

"Detective, he was with a bunch of other kids in the store, and I think they were egging him on. Besides, the owner is a chronic complainer. I don't know why he felt the need to press charges against your son. Detective, let's be serious. . ." He motioned toward Jamie's leg braces.

Mike looked wearily at the officer.

"Look, officer, I know you're trying to help, but Jamie knows he's committed a crime, and the owner of the store has a perfect right to press charges. My son has been taught that he's responsible for his actions and must face the consequences." The patrolman gave him a peculiar stare.

"What's the next move?" Mike asked.

The patrolman caught on that Mike wanted to teach his son a lesson, so he followed his lead.

"Well, now your son will get a date to appear in juvenile court, where he will go before a judge. The case is pretty much open and shut. After he's found guilty he'll be sentenced."

Mike and Jamie were silent on the way home. Mike was disturbed that Jamie didn't show any remorse. He merely stared out the window. Mike couldn't fathom Jamie's sudden anger. In Mike's early years on the beat he'd run into kids who felt the need to steal. There were always reasons for it — a kid could be crying out for help, coming from a broken home, rebelling, or just downright rotten. But Mike knew that basically Jamie was a good kid. What had gotten into Jamie's head? What was bugging him? *It's those neighborhood punks, I know it,* thought Mike.

The last few years Jamie always seemed to be in some sort of minor trouble. First it was beating up on kids at school, and now it was shoplifting. A shrink would probably claim that he was crying out because he missed his mother. Well, life is hard. Jamie had to learn how to deal with disappointments; there would be plenty of them. That's life.

Mike knew that Peggy and Katie both would have read him the riot act for being so hard, cold and pig-headed, but it was for Jamie's own good.

Even before Jamie gets up to swing the bat he has two strikes against him. He won't always have his grandmother or me to run to. He lost his mother and from the way things are going, he may also lose a father.

Mike let the matter drop for the evening. Jamie ate supper and ascended the stairs to his room in silence. Mike knew that he had to have a talk with

Jamie, but it would have to wait. Right now he had to attend to his new partner, Carl Banning. If he had learned anything in fifteen years as a cop, it was that you'd better watch your back.

Chapter 28

When he got to work Tuesday morning, Mike walked up to the desk officer and asked, "Hey, Mack, you seen Carl Banning?"

"Ryan, it's not my job to keep tabs on your partner."

"C'mon pal, give me a break! I just asked you a simple question; you don't have to bite my head off." *Has everybody suddenly gone nuts? Seems like the whole world has their shorts on too tight.*

The officer was suddenly embarrassed. He looked down at his paperwork and mumbled, "No, I didn't see him."

Mike went to his desk. He looked around the room for Dunbar. He breathed a sigh of relief when he saw the lieutenant tongue lashing a rookie in his office. Poor kid; but better him than me.

Although he was officially back on the Tamara Steele case, he was more comfortable investigating the evangelist's murder without Dunbar looking over his shoulder. There were too many loose ends in this case. Mike didn't think that jealousy could be the motive since he hadn't uncovered any love interest that would account for it.

So what was the motive? Revenge? Edmund Steele was a very wealthy man and, like most wealthy men, he had probably left a lot of casualties amongst the people he climbed over on the road to success. There's never a shortage of enemies for wealthy men. Kill the daughter for vengeance against the father? That might be worth exploring. But where to start?

Could someone in the County Seat have a vendetta against Edmund Steele? It wasn't unusual for some county official's hand to be in the pocket of major corporate wheelers and dealers on Long Island. It was a way of life; it was how business was done. If the business owners didn't cooperate with an official's greed, they often found themselves facing insurmountable roadblocks to their building projects. Payoffs were the path of least resistance — they greased the wheels of progress. Mike would start there and see where it might lead.

Mike typed Edmund Steele's name into an Internet search engine. It was amazing how much information was out there on everyone and everything. He found an article that pegged the old man's worth at upwards of $85 million, the majority of his fortune having been earned in real estate and building construction.

Scrolling down the Internet piece, he clicked a link to a *New York Times* article from several years ago. It chronicled a feud between Edmund Steele and one of his biggest competitors at the time, George Winthrop. Winthrop submitted a winning bid on a $20 million county road project. The newspapers had already run an article announcing the award, but two days before the contract was to be signed, Steele persuaded certain county legislators that Winthrop was facing "possible labor disputes that might jeopardize the project's deadline." The legislators awarded the contract to one of Steele's subsidiaries instead. Winthrop contested the award, charging corruption on the part of the legislators. The case was thrown out of court. That commenced a long and bitter feud between the two rivals.

Could Winthrop be behind the murders? Mike had nothing he could hang his hat on. He couldn't find a direct link from Tamara to Winthrop — another apparent dead end. That was the nature of police work: find leads and run them down; often they went nowhere.

Could the politicos at county somehow be related to the murders? He knew in his gut that something was rotten up at county. But what was the connection? His conspiracy theory was just that — a theory. He had no hard evidence, only jumbled pieces of a jigsaw puzzle that he couldn't put together.

Mike's suspicion of shady deals in the county offices had started with the cover-up of Katie's murder. It seemed like every elected county official wanted to sweep it under the rug. He couldn't believe that, in spite of all the sophisticated technology and information sources available, they could find nothing at all on the kid that killed her — no prior arrests, no juvenile court records, not so much as a complaint from a neighbor about a broken window. Nothing. Kids don't go from clean as a whistle straight to armed robbery and murder.

Another thing that somehow pointed to the people at county being behind the scenes, at least in Mike's mind, was the murder of Howard Carey, the County Medical Examiner. It had been strange and brutal. It had all the makings of a sensational story, yet it got very little coverage in the newspapers. They could have run the story for days on page 3, yet nothing was reported after they published the initial piece the day after he was murdered, and that appeared on page 7. After that the press was silent. Why the cover-ups? There had to be a connection, but what?

Chapter 29

Banning's sudden return after lunch from parts unknown snapped Mike back into the present. It may have been his imagination, but he could swear he smelled weed on Banning as he brushed by.

"Hey Banning, are you up to speed on the Tamara Steele case?"

Banning loosened his tie, took out a video game from his pocket and placed his feet on his desk. He didn't even look at Mike. He just said, "No, I haven't had a chance," and started playing the game.

The hairs on the back of Mike's neck stood up.

"Well," he said with obvious annoyance, "now is as good a time as any. There are a lot of details to sort out."

"Don't worry about it, I'm a quick study. I'll get to it when I have time," Banning finally responded.

Again, no eye contact. Banning was ignoring him, as if taking orders was a foreign concept to him. He just sat and played his video game, resentment written all over his face.

Mike's nose began to itch, which meant his nose for trouble was sounding a siren. There was something screwy about Banning. He was maybe twenty-two or twenty-three years old, and fresh from the academy. He couldn't be on the job more than a year. How could he possibly have made detective that fast, especially with his attitude? A rookie as green as Banning should be chomping at the bit for the opportunity to partner with a seasoned cop. Mike stared at him as he sat punching buttons on his handheld game. *I could take his head off right now, but there's enough junk to deal with at the moment. I'll have to straighten him out some other time.*

"Get up, Banning, we're going to interview Julian Giles."

"Who the h—l is Julian Giles?"

"You know, Banning, if you'd read the file you'd know who he is."

"Hey, Ryan, when did they promote you to lieutenant? Did I miss something?"

Mike was ready to pop him. *Okay Mike, calm or kill?* Pick one. He chose calm.

"Look Carl, maybe we got off on the wrong foot. Whatever it is, you can't let it interfere with the job, so let it go. Let me explain the situation with this Steele case. It has been hanging around for a long time, and the higher-ups want it to go away as quickly as possible. I need you to take up some of the slack in this investigation. Understand?"

"Now I see why your partner wanted out. I bet you two were doing more than writing traffic tickets together. But since you're such a jerk, I wouldn't be surprised if you manhandled her. Is that what happened? Did you freak out and scare her so much she had to bail out? Is that why she requested a transfer? Well, buddy, if you think you can push me around like you did your girlfriend, you better think again. "

Mike struggled to keep the lid on. "You're really pushing it, pal."

"What are you going to do, curtail my bathroom privileges? It's not my fault that your girlfriend doesn't have the hots for you anymore. You know how lady cops are — they get bored. They do their thing with one cop, get bored and hook up with another, make the rounds. I bet she has quite a rap sheet with half the precinct."

Mike's hand flew across the desk, grabbing Banning's tie and lifting him from his seat. He slammed Banning down on the desk with a loud thud and the chair flew into a file cabinet with a crash. He jumped on Banning and cocked his clenched fist. Strong hands grabbed his arm before he could let it fly.

Three detectives had run in from the next room when they heard the commotion. They pulled Mike off Banning, and a cop named John Paulson hustled him to the other side of the room.

"Ryan, what's with you? I hear you've been losing it lately. What's going on?"

Paulson was a friend. He worked with Mike at the Twenty-Seventh in New Castle. He had been Mike's partner before Peggy. They made a good team; they covered each other's back.

Mike was breathing hard. "Man, it's too bad you pulled me off that little weasel. I was about to rearrange Junior's face."

"Yeah, that's what I was afraid of. Carl Banning isn't worth a suspension," Paulson said, releasing Mike as soon as he thought it was safe to do so.

"I've got to get out of here or I might kill him. C'mon, John, I'll buy you a drink."

"My shift is almost over. Give me five minutes, okay, Mike?"

"Okay." Mike really did appreciate it. "I'll meet you at Denny's Reef down at the wharf."

Forty minutes later their cars were parked facing the huge yachts moored in the Massapequa Channel. It was already early afternoon, but the wharf was relatively deserted. Inside Denny's Reef there were only three men at the bar, sipping their drinks as they focused their attention on the large flat-screen TV mounted on the wall.

Mike and Paulson seated themselves at a table in the corner. The muffled sound of the CNN afternoon broadcast could be heard as the bartender approached their table. Although he looked annoyed, he spoke affably enough: "Gentleman, what can I get you?"

"Scotch and water for me," Mike said. "What about you, Johnny?"

"I'll have a Coke."

"Coke! Are you serious? What happened to the Jack Daniels?"

"I stopped drinking." Paulson took out a pack of gum, offering a stick to Mike.

Mike waved it away.

"Stopped drinking? That's the final omen. Now the earth is going to collide with Mars — I just know it!" He smiled. "You had the dubious distinction of being the hardest drinker in the NCPD. This will ruin your reputation! What the h—l. happened? You got religion or something?"

The bartender brought their order. Mike sucked his drink down in one gulp, and ordered another.

"I guess you can call it that," Paulson replied.

"Come on, man, you've get to be kidding."

"Mike, my life was a mess." Mike had never seen John Paulson look so serious. Paulson stared into space for a moment, then looked back at Mike and said, "Do you know I was so low that I was scoring coke from a perp? If that wasn't stupid enough, I piled on a huge gambling debt. It had gotten so bad that Julie took the kids to Ohio to stay with her Mom and Dad. Thank God she had a change of heart and agreed to come back to this area and work things out with me. We hope to reconcile."

"John," said Mike wonderingly, "I always thought you were crazy, but I never knew you to be out of control."

"Pal, I drank away all my money and I was in hock up to my ears. Then I decided that gambling was the way to get out from under the heap of debt I was buried in. I convinced myself that I was doing it for Julie and the kids.

"I found myself in an even worse stranglehold. I thought everything would be fine if I could only score big — pull a royal flush, roll a lucky seven or maybe the wheel would smile on me — then it would be all right. Money was going to solve all my problems and everything would work out. The mighty buck was going to be the cure-all. Boy, was I wrong. Instead of getting better, the monkey on my back just got bigger. My wife and kids were suffering from the strain. My marriage was already on the rocks. And the gambling that I thought was going to be the solution was the thing that finally pushed it over the edge and into the dumper. Yet I still thought all I needed was one big score. Then I could control everything — and everyone." He laughed sardonically. "I wanted to play God. It took me a long time to realize that."

"I don't understand," said Mike. "What do you mean, you wanted to play God? Hey, what's wrong with wanting a heap of money? Cops don't usually make the Fortune 500 list, so we find inventive ways to make more cash. You just went about it in the wrong way. It backfired on you."

"But, Mike," said John urgently, "it was more than wanting to provide for Julie and the kids, more than the drugs and the gambling and the women. I was dead inside! Now I realize that I was trying to use those things as band-aids to cover the wounds — the wounds that I didn't know, or at least couldn't admit, I had."

"What wounds? What the h—l are you talking about?" Mike used to think that Paulson was the coolest guy on the force, the guy who had it all, and could do it all. Now he sounded like a wimp.

"My inadequacy, man! I disappointed everyone! It was like a gaping hole in me. No matter how I tried to cover it up, it was there!"

John stared down into his Coke, remembering. "My parents had always wanted more for me. They wanted me to go into law. I was supposed to marry someone whose parents were members of the Garden City Country Club, so we could make perfect little grandkids for our folks to brag about. That was my parents' dream, and when I joined the force it broke their hearts. I felt they were ashamed of me."

Mike snorted empathetically. “Hey, my mom wasn’t too keen on my career choice either.”

John looked surprised. “Mike, no one ever tells you what to do. You always make up your own mind.”

“Well. . .” Mike didn’t want to go into his own problems. He wanted to hear more from John. “You said you’ve gotten your act together. Tell me, how did you manage to do that?”

“Things went from bad to worse,” said John. “I was in way over my head, snorting more and more coke, and losing more and more at the card table. It got so bad that the guys holding my markers were going to my house and threatening Julie and the kids. I couldn’t do anything; if I turned the sharks in it would bring everything out into the open and I would have been thrown off the force. Then what would I do? I didn’t know where to turn, so I got myself a bunch of coke and three bottles of Jack, and I headed out to the North Fork. Great plan, right?

“When I got to the outskirts of Sag Harbor, I stopped at some hell hole of a motel. I locked the door, took out my stash and proceeded to drink and snort snow up my nose. I did more lines of coke than I can remember. I should be dead.

"Somehow, in the middle of my comatose state, I managed to turn the TV on. More likely I already had it on when I passed out. Anyway, I was sitting in a stupor, watching the world from about two inches behind my own eyeballs. It was like it wasn't really me, and nothing I saw had anything to do with me — I was just an observer. Imagine; it's like doing surveillance inside your own head and no one knows you're there. It was really weird.

"Anyway, then I hear this guy's voice talking about Jesus. I wanted the voice to go away, but it wouldn't. It was a gentle voice, and it kept drawing my attention. It seemed to be calling me out of the fog in my brain. I guess I finally began to sober up, and I realized the voice I was hearing was a TV evangelist. He was preaching about the Son of God dying for our sins. He said that no matter what anyone ever did, Jesus still forgave them. I had heard about these Televangelists before, but I thought they were all phonies, running scams on the suckers watching. I don't know why, but this time I had no doubt that God had placed that evangelist on the TV that day for the expressed purpose of bringing Jesus' message to me. He proceeded to tell those who felt they were at the end of their rope to place their hands on the

TV. Then he said the strangest thing. He said that the Lord gave him a picture in his mind of a policeman who was involved in drugs, in severe debt, and was in danger of losing his family. He said that, in spite of all the things he had done, the Lord had forgiven him.

"I don't know what came over me, but I knew he was talking about me, and I placed my hands on the TV set. In that seedy motel room I asked Jesus into my heart. I asked Him to take over and straighten me out. In the midst of all the turmoil in my heart, in my head, and in my life, I suddenly felt peace — a peace like nothing I had ever experienced before.

"Gradually I began to put my life back together. I placed myself in a drug rehab program. I started going to church every Sunday. And now Julie and I are seeing a Christian counselor to help us work through our problems — excuse me — my problems. And I know, by the grace of God, that we're going to be a family again. I'm going to get my wife and kids back. I just know it!"

Mike took a heavy swig of the second Scotch the bartender brought. He drained the glass, and nervously ran his hand through his hair.

"What the h—l is going on around here? Has everybody lost all sense of reality? It seems like everyone's become a religious nut!" Mike's face flushed bright red, and his heart was racing.

John became worried about his former partner upon seeing his reaction.

"Mike, something is eating you. I can see it. You look like a time bomb with a short fuse. If you don't get hold of yourself you're going to explode. And when you do, it's going to destroy not only you, but everyone you love. Take it from me, pal, I've been there. You gotta let it out — talk to someone. I know that you're probably not ready to hear this, but Jesus is the answer! He loves you so much"— *Peggy's face flashed through Mike's mind.* John continued, "and He shares your troubles. I don't know how to explain it, but He's right there in the midst of everything with you. He takes your problems on Himself — if you let Him."

"What? What problems are you talking about, pal?" Mike's mouth had a mind of its own, spouting the usual defenses. "Don't worry about me, everything is cool." *Quick, put the mask back in place!*

John folded his arms. “No, my friend, everything is not cool. Ever since Katie was murdered, you haven’t been the same.”

Mike felt trapped. The walls were caving in on him and he wanted to run. But he knew there was no escape. John was right! Mike kept fending off the pain.

“Why does everyone have to probe?” he flared. “Why can’t everyone just leave me alone? I do my work; and I take care of Jamie and my mom. That’s all. I never ask for anything from anybody, and I mind my own business. All I want is to be left alone!”

John nodded. “Maybe that’s the trouble. You play too close to the vest. When you play everything alone it’s all on you. You know what that is? It’s pride!”

“What the h—l does that mean?” Mike moved to swig some more Scotch, but the glass was empty; he put it back down.

“Mike, you’re so busy playing the Lone Ranger, you lock everybody out. It’s like you’re wearing a neon sign: I don’t need anybody! And you get what you ask for. You end up alone.”

“Listen, John, I made my own bed. No one told me to get married and have a disabled kid. Why should I drag anyone else into it?”

"You think you've got it all covered, don't you, Mike? You've got it all under control, right? Well, what are you gonna do when it all begins to unravel and everything comes crashing down on you like it did me?"

"Man, I do have it under control. Stop bugging me!" Mike's face got even redder.

"Yeah, me too," echoed John. "That's what I thought. I had everything under control." Again the sardonic laugh. "Mike, I was lying to myself! I couldn't juggle anything anymore. The bills were mounting up and everything was falling apart. The only thing I could turn to was booze and cocaine. Yeah, a lot of good that did! Mike, it cost me everything."

"Sorry, pal, I don't want to put you down, but maybe I have more self-control than you." There was more than a tinge of sarcasm in Mike's voice.

John continued and Mike saw deep concern in his eyes. "I'm telling you, Mike, you're strong in your own strength, but it's not enough. Believe me, it's not enough! We're made to depend on God. He's our only real strength. He wants us to come to Him for help. And He's faithful. He'll be there for you. We have to lay all the stuff we try to carry by ourselves at the foot of His Cross, and He'll take care of it. He comes alongside and bears the load. He helps us get out from under. Try Him. Trust Him. I'm telling you, it's the only way you're ever going to find peace."

Mike had heard enough for today. "John," he said, "I'm happy for you. I'm happy that you found religion, that you're clean again, and that you're getting back with Julie. But as I tried to tell my partner, Peggy, this God thing isn't for me. I don't need a crutch. A man is responsible for himself and he has to deal with the consequences of his actions. The sooner people get that through their thick heads; the sooner they'll adjust to the reality of their lives and get on with it."

They changed the subject. There was some small talk about the kids as Mike swigged his Scotch. When Mike finished, Paulson said, "Well, I've got to go. I'm meeting Julie for our counseling session, and I don't want to be late."

"I know. I guess you're back with the ball and chain. Don't get her teed off or she'll beat you," Mike smiled.

John said, "No, I just don't want to be late." He didn't smile.

Mike watched him get into his car and drive off. *I guess that's another thing that happens when you get religion — you lose your sense of humor.*

Chapter 30

Mike pulled into his driveway. The house was empty.

She must have gone with Jamie to the supermarket. Mom likes to stock up early before the lines get too long.

Father and son had barely spoken since they left the Bellmore precinct three days earlier. Mike had to admit he was glad Jamie wasn't home. He wasn't sure how to handle the boy's sudden rebellion.

Mike went into the living room and walked over to his mother's old secretary, where he made out the bills and dealt with other paperwork. His mood was dark. His meeting with Paulson dragged up images of Peggy. No matter how hard he tried to let it go she was always on his mind. It was just too much.

Mike was depressed; he hadn't been depressed like this since Katie's death. He tried to shake it off and concentrate on the bills in front of him, but it didn't work. He mindlessly flipped through them, but nothing registered, just the pain.

The sound of his mother's voice pierced the blackness that engulfed him. It came from the kitchen; Mom and Jamie must have come in the back door. His mother sounded upset.

"Jamie, I'm surprised at you. That's no way to act in a public place."

"Grandma, why are you always bugging me? I wish you'd just leave me alone."

Mike took long, hurried strides from the living room to the kitchen. Reaching Jamie, he grabbed the boy's arm and pulled him towards him. Jamie almost lost his balance; Mike grabbed him with the other hand to keep him from falling.

"Hey, who do you think you're talking to? This is my mother and your grandmother," Mike said through clenched teeth.

"Michael, it's okay, he didn't mean it. He loves his old grandma." She became frightened. She had seen that same rage in her husband's eyes long ago when he used to confront young Mike.

Jamie glared at his father. "What are you going to do, handcuff me, drag me to the station and put me in the lockup. . . pig?"

Mike raised his arm to backhand his son across the mouth and everything became a slow-motion blur. His mother's scream shocked him back to reality. "Michael, for the love of God, stop!" He felt her feeble hand attempt to block the blow. His arm went limp and fell to his side. He released Jamie from the grasp of his other hand. It too fell to his side. Jamie began to sob uncontrollably and limped up the stairs to his room.

Mike grabbed his keys and headed for the door. Once he was seated behind the steering wheel of his car, he just drove, with no conscious thought on his part. It was as if he were just a passenger. Eventually he pulled into the parking lot of a club just off Hempstead Turnpike. As he stepped out of the car he could feel the bass vibration from the music blaring inside. He squeezed by the bouncer stationed at the entrance.

A fat man in a thousand-dollar suit spotted Mike and quickly made his way over. The garish light from a disco ball reflected off the large diamond ring on the man's pinky finger. "Detective Ryan, we cleaned up our act. We run a respectable place here," he said. "What's the beef?"

"Relax, Bucky, I'm off duty. All I want is a quiet drink. If that's too difficult for you, I'll find some other joint."

"Sure, Detective, anything you want. The drinks are on the on the house," Bucky said, his hand shaking as he patted his moist forehead with an embroidered handkerchief.

Mike followed him to the bar, passing a scantily clad young woman demonstrating her dubious talents on a dance pole, as leering drunks threw dollar bills at her. Mike grabbed a stool and threw a "C" note on the bar.

"Detective, I told you, it's on the house. Your money is no good here," said the fat man, smiling.

"Look, man," said Mike roughly, "I'll pay for my own drinks. I don't want to owe a low-life like you anything."

"What's eating you, Detective? I'm just trying to be friendly."

"Pal, all I want is to have a couple of drinks and to be left alone; I don't want to make small talk, explain myself or be pleasant company. Now buzz off." Bucky threw up his hands and walked away, wondering what was stuck in Ryan's craw.

Mike motioned to the bartender, saying, "Jack with a Bud chaser." The bartender brought his order. Mike put his hand on the shot glass but didn't lift it. *I'm letting everyone down. I'm letting Katie down. I promised her I'd stop drinking.* He made that promise a few years before she was killed. They were so happy together; there was no reason for him to drink. Katie's love for Jamie and her confident hope for his future, despite the boy's disability, had rubbed off on Mike. He loved his son. Jamie was a joy to him then.

The bitter memory of his hand poised to strike his son came flooding back to Mike. *How can I ever find peace after that? What do I do now?*

Mike's hand was unsteady as he downed the shot. The Jack was comforting as it traveled down his throat, leaving heat in its wake. . . all the way down. And the cold beer that followed cooled the flame in his chest. He ordered again — three more times. Finally that untouchable pain began to dissipate. He started swaying to the sultry music.

As the dancers completed their sets, they circulated amongst the crowd. One of them, a mousy young thing with auburn hair, stationed herself on the stool next to Mike.

"Hey, sweetie," she purred, "how about buying a working girl a drink?"

"Sure, girlie, what's your pleasure?" His head was spinning by now.

The evening wore on with lots of raucous laughter and lots more drinks. He couldn't remember how many. Then suddenly the room started to spin; he lost consciousness.

When he woke up he felt like the rhythm section of a reggae band was playing bongos, and a steel drum inside his head. His mouth was dry and he thought he would heave at any moment. The sun was just making its debut for the day. He was sitting on the pavement in the club parking lot, leaning against the wall of the building.

Slowly he managed to get to his feet. The car sat all by itself at the other end of the parking lot. All four tires were slashed. "Lovely," he moaned in the fresh morning air.

He checked his breast pocket and found he still had his cell phone. Mike thanked God, a knee-jerk response. *Funny how you never forget a habit you learn as a child, it's automatic.*

He scanned the phone's address book and stopped when the arrow displayed John Paulson's number. He punched the key pad and it rang three times. The pleasantness of the voice that answered surprised him.

"John Paulson."

"John, this is Mike Ryan. I'm sorry to wake you up at this hour."

"Mike! What's up, you in trouble?"

"Do you know where Bucky Fazio's place is? The Hot Shot Club?"

"On Hempstead Turnpike. Yeah, I know where it is."

"I'm stuck here. All my tires are cut. Could you help me out?"

"Give me ten minutes." Mike knew John didn't live far.

Only eight minutes had passed before John's black Silverado pulled into the parking lot. The sun gleaming off the gold Chevy emblem on the grill hurt Mike's eyes, causing him to wince.

"Mike, if you feel like you look, you've got to be really hurting," John laughed as Mike climbed into the cab of his pickup truck.

"Yeah, I really tied one on."

They pulled out of the parking lot and headed west on Hempstead Turnpike.

"You seemed alright when I left you yesterday afternoon," said John. "What the heck happened?"

Mike wasn't used to bearing his soul. He figured everyone had their own private demons to deal with, so why should they have any interest in his troubles? But John seemed sympathetic enough, and Mike knew from experience that John could keep a confidence. Besides, he'd heard confession was good for the soul. So he gave it a shot.

"Aww. . . it's my son. I don't know what to do," Mike began. He related the whole confrontation scene with Jamie.

"Wow," John said, "That's a tough one. I don't know what to tell you, Mike. Me and all the rest of the guys, we remember what a sweetheart Katie was and what a great job you two were doing with Jamie. When you lost her we were all concerned for you and your son. We know how hard it is to raise any kid, and now doing it alone. . . . It takes a real standup guy to tackle that alone. We admire you for what you've been trying to do. Hang in there, man. And speaking of hanging in, you have to do that with the job too.

We'd hate to see you blow fifteen years because of a jerk like Carl Banning."

Mike slid down so his head rested against the back of the seat.

John continued, "I was always afraid your temper would get you into trouble. You've got to keep a lid on it or you'll find yourself in a spot with no way out. Man, if we didn't pull you off Banning yesterday, he would have wound up in the hospital with a busted head, and you would have been out of a job. That temper of yours is legendary in the department, and to have that rap among cops; it's not good Mike."

Mike's wall went up. "Are cops' lives so boring that they can't find anything better to talk about than me? Obviously they don't have enough to do. Maybe if they were as jammed up with paper as I am, they wouldn't have time to be chewing the rag like a bunch of old women!" His words rang sharply in his own ears, and he was kind of sorry he spoke them. He didn't want to justify himself to John; he just wasn't up to an argument. He had earned himself one heck of a hangover, and he didn't want to make matters worse by sparring with the guy who was helping him out.

John made a left on Merrick Avenue. *That's not the right way.*

"Hey, John, did you forget how to get to my house?"

"I'm not taking you home. Not just yet, anyway."

"Okay, then where are we going?"

"To see a mutual friend."

Mike sat up, then sank back with a moan. "Pal, I'm not in the mood to socialize, not with this hangover. I feel like my head is going to explode."

"Hey, Mike, trust me on this, okay?" John glanced at Mike with that same expression of concern that Mike had seen the day before.

Mike gave him a strange look, but didn't say anything. John relaxed a little and smiled. When he pulled into Elm Street, Mike became agitated.

"Man, why are you driving me to Peg's place?"

"Take it easy, Mike, it's going to be all right."

"It's 7:30 in the morning. I'm sure she has a lot more important things to do than deal with a broken-down drunk."

"First of all, you're not a broken-down drunk," John pointed out, "and second of all she cares about you. God only knows why, but she does."

He pulled into Peggy's driveway and parked. Mike didn't move; he just sat there. John ignored him and headed up the walk to the front door. Before he could ring the bell the door opened. Mike saw her and immediately he began to ache inside. The pain was back. All that booze, and still the pain was back. He didn't know what to expect from Peggy after their last confrontation.

She rushed to the passenger window. . .

"Hey, mister, are you going to stay in there all day? There's French toast and bacon on the back porch with your name on it. Come," she ordered, and grabbed him by the arm. He didn't resist. "Your breakfast is getting cold, come on." She gave him a peck on the cheek. "Isn't this a beautiful day? God is sure good to his children."

Lightness dulled the pain inside Mike. He said, "Kid, I forgot how annoying you can be in the morning."

A group of sparrows were chirping on the dewy lawn.

"Man," muttered Mike, "tell those idiot birds to keep quiet. My head is pounding."

"Come on, Mr. Grumpy; let's get some food into you."

She placed her hand through his arm and they walked around through the yard to the screened-in porch. John steadied him from the other side. They sat him down, and Peggy served him the promised French toast, bacon and a cup of hot coffee.

Mike sat silently, sipping the coffee and hoping that he had enough control not to upchuck all over the yellow and white printed tablecloth. John and Peggy were engrossed in conversation, talking about how Jesus had blessed them during the week, and the upcoming Pentecost service. Half their conversation seemed to consist of Bible quotes that Mike couldn't follow. Frankly, all he wanted was a cold beer to settle his stomach and clear his aching head.

Finally, Mike cut into their jabbering. "Tell me, if I'm not interrupting, how do you two know each other?" Paulson had only recently been transferred to the Eighth Precinct, after Peggy was hospitalized.

"Oh," Peggy explained, "we belong to an organization called Cops for Christ, a special ministry geared just for the police, and we also go to the same church."

"Cops for Christ?" said Mike. "Never heard of it."

"Wait." Peggy hopped up and went inside, returning a moment later with a little brochure. Mike flipped it open and glanced through it.

Peggy went on, "John and I met at a CFC meeting — how long ago, John — a little over three years?" She popped a crisp piece of bacon in her mouth.

"Oh, that's just peachy keen," Mike responded with a cynical smile.

"Brother, that coffee didn't help your disposition any, did it? You've been a joy ever since I picked you up," John said.

"Man, all I wanted was to go home and hit the sack, but for some crazy reason you decided to drag me over here. By the way, why did you?"

"I'm insulted, Michael. If I didn't know better, I would think you didn't like my cooking," Peggy quipped, but her feigned pout didn't penetrate the alcoholic fog in his brain. He was still too hung over.

"Come on, Peg," he said pitifully, "how about cutting me some slack?"

"Perhaps that's the trouble, Michael. People give you too much slack." Her tone was still playful.

"Yeah? Like you? First you worried me half to death when you were in the hospital. Then you pressed me about my feelings, and when I finally told you how I felt, you dumped me because I wasn't a religious crackpot like you."

Peg stopped being cute. She took his hand and stared straight into his eyes. "Michael, it was because I love you. I was so vulnerable and afraid of being hurt. I was afraid. I'm sorry. I've missed you very much."

His love for her welled up inside. He never knew it was possible to love that much. He stared back into her eyes. For the first time in his life he was unable to dispel the honesty and sincerity of the moment with some biting Irish wit. He remained silent, gazing at Peggy.

John finally broke the spell. "Pal, if I was you, I would stop wasting time and grab this lady. But before you do, maybe you'd better do something about that temper of yours, like we were discussing before."

Still looking into Peggy's eyes, Mike simultaneously saw images racing through his mind: his hands around Kensey's throat, his hands wrenching Dunbar from his chair, one hand about to strike Opal, one hand ready to pound Banning's features out of existence, Jamie's wide eyes and Mrs. Ryan's frightened voice. . .

"I guess you're right," he admitted, no longer able to hold Peggy's gaze. "I have to do something before I seriously hurt someone, but what?"

Peggy suddenly knelt in front of him, took his hand in hers and began to gently stroke it.

"Michael, all your life people have drummed into you that you've got to be the strong one, fearless, never letting your guard down." Her voice was soothing. Peace emanated from her, a peace he had seen in her before, but still couldn't comprehend. She continued, "Society tells you that a man is supposed to be strong and fearless, decisive and responsible, someone to count on."

John put down his napkin and looked at Mike.

"You know, Mike, those are praiseworthy attributes, and God wants us men to manifest those characteristics. I think He programmed them into our DNA. We should strive to attain those strengths. My father drilled that into me from as far back as I can remember. And he did a good job. Maybe too good a job."

Mike was listening. "What do you mean?"

"I mean I didn't know how *not* to be the strong man, in control, and so on, when in reality things were beyond my control. That left me only one alternative when I found myself in that helplessness; I lied to myself.

"When my well-constructed world began to fall apart I was too proud and scared to ask for help. The great John Paulson can handle anything! That was the lie I had to tell myself. Anything else would have been unthinkable. But how do you make yourself believe your own lie? There's the rub."

Mike felt as though he was listening to a summary of his own life.

John went on, "I'll tell you how I managed it. I put that white stuff up my nose and drowned myself in booze. What else can you do when you can't look into your wife's eyes and admit that you failed? You can't admit anything like that — not if you're a man — it's just not an option. At least that's the way I interpreted what my father taught me.

"So, like I told you yesterday, I made a plan — the great plan — where I gambled away my mortgage money. Doesn't make any sense, does it? Well, it was the best I could come up with using the mush that was left of my brain. Yep, drugs and booze sure do great things. I let my marriage and my family go down the drain rather than swallow my pride and ask for help.

"You know what, Mike? I spend every moment of every day now asking for help. Know what else? I'm regaining my self-respect, because now it's based on truth, not the lie I used to believe. And now I'm free, I have a peace like I've never known before, and life is good.

"I'll tell you how all this happened. I met Jesus and I learned to humble myself before Him. I repented. Re-pent-ed! Do you know what that word means, Mike? It means I changed my mind. Actually, He changed my mind; He gave it back. I've stopped my 'stinkin' thinkin'. I repented of my sin of pride. That's what pride is, a sin. . ."

"So, what's a little sin in the realm of things? You make it sound like it's a big deal," Mike interrupted, a snide edge to his voice.

John wasn't deterred by Mike's tone. "Sin is whatever separates you from God, Mike! Don't you get it? And you know what pride is? It's what makes you think you don't need God!" John was on a roll. "I humbled myself before God and asked for His forgiveness. And He did it! He forgave me!

"Now He's teaching me how to be a man, a real man, the man He designed me to be, created me to be, and calls me to be. He's teaching me to look to Him, because He is my strength, and He is my help in times of trouble. He is the source of my entire supply, and every good thing I have comes from Him!

"So, I look to him for all my needs, day by day and hour by hour. And when I can't hear Him because I did something that pushed me far away — sin, remember? That's when I go to church, to my brothers and sisters in the Lord for help. With them I find my way back to God. He always forgives me and always takes me back. . Believe it or not, I'm getting better at this stuff as time goes on. I know that with God's help I can be a responsible husband and the right father for my kids, and some day my family can be proud of me again.

"And you know what, Mike? I'm happy. I don't have to carry the whole world on my shoulders anymore. So, Mike, now I've told you what it's like to be a religious crackpot — I believe that was the term you used. So, buddy, how's *your way* working for you?"

John was done. Peggy didn't applaud, but she wanted to. Now the ball was clearly in Mike's court.

Mike wasn't yet clear on a critical point. "But where can a guy turn when the whole crazy world is crashing down on him?"

"I just told you. Weren't you listening?" John said with a sigh.

"Yeah, but I don't know how to do that."

"Jesus says, *'Come to me, all you who labor and are heavy laden, and I will give you rest.'* It's in the Bible, Mike."

"But I still don't understand *how*."

John had once been in Mike's shoes. He tried again to explain. "Talk to Jesus, Mike. Tell Him your wants, your needs, your hurts, your troubles. Ask Him for whatever you need. Ask Him what He wants you to do — and then shut up and listen. It's called praying."

Mike took in part of John's words. "You said listen. Listen for what?"

"For the answer, pal — for the answer."

"You mean I'm gonna hear voices?" Mike looked a little suspicious.

"You already hear voices!" John reminded him.

Mike felt a pinch of fear. "But how do I know which voice is His?"

"You'll know it when you hear it. You just have to learn to listen, to pick out His voice. He gives you the answers you need. And they're usually pretty short: 'yes' or 'no' or 'wait.' "

"Michael," Peggy added, "when Jesus said 'Come to me,' it was an invitation. He said, 'I will give you rest,' included in that rest is the peace that you want — the peace that has eluded you for so long. It's yours for the asking." Peggy's hand caressed his cheek.

Mike yearned for the same peace that Peggy and John had. He slowly bowed his head. Tears ran down his cheeks. The idea of surrendering was so foreign to him. He didn't know how to process this new way of thinking.

Peggy put her arm around him, lifted his head, and looked again into his eyes.

"Michael, do you think I'm telling you the truth when I say I'm in love with you?"

"It's difficult to accept after that conversation in the hospital," Mike replied warily.

"Don't you know that I was scared, frightened that my relationship with Jesus would eventually drive us apart? We were coming from two different worlds. It wouldn't work that way. I couldn't handle loving you and then losing you," she said softly, eyes imploring. "Do you trust me, Michael?"

"Peg, you know I do."

"Do you want to ask Jesus into your life? Do you think you're ready?"

He nodded his assent.

"Then go ahead," she said, "ask Him."

Mike didn't really know what happened at that moment. The throbbing pain suddenly stopped and his head cleared. For the first time in twenty-four hours his head wasn't swimming with thoughts of Jamie, or Hanover, or Banning, or Dunbar.

In his heart he cried out, *God, help me!* Suddenly, he sensed a presence.

"Jesus," he said out loud, "I want to follow You and I ask you to take control of my life. Please Lord forgive me."

There was joy in heaven. The angels cheered as Michael Sean Ryan's name was written in the Book of Life, written indelibly with the Blood of the Lamb — Jesus. The tears welled up in Michael's eyes, slowly at first, and then the dam that held back all his pent-up hurts and fears burst. He began to weep uncontrollably. The cleansing tears flowed profusely.

Peggy held him tightly. "Michael, Jesus knows that you've had more than your share of heartaches, and that you've tried to carry your burdens without complaining. Now He wants you to know how much

He loves you. Give those burdens over to Him. Rest in the love that He has for you. Rest your heavy heart, my love." Peace surrounded the three. There was silence for a few minutes.

John looked at his watch and announced, "I didn't realize how late it was. I'd better get going. I told Julie I'd be there at 10:00 a.m. to clean the gutters for her, and it's already 9:45."

"Praise *Jesus*!" Peggy cheered. Mike had a quizzical look.

"Why are you praising the Lord for that?" he asked, "Cleaning gutters is a lousy job."

"I think Julie is sort of telling him that she needs him, and it also gives her an excuse to see him," Peggy answered. Her impish grin was back.

Mike tried to tune in. He said, "You guys are going to have to help me. This is a whole new way of thinking. It's very strange."

"Mike, you'll do just fine," John said as he hurried out the door.

Peggy put her arms around Mike again and drew him close to her.

Chapter 31

Mike's home was only a little Cape Cod style house, but to him and Katie it had rivaled the plush mansions that dotted the Gold Coast on the north shore. It was one of the few places where Mike felt completely secure. Katie was gone now and his mom had come to live with him and Jamie. Despite the hollow echoes of Katie's presence, Mike still found the house so comfortable. He'd always felt awkward anywhere else.

Peggy's place, with the pink azaleas and the breeze ruffling the bright new leaves on the trees, was now the exception. He had found a peace here, a peace that was new and foreign to him. He never wanted to leave this haven of his heart. This little piece of Long Island sod would be a memorial of this life-changing moment for him.

Reality check! The few instances that he had seen Peggy in the last couple of months paraded before his mind's eye. He recalled all the conflict and downright antagonism in their exchanges, and his need to distance himself from her. Now he couldn't help but wonder if her apparent enthusiasm stemmed from hope in their new relationship — or was she just being the stereotypical "rejoicing Christian," excited about the new convert? Doubt is an insidious thing.

Mike looked at his watch. "Wow, look at the time! I have to run."

"Do you really have to go? I have some things to do around the house, but mostly I want to spend some time with you. Please stay." He was torn between two sensations, both shock and elation. There was nothing he'd rather do than spend more time with Peggy. His desire to be near her was counter-balanced by fear and the need to run — his *protect yourself at all costs* syndrome.

"I would like that Peg, but I really have to talk to Jamie."

"You're nervous about seeing him, aren't you?"

"Ever since he was caught shoplifting there's been a gulf between us. Obviously it was there before — though I have to admit I didn't see it. When he *does* speak to me he's angry and hostile. Raising my hand and almost hitting him hasn't exactly improved the situation. Thank God my mother stopped me."

Peggy leaned toward him and spoke very intently. "Look, all the stress that you've bottled up all these years has finally exploded. It was bound to happen sometime. Fortunately, you didn't hurt him. Who knows, this incident could turn out to be something very positive."

"Positive?" Mike exclaimed. "You've got to be kidding! How could this be positive?"

"Because it has brought things out in the open," Peggy said, gathering the breakfast dishes together. "You said it yourself: the problem was already there, under the surface. Now that it has seen the light of day you can deal with it, otherwise it would just keep festering into something even worse. Besides, it brought you to the end of yourself and you finally opened up to Jesus. What could be more positive than that?"

Mike didn't respond. He couldn't take his mind off Jamie. He kept seeing the look on the boy's face.

"Sounds like the poor kid is *sooo* angry and frustrated," Peggy continued, balancing the cream pitcher atop the plates. "Maybe you're too close to the situation. Sounds like he thinks you're the enemy." She thought for a moment. "Hey. Jamie and I always had a good rapport. Do you think it would do any good for me to talk to him?"

"It can't do any harm. I can't seem to get anywhere with him, and I'm not sure my mother will let me anywhere near him after last night."

"Let me finish cleaning up here." Peggy said. "I have to run out and get some plants for the garden then we'll go to your place."

"I'll help with the dishes," he volunteered.

"You — Michael Ryan — you want to help with," she paused, "*ladies' work*?"

"Yeah, why not? I'm not a *complete* chauvinist." He removed the stack of dishes from her arms. They both laughed. The roller coaster was on its way up again. She was once more the bright spot in his life. He loved her more than ever. The darkness and the doubt receded.

Chapter 32

Mike thoroughly enjoyed the morning with Peggy, though he was a little embarrassed about her nonchalantly holding his hand as they explored various gardening outlets searching for shrubs and other outdoor plants. The change in her behavior was quite sudden. The level of affection she displayed in public surprised him, it almost seemed out of character. She was normally a very reserved person.

Peg hunted for an assortment of early blooming annuals for her little garden, taking belated advantage of spring. He offered to pay for some of the plants she admired but passed by because the price was too high. She was God's steward, and as such, she had to spend *His* money wisely.

"Strange people, these Christians," he said with a frown, but there was a lilt to his voice and a gladness in his heart. He enjoyed it every time she touched him. She told him that she had planned to attend the short noon prayer service at her church and asked him to join her. He agreed.

Mike felt comfortable in the simple church. He realized as he listened to the scriptures being read that his understanding of them had changed. The words weren't boring. Every reading could be applied to some aspect of his own life. For the first time he found himself grasping the depth of love God had for him, sending His only Son to take the executioner's bullet for the world. Mike tried to imagine himself sacrificing his own son.

After the service Peggy suggested that they drive to Jones Beach and take a stroll. They chose Field 2 and found it sparsely populated. Usually the week before Memorial Day, the place would already be invaded by hordes seeking a day in the sun after the long winter season.

It was a little overcast but they walked for a while, barefoot, the cool sand sticking between their toes. After about a half hour Peggy turned to him. "Michael, I don't want this to end, but we have some business to attend to. We have to come back down to earth and minister to Jamie.

Mike kicked the sand, as his mood darkened.

"This is really going to be difficult for you, isn't it, Mike?"

He picked up a bunch of pebbles and began throwing them one by one into the angry surf.

"I'm not exactly chomping at the bit to see him," he said. "What do you expect? Our last encounter almost sent my kid to the emergency room. He pushed my buttons and I lost it."

Peggy's hands were clasped together as if she was praying. She brought them to her lips. "Michael, let's go and see Jamie. We can't avoid it any longer."

They discussed all the what-ifs as they drove to Mike's house, but they had no real answers. For the first time since he and Katie bought the house, Mike regarded his home as hostile territory.

When they pulled into the driveway, his mother was out front watering the lawn. She completely ignored the town's water conservation program, which mandated watering only every *other* day. She watered every single day. The only thing that stopped her was the rain.

As Mike stepped out of the car, his legs felt like lead. No part of him wanted to go inside.

"Hi, Mom! Is Jamie around?"

"Exactly where were you all night? I've been worried sick. I called Jack and Sean. They put out an all points bulletin for you. If you hadn't called me this morning they'd still be searching."

Mike and Peggy stifled a laugh. "It's not nice to laugh at an old woman. You think that's funny? I was afraid you were hurt or, God forbid, maybe dead!" she chided Mike.

Her eyes flashed anger and then relief. "And you," she continued, pointing to Peggy, "don't encourage him, come over here and give me a hug. I missed you," she said as they embraced.

"Mom, I'm sorry," said Mike. "Like I told you this morning, I had a lot on my mind and had to sort things out. I completely lost track of time. I'm really sorry I worried you."

"Never mind your excuses. I'm still mad at you," claimed Mrs. Ryan, but you could see her tension dissipating into tears as she spoke.

"Aw, Ma — I'm sorry!" He wrapped his arms around her in a rare hug until she regained control. Then he gently released her. "Now, where's Jamie?"

Mrs. Ryan took her handkerchief and patted the tears at the corners of her tired eyes. Peggy put an understanding arm around her.

"He's up in his room, and hasn't come down to talk to me or even to eat," she said curtly. "I'm worried about him"

Mike and Peggy started up the porch steps.

"Michael!" shouted Mrs. Ryan, "you're not going to lose your temper again, are you?"

He turned to her.

"No, Mom. I'm okay now," he said. Mike and Peg climbed the stairs leading to Jamie's room. Mike knocked on the door.

"Jamie, it's pop. Can I come in?"

"No! Leave mc alone. I never want to speak to you again!"

His son's words hit him like a sledgehammer. Mike's heart sank. Peggy leaned close to the bedroom door.

"Jamie, it's Peggy. I've haven't seen you in weeks. I missed you, and I want to talk to you. Can we come in?"

Silence. Mike's face distorted with pain and frustration. Peggy's hand patted his shoulder.

Peggy tried again. "Jamie? C'mon, I thought we were buddies, you and me. Trust me."

They heard the clumping thud of Jamie's braces. The door opened slowly as Jamie retreated to his bed, his back to them. Not exactly a warm invitation, but it was progress. They entered the room. The TV was blaring; Mike contained his annoyance and calmly turned it off. He wasn't very pleased with his son's viewing selection, but the new voice in his head cautioned him to remain silent. He reached over to ruffle his son's hair with his usual expression of affection. Jamie jerked his head away.

Peggy grasped Mike's hand, cautioning him not to say anything.

"Jamie," she began, "your father told me you're having a bad time these days. You and I can talk about it. What do you say?" She gently smoothed back a strand of hair from Jamie's forehead.

Resentment smoldered in Jamie's expression. "Did he tell you he almost hit me?"

"Yes, he told me, and that was wrong," Peggy said. "It was a terrible mistake, and he's sorry. I have to ask you. . . honestly, do you think *you* had some part in that? Did you provoke him? You know, your Dad being a detective, he's under a lot of pressure. And since he lost your mother, honey, it's been terribly hard for him, just like it's been for you. He loves *you.* He knows you've had to deal with a lot of painful things for such a little boy."

"I'm *not* a *little boy*!"

Peggy agreed. "What I meant was that you *were* a little boy when these things happened. And even though you're a young man now, the hurts are still there. But I also know this, and you should know it too: if there was any possible way for your father to take away your pain, he would do it. He wouldn't hesitate a second, he would just do it."

Mike came to stand close, but kept his hands at his sides. "Son, I'm really sorry; I didn't mean to frighten you last night."

The boy just stared down at his own twisted hands. He couldn't look up at his father. He grimaced, his face contorted, trying not to cry.

"Pop," he said slowly, "are you sorry that I'm your son?"

The question struck like a saber through his heart. Mike could barely breathe. It took him a minute to recover.

"What? Of course not! Why in the world would you ever think such a thing?"

"Well, I thought Bobby and the gang liked me. . ."

"Who is Bobby, and what gang?" Peggy interjected.

"They're just some punk kids in the neighborhood," Mike answered. "Go on son, finish what you were saying."

"Everything was going okay. I was sort of in the gang, and it was cool. One day they let me go with them to Gino's for some pizza. Bobby made a joke, and when I laughed, my Coke went up my nose and then some stuff came out. All the guys began calling me names, they all ran away and left me there by myself. Next time I saw them they told me I couldn't hang with them anymore.

"A couple of days later, Bobby told me the guys agreed to give me one more chance. That's when we all went to Roger's. I knew you would ground me if you found out, but I thought if I didn't go, they would kick me out of the gang. Well, everyone was running around the store, and knocking things over and taking stuff. I went into the baseball department so I wouldn't get into trouble, but Bobby came over and dared me to steal the baseball glove. If I didn't they would have made fun of me again. Then everyone ran away, but I wasn't fast enough. The manager caught me, and when the police came they took me to the station house. Then you came and got me."

"So that's why you took the glove."

"Yeah, Pop," said Jamie. "I'm sorry."

Peggy did all she could to hold back tears. Feeling confident that things would be okay between Mike and Jamie, she took the boy's hands in hers.

She felt prompted to explain to Jamie about Jesus, the Son of God, who died for him so that he might live. She led him through Jesus' ministry, touching briefly on His teachings and the healings of the sick and the disabled He encountered. She summed it up with His passion and His crucifixion, ending with the resurrection promise of eternal life.

Jamie lifted his head and looked up at her. Gone was the rebellion and anger. She sat next to him on the bed, and gently stroked his hair. She felt the trembling of his hand, and knew that this wounded young boy's suffering was one reason why Jesus chose the cross.

"Now," concluded Peggy, "when Jesus went to join His father in heaven He gave His friends and disciples the Holy Spirit, who worked through them. Like Jesus, they were able to heal. Jamie, if you want me and your Dad, who loves you so very much, to pray with you, we will, and Jesus' Spirit will come into *your* heart."

"Okay," Jamie said. He sat between Peggy and Mike, who both gently placed their hands on him.

"O Jesus," Peggy began, "like Jamie, You have experienced the rejection of people who claimed to be Your friends and then turned their backs on You — people who didn't understand, and who finally abandoned You. We know You love Jamie so much that You willingly died for him. We humbly ask, O Lord, that You reveal to Jamie how precious he is to You. Let him place all his hurts at the foot of Your cross. We pray that You will wipe away every tear, and remove every hurt and painful memory from him."

Suddenly the boy became spastic. His legs began to shake, his chest rose and fell rapidly as he gasped for breath, and his heart rate soared. Finally, saliva spewed from his mouth, flying onto Peggy's face and onto her blouse. Jamie had no control, and watched in horror as the spittle flew onto his friend that he loved. His heart shriveled within him, and he was filled with self-loathing.

"Why do I do these things?" he cried mournfully. "I am such a piece of garbage!"

Peggy, ignoring the spittle on her own face, drew a handkerchief from her pocket, and gently and compassionately wiped the residue from his.

He was inconsolable, and wailed with total abandon, like the bleating of a wounded lamb. Suddenly he fell silent and cocked his head as if to listen. He was sure he heard it — there it was again — a voice like none he had ever heard before. "Son, I love you. I have made you and, to Me, you are precious amongst those I have called. I delight in you now, and in the man you will become. I love you so much that I sent my only Son to die for you. He will take away all the pain you have suffered."

An overwhelming love filled the entire room, and it enveloped Jamie. Suddenly the boy's body relaxed; he became calm. A new spirit welled up within him. He felt a freedom from his bondage. Peggy was right, he knew that *this Jesus* would always be his friend. She continued to pray silently now.

Jamie looked at his father through a blur of tears, but he saw him more clearly than ever before. He turned to him, hands limp at his sides, and buried his face in Mike's strong chest. "Dad, I am sorry about *everything* — taking the glove from Roger's, talking back to you, talking back to Grandma — everything. I'm so sorry. . ."

Mike held his son tightly. He couldn't control his emotions and he didn't care. He too cried.

Wiping his eyes, Jamie leaned back to look up at Mike and said, "Dad, if you want to ground me for the way I've been acting, it's okay. I'll clean the yard, wash the dishes and take out the garbage. You don't even have to give me my allowance for a whole year."

Stepping back, Mike couldn't help but laugh. "All you have to do is try your best — because *you're* the best. Son, I'm so proud of you," he blurted through his laughter and tears. After regaining his composure, he asked, "Hey, kid, feel like going to Friendly's for a couple of cheeseburgers and a sundae?"

"Cool, Pop! Can we take Peggy and Grandma?"

"That would be *very cool*," Mike replied

He followed Jamie and Peggy downstairs, praising God. He had never experienced such peace. For the first time in his life, he didn't feel the weight of the whole world on his shoulders. God *is* good.

Chapter 33

Henry Chambers' Memorial Day weekend wasn't very memorable for him. Oh yes, there was the annual parade organized by the Chamber of Commerce with the usual assortment of little league teams, scouts and marching school bands. Every beat on every drum in every band seemed to pound on his head as he tried in vain to nurse his hangover. He could have tolerated that; he was used to dealing with hangovers. What he couldn't tolerate was Barbara, his wife, and their four kids. The time he'd had to spend with them was the worst part of the weekend.

Tuesday morning his head still throbbed, but he couldn't wait to get to the office. He arrived an hour early. Somehow he had managed to survive the three days with Barbara and the brats. He would rather have flown down to St Croix with Debbie. Debbie understood how to treat a man. All Barbara cared about was her kids, his money, and the various charities to which she gave his money.

Hank's vest was annoying him. The stupid thing kept riding up and he had to keep pulling it down. He consumed four hot dogs at the parade, washing them down with a pitcher of beer. But it was Memorial Day, and just like the Fourth of July, he had to put on a patriotic face. The Democratic base expected it.

If his difficulties with women had been his only problem he could have handled it and his life would be manageable, but his responsibility to the party was all-consuming. Sometimes he regretted being the Democratic Party boss for Nassau County. He resented the bureaucratic Neanderthals and party hacks he had to deal with on a daily basis. And since the Democrats catered to what he considered the dregs of society — the poor and downtrodden — he was forced to hold hands with the leaders of every minority group and their liberal do-gooder advocates. Though he wasn't very happy with his biweekly paycheck, amounting to only sixty grand a year, the job had its perks. He liked the status; he liked driving a county car and breaking bread with the liberal elite.

His shapely secretary, Laura, walked into his office with a latte and a copy of the *Wall Street Journal* plus two other dailies tucked under her arm. He appreciated her. She was good at her job.

"Morning, Hank, how was Memorial Day?"

He grumbled something, sipping the coffee she handed him.

"That good, huh?" she teased.

He scanned the front page of the *Journal* without comment.

"You want to go over the line-up?"

"Do I have to?"

"Your subjects await you," she said with a slight bow.

"Okay, if you insist on torturing me."

"Well, you have Eddie Forrest at ten; Tim Adams of the Freeport Coalition at eleven; and. . . oh, Jake Gottlieb of the Jewish Alliance around quarter to. . . Barry Roth from the Nassau County Rights of the Disabled is after lunch, and George Winthrop brings up the rear; he's at three."

"Laura, get rid of Barry Roth. I'm in no mood for him."

"But Henry, the guy's driving me crazy. He calls about forty times a day. Besides, I hate lying to these people."

"Why? Are you a holy roller or something? Lying is part of the job."

"C'mon. I work hard for you."

"Yeah, I know. I'm sorry. It's just that I really can't take his garbage. I don't know what these people want. All Roth does is complain that there aren't enough jobs for *cripples*. Those people can't really do anything anyway. Every time I have to make an appearance at one of their meetings I want to puke. You should see them. Half of them can't even sit up; their arms waving all over the place. And some of them — well, you can't understand a single word they say."

"The County Executive *did* promise them jobs."

"Yeah, he promises and *I* have to deliver!"

"That's because you're Henry Chambers, the great miracle worker," Laura smiled.

"Thanks a lot. Okay, send the first one in. Might as well face the music."

He watched as she turned towards the door, and wondered if he was due for a new mistress. But Laura was high maintenance. If he made her his new love interest she'd be very difficult to dump when he got tired of her. She'd been around the block a few times and wouldn't be satisfied with a gold bracelet from Zales — no, she would require substantial compensation, and that wasn't part of his itinerary.

His morning went by in a blur, with all his attention concentrated on the meeting with George Winthrop at 3:00 p.m.

George Winthrop's father, Kenneth Winthrop, had been a sergeant in the Marine Corps. He saw heavy combat in the Pacific during World War II. The young Kenneth was captured behind enemy lines and, despite being severely tortured, refused to give the Japanese the location of his platoon. The Japanese position was soon overrun and he was rescued, but not before his captors rewarded his stalwart loyalty and dedication by cutting his right arm off at the shoulder with a samurai sword. Somehow he survived. Two weeks later Truman ordered the atom bomb dropped on Hiroshima and Nagasaki.

During the three months Kenneth spent recuperating in an army hospital he decided that, since he had lost his arm for his country, the country owed him. His recovery was sheer grit and determination on his part. He applied that same determination to acquiring as much wealth and power as was humanly possible.

Kenneth Winthrop was a visionary. He had an uncanny ability to see into the future, not through any kind of magic or divination, but through careful analysis of social, business and economic trends. He observed and scrutinized the rapidly changing postwar New York City. It was not only booming, it was bulging, ready to burst its seams. The population pressure of the recently returned GIs was more than apparent to many, but he was the one with the foresight and the plan to take advantage of the opportunity. He knew what to do. All he needed was the means.

He worked two jobs, — sixteen hours a day — invested shrewdly, and lived a miserly life. He had no time for women; his lust for wealth superseded all other pursuits. In the span of eight years following the end of World War II, Kenneth amassed the astronomical sum of $150,000, a considerable fortune in that era.

Unlike the mantra of a century before, “Go west, young man,” Kenneth cast his eyes eastward to a two-lane strip of road on the south shore of Long

Island. It was the fifteen-mile section of Sunrise Highway that stretched from Rosedale to Wantagh. He begged, borrowed or stole every additional dime he could get his hands on to purchase every available lot on either side of the road. He was one step ahead of the merchants that flocked from Manhattan and Brooklyn to build retail stores, restaurants and motels to service the area's flourishing population. All the new construction was on land leased from Winthrop Realty.

At age fifty Kenneth finally allowed himself to be distracted by a lovely young brunette named Agnes Braun. They married and a year later Agnes died in childbirth. Kenneth named his infant son George. The World War II veteran passed away, at the age of sixty-six, leaving an estate worth approximately one hundred fifty million dollars to his sole heir.

Unlike his father, whose ambition was to accumulate as much wealth as possible, George's lust was for power itself: power beyond what his father had ever dreamed of. He didn't care what methods he used in achieving his goal.

George used the large fortune he inherited to storm the gates of Nassau County politics. He salivated over the power he could wield over the Office of the County Executive. He bullied other county politicos into granting county contracts to his own construction company. He secured his power base by twisting arms, and placing his stooges in various strategic county positions.

George's chief rival in this political and financial chess game was Edmund Steele. The victor would be the most powerful mogul on the Eastern seaboard. While George Winthrop was obsessed with the office and the title, Steele was interested in using the power of money to engineer institutional changes and social projects that would benefit the county residents.

The centerpiece of George's plan, and the platform from which he planned to reign supreme, was a sports stadium complex that would include a football stadium for a National Football League franchise with an adjacent casino. Everyone knew a lot of money would change hands. Why let all that money leave with the crowd? Why not combine the glitter and hype of a competitive team with the fever of a roulette wheel? George saw this as the perfect win-win opportunity — *for him*. He chose the parcel of land where the old Roosevelt Raceway once stood as the site for the project. The concept project was dubbed The Merrick Plan.

The Merrick Plan generated considerable interest and George started to put his ducks in a row to get approval and launch the project. But he was not the only one eyeing the Roosevelt Raceway property. When old man Steele's idealistic daughter, Tamara, heard that gambling was part of the proposed Merrick Plan, she was appalled. She developed her own plan for the property and asked her father to intervene on her behalf. Tamara had a heart for the poor and the elderly. She proposed a plan for the county to build subsidized housing on that land with a small plot set aside where she would build a church for the community with her own funds. When county officials informed Winthrop that his plan wasn't a slam dunk — that Tamara Steele had convinced her father to oppose the Merrick plan — he was furious, and went into a fit of rage. He despised these religious fanatics.

Chambers looked at the clock on the desk. *Unbelievable, three o'clock already*. Of all the people he had to talk to, Winthrop was the one he dreaded most. He could hold his own with most people, but George Winthrop was different. Winthrop scared him.

Laura stuck her head in his office. "Hank, your three o'clock is here."

Frantically, he shoved his half-eaten corned beef sandwich into the wastebasket, and hurriedly swept the crumbs off his desk.

"Well, Laura, what are you waiting there for? Tell Mr. Winthrop to come in."

"Right this way, Mr. Winthrop."

Hank almost tripped over himself as he half-ran around his desk to greet George Winthrop, shaking his hand profusely.

"George, how are you? Come right in."

Hank led him to the leather couch opposite his desk.

"George, how's your family? How are Ginger and the kids?"

He could see the malice in Winthrop's eyes. It was obvious that small talk was not on his agenda. Henry shot back towards his desk. Frozen with fear, he couldn't think of anything else to say.

"Chambers," snarled Winthrop, "every time I see you, you waste my time. *I'm losing money* and I don't *like* losing money! Have you heard from the County Executive yet?"

"I'm sorry, but the County Executive was supposed to get back to me in regard to. . .?" Chambers drew a total blank.

"The Merrick Plan, you moron!"

Chambers stumbled back against his desk. The venom in Winthrop's voice paralyzed him. He couldn't wait for Winthrop to leave. The bottle in his bottom drawer was calling out to him.

"Bower told me that he hasn't forgotten you," Chambers babbled.

Winthrop's face reddened with fury.

"Who do you think you're talking to? I am not some idiot loser begging, hat in hand, at the County Executive's door. I want answers and I want them now! If I don't get them I'll have you picking up trash on Long Beach Boulevard. Do you understand me?"

"I'm sorry, George," said Chambers, "but we have to tread lightly. Edmund Steele desperately wants that land now so he can build a low-income housing development as a memorial to his daughter, Tamara."

"I don't care what Edmund Steele wants. What I do care about is this cop, this Michael. . ." he paused, "what's-his-name!"

"You mean Detective Ryan, the one who was on the Steele case for a couple of weeks until he was suspended for possible sexual harassment?"

Winthrop crossed his long legs and stroked his graying goatee.

"Yeah, Ryan. I hear he's a loose cannon. He's got it in for Mark Carter's son."

"Well, George, the kid *did* kill Ryan's wife."

"Don't say that again, you imbecile. Don't you know how big a contributor Mark Carter is to the party? We can't allow that kind of talk. There's no evidence against the kid. Anyway, the family has him hidden somewhere in Canada."

Chamber's hands began to perspire and he didn't know what to do with them. He spotted a letter opener on the desk and picked it up, grateful for something to keep his nervous hands busy.

"I want to know more about Ryan and this woman, Hanover," said Winthrop.

Chambers drew a deep breath and began to lay out the details of the alleged assault and the status of the hearing.

"Why the h—l is Ryan still on the Steele case?" demanded Winthrop. "He should have been suspended, or at least on desk duty while the charges are pending."

"Well, Hanover keeps changing her mind. First she drops the charges and then has her lawyer reinstate them. Poor Dunbar. . ."

Winthrop slammed his walking stick on Chamber's desk. "I don't give a rat's behind about that fool, Dunbar! I want Ryan off the Tamara Steele case. He's nudging too close."

Chambers couldn't understand Winthrop's interest in the Steele case. He was curious, but not curious enough to ask questions and risk incurring Winthrop's wrath any further. Winthrop massaged his beard and once again mulled over the information presented.

"Who is presiding over the Hanover case?"

"Richard Roth. Why?"

"Does anybody own him?"

"If you mean is he in somebody's pocket, I have to say I don't think so," said Chambers. "He's a boy scout, does everything by the book. No skeletons in his closet that I know of."

"Well, Hank, start digging. Everyone has a past."

"I think Roth is squeaky clean."

Winthrop snorted. "One thing I've learned from being in politics is that everyone has his price."

"George," fumbled Chambers, "I think the County Executive will want to tread very softly on this issue."

"I don't care about Samuel Bower! He's an idiot!" Winthrop's eyes showed a reddish tinge. "We have to find some way to burn that cop. I don't want anyone or anything to impede the Merrick deal."

"Well, we have something else in the mix to our advantage. Carl Banning is Ryan's new partner. I hear they're at each other's throats," groped Chambers.

"So?"

"Banning is indebted to the party. We provided a house for his parents in Baldwin Harbor, and we made Banning a detective right out of the academy. He'll do whatever we tell him. All I have to do is call."

Winthrop reached over Henry's desk and grabbed the handset. "No time like the present." He handed him the phone.

"We have to be careful, George."

"Careful?" "You're such a gutless wimp!"

Winthrop grabbed an ash tray from the end table and flung it at the plate glass window. It sounded like a gunshot.

Laura burst into the office; her fearful eyes darted around the room trying to take in what was happening. "Henry, what happened?"

Winthrop spun around to face the frightened woman. "Get out of here, you tramp!"

"It's okay, Laura, I don't need you anymore today. Why don't you take the rest of the day off?"

Laura turned and stormed out of Chambers' office.

"I don't care about Edmund Steele!" Winthrop shouted, turning back to Chambers. "I don't have to be cautious or subtle with him. That's just what we need in this county, more religious fanatics praying all the time, and encouraging the bloodsuckers who sit on their behinds collecting their welfare checks and watching Jerry Springer. Get Banning on the phone and tell him it's time to start paying his debt."

Chambers hesitated. He needed a shot from that bottle in his drawer more than ever.

"Tell me, Hank, who's responsible for making you one of the most powerful men in Nassau County?"

"George, you know how grateful I am to you."

"Well, show me. Dial."

"But we have to wait for the rest of the pieces to fall into place. It would be risky to act prematurely," Hank implored.

"I *refuse* to wait any longer! I'm warning you, Hank, something had better happen by next week. You know I have plenty on you and Bower. If Steele gets the go-ahead and it locks me out of the Merrick Plan, you can be sure that I'll go to the *New York Post* with everything I've got. I'll blow the whistle on you and everyone else in the party!"

As soon as Winthrop stormed out, Chambers pulled open the bottom drawer of his desk. He sat down and took a big swig straight from the bottle.

Chapter 34

Mike felt like he was walking on air. Peggy had given him a CD of worship songs, and suggested that Mike read the Gospel of John and the Book of Acts. As he devoured John's Gospel, John 3:16 took root in Mike's heart: *"For God so loved the world that he gave his one and only Son, that whoever believes in him shall not perish but have eternal life."* Jesus' pure love took hold of him and enveloped him. The Book of Acts unveiled the establishment of the church by the power of the Holy Spirit, and Mike could feel the Spirit changing his pain-filled view of the world.

He walked into the squad room and braced himself — but the dread he usually felt at the beginning of each day failed to appear. He felt the Spirit gently urging him to some action. *What, Lord? What are you saying?*

The first thing he saw was Carl Banning's feet on Peggy's desk. Then he encountered the annoying attitude so apparent on Banning's face — smug, cocky and condescending, all at the same time. Mike felt immediate heat in his blood. He wanted to jam those gigantic feet down Banning's throat. He couldn't believe how quickly his mood had swung; he was determined not to swing with it. *I don't have to do this anymore. I need to put my temper behind me. I no longer have to regard every person I encounter as a threat or an enemy. As Jesus' disciple I am called to love them.*

Now he understood the urging of the Spirit. The Master commanded him to seek forgiveness. There was no room for rationalizing. The voice was sure and unyielding. "*Forgive one another. Forgive as I have forgiven you.*"

The command was hard. Mike struggled in his soul. *Lord, do you also expect me to forgive the callous monster that gunned Katie down*?

The voice in his head — in his heart — encouraged him. *Take one step at a time, son.*

."Look, Carl, I was out of line the other day I want to apologize."

"You're a maniac?"

Mike felt awkward standing in front of him.

"Stay away from me, you crazy moron," Banning warned as he bolted upright in his chair.

"But you don't understand. I want to start over — on the right foot this time. Forgive me." Mike was surprised at the peace he felt as he spoke the words.

"Uh. . . right. It's okay. Let's just do our job and leave it at that," Banning said, humoring him.

Mike recognized the look on Banning's face. *It's the same expression I had on my face the first time Peggy spoke to me about Jesus' love for me. We had just become partners.* Mike understood where Banning was coming from. He shrugged his shoulders, silently said a prayer for Carl, and then booted up his laptop. Banning left the office.

The next few hours were routine. His cell phone interrupted him at 11:30 a.m.

"Mike, it's Dave."

"How're you doin', man?"

"Busy, Mike, how is everything with you? I called because Judge Roth wants us to resume *The Hanover Case Part II.*"

Mike heaved a gigantic sigh, "I thought Hanover's lawyer said she dropped the charges and the whole thing was over."

"Apparently not."

"Why not?"

"Their mystery witness has materialized and he's prepared to testify that he saw you molesting Opal Hanover. They've reinstated the charges. We're back on the docket with Roth."

"That's crazy. If someone was around, and I'm not saying there was, he or she was nowhere in the vicinity of Hanover's office. I may sound paranoid, but I think this thing goes beyond Hanover. Someone is trying to frame me and put me out of commission."

"That may not be too far-fetched. I have a guy who does some investigating for me. Let me call him. When we have something I'll call you to kick this thing around."

"Okay, talk to you then."

Mike was grateful that Banning had left the office. Prior to Peg and John's counsel he would have been perfectly happy to immerse himself in resentment against Banning — it would have been familiar and comfortable — but this repentance scene was new territory for this street-hardened cop. Seeing Banning tomorrow would be soon enough. Besides, Mike was more comfortable working alone now.

He saw the box in which Banning had put the things from Peggy's desk. He took it down from the filing cabinet and rummaged through it. He found her old memo pad. He scanned the pages and came across notations regarding the former medical examiner, Howard Carey.

Mike grabbed a legal pad and started listing all the deaths that were related, directly or indirectly, to the Tamara Steele case. He placed Tamara's name at the top of the page, and drew a line to the right-hand margin. Under it he scribbled the cause of death: multiple stab wounds.

Halfway down the page he printed Cora Smothers' name in bold letters. Cause of death: hanging. Everyone seemed to be relieved that Cora had left a suicide note confessing to Tamara Steele's murder. The Crime Scene Unit, however, had proved Cora's death wasn't a suicide. The chain of the chandelier around which the rope was looped was too short. There was no way she could have gotten up high enough from the chair that had been knocked over beneath her to have reached that chandelier. Her death was a murder. Someone else had strung her up and used the chair and the note to make it look like a suicide.

Peggy must have discovered and noted the CSI report the day she met the mysterious Juan at Reggie's dive in Roosevelt. *She never had time to tell me about it,* he thought remorsefully.

No wonder Dunbar had ordered Mike back on the Steele case again; the CSU report would have made reopening the case a necessity. Dunbar and County Executive Bower had been all too eager to close the Steele case after Cora's death. From the very beginning of this case, Mike and Peggy had encountered too many curve balls. It reminded him of how Katie's murder was swept under the rug. *Could there be a connection? Am I being paranoid? Maybe I'm just losing it!*

"Don't lean on your own understanding." There it was again — a scripture verse. Ever since Mike invited Jesus into his life, God was interwoven into every conscious thought. Part of himself was immersed in prayer while another part dealt with the world around him, and yet the two were inseparable. Mike spent all Memorial Day reading the Bible, and

now scripture verses seemed to pop into his head. With these words, he decided to ask God for some answers in this confusing case.

He turned back to his computer. He intended to put Tamara Steele's name into the Internet search engine. Instead he found himself keying "Edmund Steele." Near the top of the search results was a link to an article in the *Newsday* archives. He clicked it and the article popped up on his screen. The headline read: *Race for the Raceway*. He began scrolling through the text:

> *Edmund Steele, wealthy financier, has been battling his business rival and arch political adversary, real estate giant George Winthrop, for rights to a parcel of land just west of Merrick Avenue in Westbury, the former site of the now defunct Roosevelt Raceway. Mr. Winthrop envisions a mega arena, which would house a professional football franchise and a casino. Winthrop claims that the tax revenue garnered from the Merrick Plan would enable Nassau County to become the wealthiest county in the world.*

His adversary, Edmund Steele, wants to earmark this same area for low-income housing. Steele's proposed project is the vision of his daughter, Tamara Steele, the renowned evangelist. Miss Steele maintains that Nassau County is the richest region in the nation, with no compassion for the poor. Miss Steele has greatly influenced her father, who has pledged his complete moral and financial support to fulfill Miss Steele's dream of affordable housing for the poor and downtrodden on the site in question.

George Winthrop responded to the comments of his nemesis by accusing Edmund Steel of being a socialist. He further insists that his adversary is hostile towards people of wealth and is part of a conspiracy to make the central government rule the lives of the people. Mr. Winthrop went on to vilify welfare recipients, whom he accuses of "using 'victimhood' as an excuse for their inability or unwillingness to join the workforce." He vowed to do everything possible to wrest the property from Steele, and bring his own "Merrick Plan" to fruition.

Mike needed more information. He typed "George Winthrop" into the search engine. He followed the resulting links to financial sites and news archives. One of them brought him to a society page article. He scanned the text: "To the left of the bride are her uncle, George Winthrop; his sister, Rachel; and their cousin, Miss Opal Hanover. . ."

This George Winthrop seems to be smack in the middle of everything, thought Mike. *He has a possible motive for the murders, and Opal Hanover is his cousin! Maybe I've been watching too many suspense thrillers. I need a reality check from people I can trust.* He called Peggy and John. They agreed to meet at Peggy's house that evening at eight o'clock.

Opal Hanover felt as if she were in a trance. She was just going through the motions at work. All her attention was focused on the destruction of Mike Ryan. His rejection tormented her. Opal Hanover wasn't used to men snubbing her. She was the one who dumped them, not the other way around.

She was attracted to the detective; he should have jumped at the opportunity to have an affair with her. If he hadn't been so blinded by his pride and pigheadedness, he would have been dazzled by her.

Then, when she grew tired of him she'd kick him to the curb like all the rest.

She was furious with herself for twice losing her composure with him. Her mother would have been scandalized if she knew she had not conducted herself in a manner becoming a lady. But mother never understood that a woman had needs; she had always suppressed her needs — until they finally overwhelmed her. The bottle of sleeping pills was her only way out. Poor mother.

Opal was certain of one thing; she was going to see the ruination of Michael Ryan. She would not tolerate his affront to her twisted vanity. He would regret the day he brushed aside Opal Hanover. Just wait.

Chapter 35

The reserved secretary stuck her head in the door and announced, "Sir, your two o'clock is here." George Winthrop didn't lift his head, but continued to read the contracts and affidavits awaiting his signature.

"Please tell him to give me a few more minutes."

George was disgruntled at having to clean up other people's dirty work. He thought Chambers should have dealt with this Steele situation a long time ago. But Chambers was too busy juggling his love life and guzzling booze to take care of business. Winthrop sighed and picked up the phone. "Harriet, you can send in Mr. Banning."

Among his other attributes, George Winthrop possessed a photographic memory. He rapidly scanned the file on Banning that was on his desk. Banning entered timidly. By the time the detective had taken a seat, Winthrop had committed the significant events of his file to memory.

"Mr. Winthrop, how are you today?" Banning offered.

Winthrop could hear the tension in the young detective's voice. He had long ago deduced that most people who solicited jobs and political favors from the party possessed neither ingenuity of any significance, nor personal courage. There didn't seem to be anything to distinguish Carl Banning from the rest.

"Carl, how is the force treating you?"

"Great, sir, just great. Again, I want to thank you for this opportunity," Banning replied. Although he was still unsure of himself, he was inwardly elated that such an important and powerful man would take so much interest in him.

Winthrop waved his hand in dismissal of the expressed gratitude.

"Carl, I told you many times, don't mention it. Knowing that a loyal Democrat like you is protecting the constituents is reward enough."

"Mr. Winthrop, I'll do anything — anything at all — to help you and the party. I would be grateful for the opportunity to show my appreciation."

Winthrop opened a leather-bound box and handed it to Banning. "Take one, Carl. These come all the way from Havana."

Banning took a cigar from the box. "Thank you, sir. I'll smoke it later."

"I'm told you have a partner by the name of Mike Ryan. What do you think of him?"

Banning just stared at the plush rug and didn't respond.

"What's wrong Carl? Aren't you and Ryan getting along?"

"Well, sir, I guess he misses his former partner. I think there was something going on between them."

"Oh, yes, Younger — Detective Margaret Younger," Winthrop said with a malicious glint in his eye. "Well, that's too bad. Apparently Ryan likes to go his own way and isn't very good at following orders. He's not one of us. In fact, Carl, Detective Ryan is the very reason I called you in. I'm going to take you up on your offer. We need to gather evidence against him so we can get him suspended from the force. He's not a team player. We need someone like you, who knows where his loyalties lie."

Banning's hands began to shake and his voice quivered. "Sir, I don't want to get a fellow police officer in trouble."

"Carl, Ryan is stepping on the toes of many important and loyal people in our party, a party committed to the growth and welfare of the people in this great county. The party, may I remind you, has worked very hard to get your mother and father into senior citizen housing, and helped you along in your career. We've opened doors for you, young man."

"Again, sir, let me tell you how grateful I am to you."

"Evidently not grateful enough. We mistakenly believed that you would be more than happy to reciprocate the favors we have extended to you and your family. You gave us the impression that you would help safeguard our party from those who are trying to undermine our efforts."

Fear showed in Banning's eyes and his hands shook even more than before. "I do want to help with all those things and more, sir, but what you're asking of me could cost a fellow officer his career. It could ruin his life."

"Let me ask you a question. Do you think that our party is the one that could make its citizens more prosperous and happy, and make Nassau the premier county in the entire world?"

"You know that I do."

"Then, young man, be a part of the magic. Help us bring this *cancer* down."

Banning thought for a moment, then leaned in toward Winthrop's desk and asked, "What do you want me to do?"

Chapter 36

Tamara Steele's unsolved murder was six and a half weeks old. The murders of Cora Smothers and Howard Carey were also still pending.

In his mind, Mike had begun to call the three cases "the evangelist murders."

John's car was already there when Mike pulled into Peggy's driveway that evening. The front porch light went on and the front door opened as Mike turned off his headlights and killed the engine of his Mustang. He could see Peggy's face behind the screen, smiling, and the tension of the day immediately began to melt. He gave her a kiss of greeting.

She led him toward the kitchen. "Come," she said, "we were just having coffee."

"Can we have the coffee in the den?" he asked as he shook John's hand. "I can't wait to show you what I found. Maybe you can help me make some sense out of it."

They each pulled up a chair around Peggy's computer. John and Peggy watched silently as Mike navigated his way to the sites he had visited earlier in the office.

"Bear with me, guys," said Mike. "Maybe I'm paranoid but, hopefully, I'm not completely off my rocker. I've been doing some research, and. . . I don't know, but I think the Lord is leading me to people who are not on our list of suspects. John, that book you gave me. . ."

"*Discernment*?"

"Yeah, Discernment, Great book, by the way." Mike was distracted when he noticed Peggy and John nodding to one another. He just looked at them, shrugged his shoulders and returned to the screen he was viewing.

As he pulled up the articles, he explained what he had found on Winthrop and his rivalry with Edmund Steele over the Merrick Avenue Plan. "So, I was thinking that the murder at the mansion on Good Friday night might actually have been related to the struggle between Winthrop and old man Steele."

John completed Mike's thought: "And you think that Tamara Steele was just caught in the cross-fire," he summarized.

"Tamara," Peggy said, her eyes suddenly sad, "was just an innocent victim."

"Maybe Winthrop thought having Tamara out of the way would dampen the old man's enthusiasm for the housing project. Maybe he would lose interest altogether," Mike offered.

"So you believe George Winthrop stabbed Tamara, shot Howard Carey, and murdered Cora Smothers and tried to make her murder look like a suicide?"

"Well, yes and no. I'm not sure how they all tie together. I think Winthrop may be behind all this, but I doubt that he's a do-it-yourself murderer. I'm sure he had someone else do his dirty work," Mike said as he began navigating to a different Web page.

"How about Julian Giles and Billy Kensey? Are you taking them off the list of suspects?" Peggy asked.

"No, there still could be blood on their hands. I'm not sure yet." He paused, his attention being drawn back to the screen.

"Ah, here it is," he said as the society page article came up. "Look at this," scrolling down to the text he was looking for: "*Standing to the left of the bride are her uncle, George Winthrop; his sister, Rachel; and their cousin, Miss Opal Hanover.*"

"See that?" Mike continued. "It says that Opal Hanover is George Winthrop's cousin!"

"Isn't she the woman who's accusing you of attacking her?" John asked.

"Exactly!" exclaimed Mike. "As a matter of fact, we have a hearing before Judge Roth tomorrow morning. But don't you see? It's too much of a coincidence. Winthrop seems to be in the middle of everything. It's like he's got a spider web around me."

"Let me see something," John said, leaning over and taking the mouse from Mike's hand. He scrolled up the page to the top of the article where a picture of a wedding party was displayed. "So that's your little temptress," he said, smiling and pointing to Opal Hanover. "Not too bad, Mike."

"Cut it out," Mike said, retaliating with a good-natured poke in John's ribs.

"Look," observed Peggy "that's Rachel Giles, Julian's wife! Didn't it say, 'George Winthrop's sister, Rachel'? I didn't know she was related to Winthrop!"

Mike squinted at the screen, "Yeah, looks like her. Years younger of course, but it sure looks like her. I was suspicious of Giles before, but this plants him firmly back on the suspect list. I'm going to have to dig into this more deeply. I'm not sure if we're moving ahead or backwards!"

"Mike," John interjected, "the woman who accused you of attacking her, what was her name again?"

"Hanover, Opal Hanover."

"Opal Hanover, why does that name ring a bell?"

John searched Hanover's name on the Web. In a matter of seconds he had the results. His eyes scanned the list.

"Here it is. *New York Times* article, October 23, 2003." He clicked the link.

Peggy and Mike peered over his shoulder:

"Miss Opal Hanover was arraigned today on charges of perjury for testimony she gave in a rape trial in which she was the plaintiff. She had alleged that Thomas Flannigan had forced himself on her and sexually molested her. The defense produced not one,

but two eyewitnesses that testified that Miss Hanover was the aggressor. Mr. Flannigan was acquitted of all charges brought by the plaintiff.

"When reporters outside the court asked Miss Hanover's attorney to comment on the perjury charges against his client he would only say that he could not comment on a pending case. He then pushed his way through the crowd and led Miss Hanover to a waiting limousine."

Peggy hugged and kissed Mike. She was sure that, in light of this new information, he would be completely vindicated.

John's voice interrupted them. "Well Mike, I have to tell you, I don't think you're paranoid at all. Some people have made it extremely difficult for the two of you to remain on this case. Just look at what has happened. Peggy, you were attacked and left for dead. Mike, you get embroiled in a sex scandal that pulls you off the case. It has been one roadblock after another."

"Wow, it just dawned on me," Mike said, continuing John's line of thinking, "do you think Dunbar and the County Executive could be involved?"

"Well, didn't each of them give you and Peggy a hard time for not hanging Tamara's murder on Cora

Smothers? Looks to me like they were trying to derail the investigation."

Mike looked at Peggy for confirmation.

"Dunbar became extremely angry when I suggested that Cora was murdered. I thought his reaction was totally inappropriate under the circumstances," Peggy responded.

"But why would the lieutenant derail the Steele investigation? What incentive would he have? He has to be receiving orders from someone higher up."

"Yes, John, and he's at the top. He resides at 405 West Street," Peggy replied.

"So if we're right, and money related to the raceway property is the motive," added Mike, "then it seems that the movers and shakers in Nassau County all have something in common — their hands are in the cookie jar."

Chapter 37

Wednesday morning celebrated God's creation in all its glory. The fragrance of late spring filled the air and a profusion of bright pinks, reds, yellows and greens delighted the eye from a pallet only He could prepare. Winter can be dull and gray on Long Island, but springtime bursts into bloom in full array with all the cultivated flower beds and manicured lawns. This particular day in May reflected God's finest. Even the grounds of the courthouse at Franklin Avenue and Old Country Road were magnificent.

But all this beauty was lost on David Kennedy. His full attention was focused on getting his brother-in-law exonerated.

Mike met David on the courthouse steps. He told him about the charges Opal Hanover had brought against Thomas Flannigan back in 2003 and her perjury conviction.

"I see you've been doing your homework. That coincides with what I dug up on her. The woman is whacko!" said Dave. "Listen, Mike, one other thing before we go in. You have to control yourself. Judge Roth has very little patience with volatile people in his court, and I think you already used up your *tantrum* quota. Okay?"

"Don't worry about me," said Mike quite seriously. "I know I am righteous in God's eyes. He knows I'm innocent and that's all that counts, so I really don't have to prove myself to anybody."

Dave stared at him. "Oh, yes, you do, pal! If you want to walk out of there a free man, you're going to have to prove your *righteousness* to Roth, and don't forget it!"

Dave was amazed at the change in his brother-in-law since the last Hanover hearing. What happened to the defensive, impulsive, volatile and unreasonable man his sister had married? Mike's reliance on God and his resignation without travail to whatever the outcome would be was beyond Dave's comprehension. He himself had never really bothered with the concepts of God or religion, but this Jesus stuff apparently had effected a very profound change in Mike. *Maybe,* he thought, *it's worth looking into.*

Chapter 38

Billy Kensey was running into hard times. He thought that Tamara's death would help his career. Strangely enough, it did just the opposite. His hit single had dropped on the charts to number fifty. Concert dates were cancelled with no explanation and that *idiot manager* never returned his calls.

And to make matters worse it seemed that Tamara's will would be tied up in probate forever; if old Steele had his way. Edmund Steele had disliked Billy from the day he met him; yet Tamara married him despite her father's vehement protests. The old man was convinced that Billy had hired some thug to murder his daughter.

Kensey was less than broken-hearted over his wife's death. He felt she was always watching him, waiting for him to slip up, always judging and correcting him, an embarrassment to her. Well, if that's what she thought, so be it; he wasn't going to disappoint her. He had cast aside his pretensions at being a Christian and determined to live up to her expectations at every opportunity. He arrived at every fundraiser or religious event either stoned or drunk and invariably there would be some star-dazed groupie on his arm.

In reality, Tamara never reacted to his behavior. She never confronted him. She would merely look at him with pity in her eyes, as if he were a wounded animal. Without a word to him, she would just pray. It infuriated him.

As for Tamara's friends and members of the church he felt he was a target for their piety.

But what was he to do? He sat on his couch staring at the mountain of snow on the glass coffee table before him. He sorted out a line of the white particles with a razor blade. *Soon,* he thought, *all of this will be a distant memory. That Jesus of theirs is merely a psychological crutch. Who needs him? Not me!*

Chapter 39

Mike and David took their seats in the courtroom. Within five minutes Opal Hanover and her attorney arrived. Ever aware of the importance of packaging to make an impression, she was dressed very conservatively. She and her attorney seated themselves at the table opposite the defendant's. A few moments later Judge Roth took his position on the bench.

"Okay, attorneys," he said matter-of-factly, "let's see if we can resolve this mess."

Mike still felt that Roth was really turned off by the case and would try to dispose of it as quickly as possible.

"Mr. Benedict, you indicated to me in my chambers that you have a witness."

"Yes, your honor, we call Charles Davenport."

A shabbily dressed man of about thirty ambled slowly forward. He appeared confused and disoriented. The environment was strange to him and he looked around as if seeking someone to help him. He was quite obese and was breathing heavily from the exertion of the short walk to the witness stand. When the man was finally seated, the court officer began the swearing-in process. "State your name for the court."

The man looked lost, and in desperation, looked at Judge Roth for clarification. Roth, sensing the man's confusion, attempted to assist him.

"Sir, please tell us your name," he said gently.

The witness raised his eyebrows and smiled at the judge. "My name is Charlie Davenport and I have a job at the Wilson Academy."

"Mr. Davenport, we're going to ask you some questions. Do you promise to tell the truth?" Roth paused, then continued as gently as before, "The whole truth and nothing but the truth?"

The witness said, "Okay."

"Please, just say yes or no."

"Okay."

"Yes or no, Mr. Davenport?" said Roth, repeating the instruction.

"Okay. Yes."

"You may proceed, Mr. Benedict," the judge said.

"Thank you, Your Honor." Benedict turned to the witness, "Charlie, my name is Mr. Benedict. I wonder if you would help me."

"Okay, I'll try real hard."

"Do you know the plaintiff? The lady sitting over there?" Benedict asked, pointing to Opal Hanover.

"Sure I do, that's Opal. She's the prettiest girl in the school. Hi Opal; you look pretty today," he said as he smiled.

Opal Hanover looked embarrassed; she shifted in her seat.

"Do you know anyone else in this room?" Benedict continued.

Charlie's face was distorted as he squinted, scanning the courtroom. It took a minute before his eyes lit up.

"Oh yeah, I seen that guy before," he pointed to Mike.

"Charlie, you're doing very well. Now just two or three questions more and you will be done. Where did you see that man?"

Charlie raised his hand and placed it on his chin as he screwed up his face in thought. It was a few seconds before a light came on in his eyes.

"I know; I know," he shouted with enthusiasm. "He was in with Opal in her room."

"And what were they doing in the room?"

He started to laugh sheepishly.

"Charlie, is there something funny?"

He turned crimson. He covered his face with his hands.

"Charlie, what did you see Detective Ryan doing with Ms. Hanover in the room?" Benedict asked again.

"Well, he was doing some stuff to Opal."

"What kind of stuff, Charlie?"

He flushed again and cast his eyes down in embarrassment, "Stuff like I do to Cynthia sometimes."

"And what do you do to Cynthia sometimes?"

"I can't tell you 'cause I may get in trouble."

The attorney took a deep breath and continued patiently, "Charlie, I promise, you won't get in trouble."

"Well, okay, I try to kiss her," he hesitated, embarrassed again. He couldn't take his eyes off the floor. He continued, "And I pull up her dress to see her underwear." His face was bright red and he smiled sheepishly.

Benedict pointed towards Mike. "So, Charlie, you're saying — look at me, Charlie — that man," he pointed to Mike, "did the same things to Opal that you do to Cynthia?"

"Yes."

"Now, Charlie, this question is a very important one. Was Opal happy that the man sitting over there was doing these things to her?

"No, she wasn't. She was screaming and tried to push him away from her."

Mike couldn't believe what he was hearing but he just sat there calmly, confident that somehow he would be vindicated.

David leaned over to his client and whispered in his ear.

"Do you remember seeing this man?"

"I don't know. Maybe, I may have seen him sweeping the floor some time."

David looked at his notes and knew that he had to tread carefully as he cross-examined. It wouldn't be easy to get accurate testimony from a witness like this. He knew Benedict would be on his guard. He slowly approached the witness, wearing a friendly smile on his face.

"Hi, Charlie, my name is David. I'm here to help that man over there," he said, pointing to Mike. "His name is Mike. Do you know that Mike is a policeman?"

"Oh, no! Is he going to take me to jail because of what I did with Cynthia?"

"No, no, Charlie, you're okay. Mike's not going to take you to jail. You are a good man, and there's no reason for Detective Ryan to put you in jail. But if you don't tell the truth, Mike may have to go to jail. Do you understand?"

"Your honor, this is ridiculous," Benedict interrupted, "Mr. Kennedy is laying a guilt trip on this poor man. He's bewildered enough."

"Mr. Benedict, he's your witness." Judge Roth's voice reflected jaded patience. "I allowed you a lot of leeway with this witness for the sake of getting to the bottom of this case. Under the circumstances, for Mr. Kennedy to emphasize the gravity of this matter is not out of line. I will allow him the same latitude I gave you. Please sit down and maybe we can get through this before the next millennium."

"Okay, Charlie," Kennedy resumed, "let's try this again. Listen very carefully. What time do you work at the Wilson school?"

"Well, I go to Miss Adams at one o'clock and we finish at five o'clock. Miss Adams teaches me how to do my banking, and to wear clean clothes, and to be nice to people and. . ."

"That's great, Charlie, but we want to know if you work near Miss Hanover's office."

"At five o'clock I sweep the floors. Then I'm allowed to go home at seven-thirty."

"Charlie, the night you saw Mike, do you remember if Opal's office door was opened or closed?"

Nervously, Charlie wrung his hands, then glanced at Opal Hanover. David could see the question upset him. He decided to take a different tack.

"Charlie, nobody here wants you to be upset or angry with yourself. You're doing a good job. Now I'm going to ask you a different question. Maybe even an easier one. Tell us how long you have known Opal Hanover."

"I know her for a long, long time."

"Your honor, I haven't a clue where Mr. Kennedy is going with this line of questioning," Benedict interjected. "I'm sure you haven't either."

"I beg the court's indulgence," David replied. "With a little patience everything will become clear."

"Okay, Mr. Kennedy. But I warn you the court has you on a short leash."

"Thank you, your honor. Charlie, you told us that you knew Opal for a long time. Now why is that?"

Charlie looked at Opal and began to perspire.

"Opal's mother is my Aunt Mary. Opal and I used to play together. We used to play hide 'n' seek. Opal found me all the time," he began to giggle.

Mike turned to look at his adversary. A whole range of emotions, from intense embarrassment to seething anger, raced across her face. Her eyes darted from Charlie to Mike, to the judge.

"Hey, Opal, was that okay?" Charlie asked. "Did I say what you wanted? I tried to remember everything you told me. Did I do good?"

Benedict sprang to his feet.

"Your honor, I ask that you disregard what the witness has been saying. It's obvious that he has diminished capacity, and in his state of agitation we concede that his testimony is unreliable. I ask that you disregard it."

"That was rather feeble, Mr. Benedict," responded Judge Roth. "I told you before that you can't have it both ways. You presented him as a credible witness. I agree — at this point he is credible, like it or not!"

Hanover fumed as she stared at her cousin, "You blithering idiot. You can't get anything straight in that mush you call a brain. I hated my mother for making me play with you. I can't stand you!"

"Order, order," Judge Roth commanded.

"And as for you, Mike Ryan, how dare you reject me. You should have been thankful that I even *considered* letting a low-life like you have me. What was I thinking?"

"Mr. Benedict, I order you to control your client."

Benedict tried to calm Opal down, but she ignored him. Her eyes locked on Mike and she suddenly flew across the aisle at him. Something flashed in her hand and he barely had time to react. He raised his left arm to block her. He felt searing pain and blood spilled from his arm onto the table, the same blood that now dripped from a letter opener in her hand. As she raised it to strike a second time, the determined hand of David Kennedy grabbed her wrist and twisted it, forcing her to drop the weapon. A court guard responded quickly, forcing Opal's arms behind her back and cuffing her in one smooth motion. As he dragged her off, she screamed expletives and kicked wildly. Charlie cried as he watched her being taken away. His eyes begged forgiveness.

"Thanks, brother-in-law," Mike said, "you really saved my bacon. Does this mean I can't make fun of your barrister skills anymore?" he quipped with a big grin that suddenly turned to a grimace from the pain in his now-throbbing arm.

Peggy drove Mike home from the Emergency Room where he had received a tetanus shot and seven stitches. Mike was filled with gratitude because he was vindicated. More than that, he was elated that the scriptures he read were true. Now he knew for sure that the Bible wasn't just an ancient book of feel-good platitudes, but instead the living word of God. The Bible contains everything we need to know for salvation, plus wisdom for living. It is filled with promises for the children of God and assurance of the plans He has for us, plans to prosper us and not to harm us, plans to give us hope and a future.

Mike basked in an inner peace that was still new and strange to him.

For the first time in his life Mike felt compassion for someone who had tried to harm him. He felt sorry for Opal Hanover and earnestly prayed for her. He couldn't believe the major attitude change that had taken place in him.

Chapter 40

Carl Banning felt intimidated the first time he met Mike Ryan. Ryan wasn't a particularly imposing figure, and Banning was sure he could hold his own in a physical encounter. No, it was Ryan's self-assurance that intimidated him. Ryan exuded confidence.

At the same time, Banning was painfully aware of his own fearfulness. And he wished, oh, how he wished, that he had the guts to tell George Winthrop what he could do with his patronage. Banning would love to be the hero, rejecting corruption and championing the golden rule like the heroes of his grandfather's classic movie collection. But he had no delusions about himself; that kind of courage just wasn't in his character.

And there was Gloria to consider. He couldn't lose her. He knew that if he betrayed Winthrop and the county Democratic machine they would destroy him financially, and Gloria would give him his walking papers. Being a hero wasn't going to support her in the manner to which she was accustomed. He had no delusions about her either. She was a creature of comfort, and her comforts were becoming increasingly expensive. Still, he couldn't let her go.

Besides, Ryan was really just a bully, *right*? The "quiet strength" routine didn't fool Banning. Ryan just threw his weight around and abused his authority as a cop. The very thought of it made him angry. What gall! He was convinced that everyone hated Ryan. Why else would the bosses be so eager to get rid of him? So, in a sense, by messing with Ryan's head, he would be performing a public service. That was adequate justification for Banning.

Maybe he was being a hero after all. The thought energized him. It strengthened his resolve to do what Winthrop asked. There was no need to risk losing Gloria, the most beautiful girl in the world, or to jeopardize his parents' security. He had convinced himself that this was now a noble quest. *Down with Michael Ryan!*

Chapter 41

Every time Peg thought of the Lord's faithfulness her spirit would soar. *He is so good.* She would close her eyes, feel His presence and just bask in His love.

Her mind wandered back to the first time she had laid eyes on Michael Ryan. Lieutenant Dunbar introduced them when he assigned her to be Michael's partner. She found herself immediately attracted to him despite all the things she heard about him. He had a certain boyish charm. Yes, he was brash, a bit of a smart aleck, frequently sarcastic and just as unpredictable as they said; but underneath all that, there was something good and decent. As she got to know him she found that he was an honest man with a lot of integrity and a very strong sense of right and wrong. He was also a very caring father and dedicated to his family. She liked what she saw.

She knew he was still grieving the loss of his wife, a deep wound that would take a very long time to heal. He was able to function but he was far from whole. He built a wall around his heart to protect the wound. Daily she watched him suffer the pain of love lost and all his hope for his family's future. Her heart went out to him, but it was more than pity. In a very short time she found herself in love with him.

She sensed that he was angry with God for allowing the tragedy that took his Katie away and then suffering the injustice of having her killer go free. That anger was a wedge between him and God. It was also a wedge between them. As time passed her love continued to grow, though she saw no hope for anything more than a deep friendship between him. She longed for something beyond their professional relationship. It was torment for her.

In her prayer time she would beg the Lord for an answer. Why would He allow her to suffer like this? The Holy Spirit led her to Paul's Letter to the Romans, chapter 5, verses 3 and 4: "We also rejoice in our sufferings, because we know that suffering produces perseverance; perseverance, character;

and character, hope. And hope does not disappoint us, because God has poured out His love into our hearts by the Holy Spirit, whom He has given us." She understood it in her head, and only partly in her heart, but she accepted it. She had to let go and pray for the Lord's will in Michael's life and in her life; she had to trust God.

The scripture came to mind: "Know therefore that the LORD your God is God; he is the faithful God, keeping his covenant of love to a thousand generations of those who love him and keep his commands." It referred to the Jews being led out of captivity after four hundred years in Egypt. Each of the four years waiting for God to move in Michael's life had seemed like a hundred years to her. Nonetheless, God is faithful. With a heart full of gratitude she gave thanks.

Then she excitedly primped her hair one last time and prepared to leave for dinner. She had to meet Michael in about twenty minutes. She spent this Friday counting the hours until they would be together again. She was full of joy.

The doorbell rang. "Oh heavens! Who in the world can that be? I have to get going. I don't have time for this," Peggy said out loud but to herself. Her face reflected her annoyance as she scurried to the door and peered through the peephole. It was Rachel Giles. There was someone else with her, but Peggy couldn't see who it was.

"Rachel, what a surprise!"

"Margaret, how are you? Could we come in?"

"Well, as a matter of fact, I was going to meet someone."

"We will only take a few minutes of your time. I would like you meet my — who are you to me, Fred, friend or bodyguard?" Fred, handsome in a conventional way, and obviously much younger than Rachel, smiled politely at Peggy, but stood silent.

Peggy opened her mouth to protest, but before she could utter a word Rachel and her companion had maneuvered themselves into the foyer.

Chapter 42

Even though what Mike called "the evangelist murders" weren't close to being solved, Mike felt a peculiar peace. Peggy and John had prepared him for moments of exhilaration upon giving his heart to Jesus, but he hadn't dreamed this glorious mood would last.

His date with Peggy added to his excitement. He and Peggy were going to celebrate by having dinner at Yancy's Pier on Freeport's Nautical Mile. The restaurant was a departure from the various greasy spoons he and Peggy once frequented. He wondered if he'd know what fork to use in such a fancy joint and prayed he didn't make a total fool of himself.

Even though he was going to be with her in less than two hours, he still felt the urge to hear her voice now. He took out his cell phone and punched in number one, connecting him to her phone. There wasn't any answer. Anxiously, he tried her home telephone, and got the same result. He felt a little depressed. *She's probably in the shower, getting ready.* Mike knew he was being foolish.

Mike laughed at himself. He waited fifteen minutes and redialed her numbers. Still no answer.

He didn't see any use in thinking about Peg again until dinner. He returned to the frustrating case he was working on. Back at his desktop, he redirected the cursor to a *Daily News* blog. In a piece dated March 17, 2002, he spotted a picture showing George Winthrop with his arm around Rachel Giles.

He grabbed a sheet of computer paper lying on the corner of his desk and jotted down three names: Julian, Rachel and George Winthrop. "I guess it's time to go to the church to check on some leads," Mike hummed to himself.

Mike drove to The Good Shepherd in Valley Stream which was the church Tamara Steele had pastored until her death. The administrative offices were in the church building. He opened the double doors and stepped onto a plush red carpet. On his right hung a large and beautiful painting of the fallen evangelist.

Even though its leader had been struck down, the church was ablaze with ferocious clerical activity. Phones were ringing off the hook, printers were printing and fingers were frantically punching laptop keys. The office resembled the campaign headquarters of a presidential contender on election night.

Mike walked up to a receptionist and flipped his badge. "Excuse me, could I speak to the office manager." The attractive young woman directed him to a cubicle in the middle of the room where a middle-aged woman was deep in conversation on the phone.

He entered the cubicle and stood in front of the desk. Although he was sure she was aware of his presence, the woman didn't acknowledge him. He stood before her, rocking to and fro, forcing himself to remain patient while she continued her conversation.

She finally freed herself from the phone and presented him with a broad smile.

"Good afternoon," she said. "How can I help you?"

"Detective Mike Ryan here. I'm on the Tamara Steele case. I have a couple of questions."

Her affable smile was suddenly transformed into a scowl.

"I thought you were a contributor. I already told Peggy Younger all I knew. Frankly, I don't have anything to add to it."

"I appreciate your cooperating with Detective Younger. But I'm approaching the case from another angle."

Her eyebrows narrowed.

"There was a rumor that Miss Steele and Reverend Giles were involved."

Mike knew that he had struck a chord, for the woman began to nervously shuffle papers around. Quickly, she stood up and said, "Detective, please follow me."

They went to a conference room at the end of the office. She closed the door. The conference table was long, but she sat adjacent to him and said, "By the way, my name is Marion Adams. As you were told, I am the office manager, how can I help you?"

"Miss Adams," Mike began, "I'm told that you have been associated with The Good Shepherd for fifteen years."

"Yes, this has been my place of worship for a long time. Next month, I'll be a member of this blessed community for sixteen years. Ten years ago the church elders made me part of the staff," she proudly announced.

"In that time I bet you have come to know all kinds of secrets about your fellow congregants."

She threw Mike a piercing glance. "Detective, these holy people are my brothers and sisters in the Lord. Some have brought me into their confidence, relating intimate moments in their lives. I will never betray their trust."

"Miss Adams, I assume you loved Miss Steele and want the person who brutally stabbed her to death to be brought to justice. Although I'm only a baby Christian I know that God, too, wants the murderer to pay for this crime."

Miss Adams took her handkerchief and began dabbing her eyes. "Of course I want justice. Tamara was such a beautiful person of God."

"Tell me," said Mike, "do you know George Winthrop?"

"He's not a member of our church, but I've seen him a few times attending our services. The Lord doesn't want us to judge others, but I can't help thinking that he's a very nasty man."

"Miss Adams, I've heard the same thing. Could you tell me if he was close to Rachel Giles?"

"You do know, of course, that they're brother and sister."

"Yes I know. I read about their relationship."

"They don't seem very close. I think that Rachel and her husband view George Winthrop as crude and try to disassociate themselves from him." She moved her chair closer to Mike. "But I'll tell you who Winthrop was really chummy with. . . Cora Smothers."

Mike was beginning to see all the pieces of this complex puzzle suddenly coming together.

"In what way did they appear chummy?"

"Well, I once heard them making plans for dinner. I tried to warn her as a sister in Christ that Mr. Winthrop was a married man and that she should discourage anything serious. I also reminded her that he really wasn't a Christian."

"Miss Adams, you've been very helpful. Thank you very much."

Chapter 43

"Well, anyway, let me explain about the bodyguard, it's really very funny." Rachel stood in the doorway, preventing Peg from stepping out of her foyer. "Julian thought I needed a bodyguard. Isn't that a hoot? Some of the members of his congregation think he's having affairs. These people never stop expressing their fury. He thought they would direct their anger at me; thus the bodyguard."

While Rachel continued on about the bodyguard, Fred moved suddenly in back of Peg and got a choke hold on her. Then Rachel took a handkerchief soaked in chloroform from her handbag and covered Peg's mouth. Peg's surroundings gradually faded as she collapsed into Fred's arms.

When she regained consciousness her head felt as if she had been struck with a sledge hammer, her hands were tied behind her back. She couldn't see anything; she felt some sort of cloth around her eyes. While blindfolded, her other senses became activated. She guessed by the roomy feel of the backseat that she was being taken somewhere in a sport utility vehicle. Although still feeling groggy, she tried to recall the circumstances that resulted in her abduction.

Peg felt herself roll back into the seat, as if the car were climbing up a steep incline. Soon the vehicle came to an abrupt halt. Then a firm hand helped her out. She tripped and almost fell. Her fall was broken by a man with hairy arms. She was directed to lift her leg onto a step and she heard a door opening. She was made to walk up a few steps, and cross a doorsill. Once they had each entered the room, she was pushed into an overstuffed chair and the blindfold was removed.

"Welcome to my summer home, Peggy."

Peggy's vision continued to be marred by the blaring light. She squinted, trying to focus. At first she didn't recall the high-pitched voice, but as her surroundings became more stable, so did the bodies and furniture in the room.

"I only invite special people like you and your *friend* Tamara here. Oh, what am I thinking? You and Tamara were always too busy to come up here. Besides, you two were too good to be bothered with the likes of me."

Rachel Giles, that's who the voice belonged to. Rachel stood in front of Peggy, wearing a long blue silk dress. The color accentuated the blond highlights of her hair.

"Rachel," said Peggy, "I don't understand."

"You don't understand. . . you don't understand! You and your dear friend Tamara never understood."

"Please, Rachel, tell me. Why am I here?"

Rachel's neck vein became pronounced. "Don't tell me that you don't like my hideaway."

Peggy's face must have shown her astonishment. "I've always tried to show love towards you, and I know Tamara admired you."

"You and your *precious* Tamara thought you were so special and magnificent."

Rachel's eyes practically bulged as she walked over to a makeshift bar where she poured a healthy drink of what looked like gin or vodka.

"Rachel," she said, "I really don't know what you're talking about,"

Rachel briskly walked towards Peggy and her steel-like arm slammed her prisoner's mouth. Peggy's lip began to bleed.

"You deserve that and more. Even though you're my prisoner, you're still so prideful, so full of yourself." Rachel gulped down the contents of the tumbler, walked over to the bar and added more to her glass.

Peg's mind cleared a little and she said, "Tell me the reason you're holding me prisoner."

"You're in no position to tell me what to do. Detective Margaret Younger, I don't have to tell you anything."

Peg saw Rachel grinding her teeth. She took another hearty gulp from her drink. She picked up a broom that was resting against the wall and jammed the handle into Peg's stomach. Trying desperately to regain her breath, Peg moaned in pain and said, "If you'd just drop me off somewhere, I'll call someone to come and get me. I promise I won't press charges and no one will ever know."

"And please tell me, what will the D.A. do about my other crime?"

"Rachel, I don't understand."

"Oh, you don't understand. In fact you never understood anything. How in the world you and the rest of the nation thought Tamara Steele was the modern Joan of Arc leading everyone to the land of milk and honey. It's always been a mystery to me. I saved my brothers and sisters from the lies and deception she wrought. I'm the one who should be crowned *savior of the world.*"

"You killed Tamara! Oh, my sweet Lord, I can't believe it."

"Yes, I'm proud to say I rid the world of that hypocrite!"

Peg gasped. She couldn't believe her senses. Maybe the drug was causing her to hallucinate. It just failed to compute. How could a fragile, seemingly gentle person like Rachel be capable of such a brutal murder?

"I can't believe you did this!"

"I bet you can't believe that harlot had an affair with my Julian either?"

"She had *what* with Julian?"

"You heard me. Your saintly evangelist committed adultery with my husband."

"If there *was* an affair, how did you find out about it?"

Rachel walked over to Peg, grabbed the broom-stick and jabbed her again. Peg doubled over and winced with pain, using all her strength to remain upright in the chair.

"You just ask too many questions." After her fourth drink, Rachel's tongue became thick and she was having a difficult time steadying her steps.

Peg gradually tried regaining her breath. "Rachel, what have you got to lose in answering me? If the Lord doesn't choose to intervene, you and I know that I'm not going to see the light of day."

"You don't know what I'm going to do."

"Rachel, come on. Maybe the murder wasn't entirely your fault. You were so distraught by Julian's behavior, maybe you weren't responsible."

"Well, Tamara had to be stopped, her and her millionaire father. Both of them thought they could push everyone around, flashing thousand-dollar bills and buying people off. Thank God George told me about how she wrapped my husband around her little finger."

So Michael was right! He said that the moguls had something to do with Tamara's murder. Imagine using a woman like Rachel to satisfy their greed.

Fred had been standing to one side the whole while, hands clasped behind his back, trying to look blank but looking faintly sick. He walked over to Rachel and spoke softly, "Rachel, you're tired. Maybe you want to lie down." Looking at him, anyone would have surmised that he wasn't comfortable advising Rachel on anything. There was an understanding that she gave the orders and Fred took them without a hint of contradiction.

Rachel's eyes focused on Fred. "How dare you patronize me? Why don't you say what you're thinking? You think I've had too much to drink."

Fred started wringing his hands, his voice quivering. "No, Rachel! It's just that you've been through many traumatic experiences, I don't want you to overburden yourself."

Rachel staggered over to him, pushed him onto a couch, sat on his lap and ran her hand through his bushy light brown hair.

"Isn't he the cutie? And he's all mine. I'm too good for Julian anyway."

"Rachel," asked Peggy with determination, "did George want Tamara dead?"

Rachel left the man's lap. "Freddy," she commanded, "Peggy bores me. Grab her and throw her in the basement. I haven't made up my mind what to do with her yet."

Chapter 44

Mike looked at his watch. It was ten minutes after six. *This darn case! I'm gonna be late.* He rushed home showered, shaved and changed. He put the car through its paces as he sped along, weaving through traffic to the restaurant.

He took out his cell phone and punched in Peggy's number. After a few rings he heard her voice mail greeting. She wasn't in. *Did she forget our date? Or worse, did she finally come to her senses and decide Michael Ryan isn't for her after all?*

He sat in his car for three hours, checking his watch every few minutes. All the while he was wondering what he had said or done to make her have a change of heart. Finally he drove home.

He heard nothing from her the rest of the evening. He called her the next morning and still got no answer. The rest of the day he spent coping with doctor's appointments for Jamie and his mother, the month's bills and left over paperwork.

The whole while, he thought of Peggy. *Well, at least she introduced me to the Lord, and she gave me of a week of joy believing she was going to be a permanent part of my life and Jamie's. She cut out of my life before and I survived; there's no reason why I can't do it again. I guess it'll be uncomfortable at church, but I won't give it up just to avoid her. The Lord and the other kids at church have already become too important to Jamie.*

He awoke Sunday morning and still hadn't heard from Peggy. He tried his best to be cheerful for Jamie. Soon they were dropping Mrs. Ryan off at her church and proceeding on to The Good Shepherd.

In spite of his depressed mood, Mike had to admit that the Lord was blessing him. The May sky was painted a beautiful blue and the reds and yellows of the flowers sang the glory of their Creator. No matter how he tried, Mike couldn't remain in his dark world.

Mike arrived at The Good Shepherd. He looked around… still no Peggy.

He found himself actually looking forward to the sermon. Last week's had been given by Pastor Evans. Though the minister possessed an uncanny intelligence, he still had the ability to simplify his theology enough to speak to the congregation in user-friendly terms. After the opening hymns and prayers, Pastor Evans took the pulpit.

He selected St. Paul's description of love in Paul's First Letter to the Corinthian Church, chapter 13. Mike, as he listened, received a peculiar feeling that the Lord spoke directly to him through Pastor Evans. The fourth verse reverberated in his consciousness:

> *Love is patient, love is kind. Love does not keep a record of wrongs.*
>
> *It is not rude. It always protects, always trusts, always perseveres.*

Mike had the impression the Holy Spirit was showing him that there wasn't a hook to love; that perfected love is always giving to another person. The perfect illustration of this love was embodied by the cross.

As the sermon continued, Mike found himself wondering whether he had exhibited love toward

Peg. Had he been patient with her? Did he trust her? Did he protect her from various insults and hurts, or was he one of the perpetrators?

After the sermon, the worship leader led the congregation in a few spirited praise songs. The service ended and most of the worshipers headed to the church basement for the weekly fellowship. Although he didn't feel much like socializing, Mike knew Jamie wanted to hang with his new found church friends so he followed him downstairs.

Mike grabbed a cup of coffee. He felt awkward without Peggy; socially she acted like a buffer for his shyness. Adding to his discomfort, he feared running into her, though he hadn't seen her during the service. *What would he say? How would he act?*

Suddenly he felt a hand on his arm. "How are you this fine Sunday?"

"Hello, Mrs. Younger," said Mike. "You and Mr. Younger haven't returned to Kansas City yet?"

"No, we were planning to stay a little while longer."

After exchanging pleasantries, Mrs. Younger asked. "Have you seen Margaret?"

Mike didn't want to explain to her that Peggy apparently wanted to end their relationship. "No. We were supposed to have a date Friday night, at least I thought so. But I must have gotten the day wrong because she didn't show up."

Mrs. Younger's face fell and she said, "Strange. Margaret and her girlfriends usually meet at Sammy's for breakfast before Sunday service, and since I'm visiting they invited me but Margaret didn't come. She usually calls if she is going to be tied up. Mrs. Younger turned to Peg's sister and asked, "Fran, when did you say that you spoke to her last?"

"Mom, it was Wednesday. That's when she and I set up the plan to meet yesterday for lunch while you and Dad were in Manhattan at the Metropolitan Museum of Art."

Mrs. Younger's normally affable face turned pale. "But she didn't meet you, either. This seems very strange to me. Henry, something must be wrong."

"Tina," said Henry soothingly, "I think you're getting excited over nothing.

"Mom, you know Peggy, she probably has a lot on her mind what with her detective work and her *new boyfriend.*" Here Fran winked at Mike. Mike tried to smile.

Mrs. Younger's expression twisted. "I want to know why no one has heard from her and I want to know now."

The atmosphere became tense. Mr. Younger's brow wrinkled. Fran's eyes widened. They all turned to look at Mike.

He stood still.

Steadying his voice, and trying not to frighten them, he said, "I'm going to the precinct. Stay by your telephones. I'll try to keep you posted."

Mike went over to Jamie.

"Kiddo, I'm sorry, but your fun has to be cut short."

Jamie had made a quantum leap to maturity since Mike and he had joined the church. He said without protest, "Right Pop. Catch you later guys." He gave each of his new friends a fist bump and left with Mike.

Mike trusted his son's newly adopted maturity. As they drove to pick Mrs. Ryan up from her church, Mike explained that Peggy could be in trouble. "She might have been involved in an accident," he told his somber son. "I'm going to the precinct to call all the hospitals in the metropolitan area."

"Pop, can I do anything?"

"Pray."

Peggy thanked God for Fred. He disobeyed Rachel and treated Peggy more reasonably when Rachel was out of sight. She concluded that he wasn't evil, just very misguided.

Peggy had fallen asleep on a small old bed stored there in the basement. She awakened with no way of knowing how much time had passed. Her stomach still wretched from Rachel's jabbing her with the broomstick. When Rachel had finally left the basement, Peg felt free to moan in agony. The basement windows were small and were situated eight feet from the floor, making it virtually impossible to ascertain the time of day. However, she was able to see a patch of lawn that was dimly lit, and she figured that it was either twilight or early morning.

Her stomach growled from hunger. Even if they offered her food now, she wondered whether she could eat it without getting sick.

Peg decided to pray: *O Lord, I'm frightened. Forgive my weakness. You said in Your word that You would never leave me or forsake me. You also promised that You have a plan for my life. I can't believe that Your plan is to have me die in this dark damp basement. Why did you bring Michael and Jamie into my life?*

She was so thirsty, her mouth felt like cotton. She would never have thought that Rachel could be so vicious. *How could I have been so blind?*

Peggy questioned her own discernment.

She heard the basement door opening, the click of high heels; Rachel stood before her.

"Are we comfy, dearie?" Rachel leered. Peggy judged that Rachel had been drinking again, so there was no use reasoning with her. She decided to remain silent.

Rachel snarled, "Tell me, Detective, do you want to talk to me now?"

Peggy merely stared at her, offering no response.

"Well, Detective? Nothing to say? You and your buddy, Tamara, never used to be at a loss for words."

Peg prayed. The Holy Spirit brought her mind to another scene of interrogation. She envisioned the Son of God before Herod. Her Lord quietly endured the scorn, mockery and cynicism of a pagan, who was morally bankrupt. Peggy prayed that she could have a portion of Jesus' courage.

Peggy lowered her eyes. As she did so, she spotted a two-by-four lying against an adjacent wall. She prayed that Rachel would overlook it. But Rachel staggered a little, noticed the beam, picked it up and stood before Peg. Peg held her breath as the beam collided with her left shinbone. She writhed with pain. For the first time in her life, she felt totally abandoned. The blow was so brutal, she passed out.

When Peggy regained consciousness, she heard the peal of hysterical laughter — the laughter of a madwoman, a psychopath. In spite of her unflinching faith, she now doubted if she'd ever see Mike again? Would he or her family ever find out what had happened to her?

Slowly, she tried to gain her bearings. Peggy couldn't imagine being free again, and that uncertainty also included her faith in the Lord. Would she ever be delivered from this prison, this pit of death? In her desperation the ninth verse of the Forty-Second Psalm rang in her ears:

> *I will say to God my Rock,*
> *"Why have You forgotten me?*
> *Why do I go mourning because of the oppression of the enemy?"*

Peggy never felt so alone. She no longer had joy, hope, or promise living in her heart. Where was her Heavenly Father, the personal God who had always cradled her in His arms when she felt threatened? She moaned a verse from the Sixty-Third Psalm:

I seek you; my soul thirsts for you.

She escaped her garden of sorrows by submitting to a deep sleep.

Mike hung up the telephone on his desk at the precinct. No hospitals in the area had Peggy listed as a patient.

Mike felt in his gut that Peggy was in grave danger. He had stopped wondering how a class act like Peg could even give a second thought to a loser like him, his mind was now fully alert and in cop mode. As a cop, his thoughts naturally led to negative conclusions.

He didn't know why, but George Winthrop came to mind. Would he know anything about Peggy's disappearance? By a mysterious and instantaneous inner process, Mike decided that he needed to pay the political mogul a visit.

A memory was nagging him. He found the digital camera he had used to take photos at Cora Smothers' place the morning her murder was discovered. He had noticed some carbon copies of letters typed on her stationery then, stacked on a small out-of-the-way stand. It was pictures of those papers he was snapping when Dunbar interrupted him. Subsequent events had distracted him from examining the photos. He examined them now.

Mike arrived at Winthrop's office around 10:15 a.m., carrying a small briefcase.

"Morning," he said to the receptionist. "Detective Ryan to see Mr. Winthrop."

The perky receptionist looked up from her desk.

"Good morning, Detective. Do you have an appointment?"

"No, but I have to see him."

"I'm sorry, but Mondays are very busy for Mr. Winthrop."

"Miss," exclaimed Mike, struggling to contain himself, "I know you have a job to do, but I must see him now!"

Mike moved past her and briskly walked by another attractive assistant

"Sir, I can't have you go in there; Mr. Winthrop is with someone."

Mike didn't skip a beat and pushed in the heavy door. The assistant nervously ran past him, and faced the commanding figure sitting opposite his appointee.

"Sir, I couldn't stop him."

"Who the h—l do you think you are?" growled Winthrop. "Didn't anyone ever teach you office etiquette, not to barge into business meetings unannounced?"

Mike briefly met the eyes of a nervous man, seated in the chair facing the desk and wearing horn-rimmed glasses.

"Friend," said Mike, "I'm sorry to interrupt your time with Mr. Winthrop, but maybe you can reschedule with his assistant." The harried man dropped some documents that he had been holding on his lap, nervously picked them up, and shoved them into his attaché case. He stood up squeezing past Mike, and sped from the office.

Winthrop angrily rose from his seat. Smoke seemed to escape from his bald head. But this new adversary, undaunted by his host's demeanor, nonchalantly sat in a vacant chair.

"I'm going to call security and have you escorted from the building," Winthrop snarled.

Winthrop reached for the phone and Mike rose from the chair, knocking the receiver from Winthrop's hand.

"Winthrop, why don't you just get comfortable? You and I are going to have a little chat."

"You punk, if I was a couple of years younger I would eat you for breakfast."

"First of all, you're not a few years younger, and second of all it's lucky for you that I just became a Christian. Finally, with all I've dug up on you, by the time you're released from Attica, pabulum will be your steady diet."

"Who the h—l. are you?" Winthrop's tone remained arrogant.

"Oh, I am sorry, *Mr. Winthrop,* how unprofessional of me. I'm Detective Michael Ryan, of the Nassau County Police Department."

"You know, Ryan, or whoever you are, I can make your life miserable."

"I could talk to you all day, Winthrop. Your conversation is so scintillating. But we're both busy men. I have crimes to solve and you. . . well, what do you do, really? Oh, I know; you count your money."

"You're a real wise guy, aren't you?" Winthrop's broad jaw was thrust forward.

"Okay, let's get to it." Mike slammed a file on Winthrop's desk. "Open it," he ordered.

Winthrop reddened, and beads of sweat formed on his narrow forehead. He was visibly shaken.

Mike pressed on. "What about this feud between you and Edmund Steele and the Merrick Avenue Plan?"

Winthrop wiped his mouth with the handkerchief from his breast pocket. "What's it to you?"

"You seem pretty shook up, Winthrop. I'm merely interested in what motivates rich moguls to claw at one another. If you have difficulty with my questioning, try this one on for size. I heard that you were cozy with Cora Smothers." Winthrop's iron hands now were trembling.

"I don't know what you're talking about. I'm a married man."

"So now you've become *Mr. Clean.* You know, I'm really trying to be patient with you, an attribute that has always been very foreign to me. But I've been asking you a series of questions and you haven't answered one." The contempt that curled Winthrop's upper lip made Mike's voice drop to a low intense pitch. "I have dual personalities, Winthrop. One is polite and restrained. But the old Mike, you don't want to mess with that dude. He's prone to violence when provoked. You see, if he took me over, he would already have dragged you out of that chair and danced on your face with his fists. In fact" — Mike leaned forward, jamming his fists onto the top of Winthrop's desk — "I feel the old Mike taking over at this very moment."

Winthrop shrank back slightly. "Okay, okay, I had dinner with Cora. So what?"

Mike said, "I doubt if I can hold this old Mike off any longer."

Winthrop folded his arms. "I don't know what else to tell you."

Mike took a deep breath, opened the file on Winthrop's desk. "Here, read this."

Winthrop held the piece of paper in his cigar-stained hand and began to read.

The silence was deadly. A moment passed without a word or a motion from Winthrop.

Mike retrieved the note from him. "For someone who is always barking orders and giving ultimatums, you're surprisingly silent. Let me create a scenario for you. You figured with help from the County Executive and a few hacks from the legislator you had the Merrick deal in your pocket. But Tamara

Steele spoiled everything when she wanted the property for low-income housing. She went to her father for help. Steele placed a bid that was lower than yours. You were afraid that the County Executive would be forced to award the contract to Steele. You had to enlist someone who would monitor Edmund Steel and hopefully get something on the old man to force him out of contention."

Winthrop did his best to look bored.

"So a business deal went south," he said. "I've made millions and lost millions; that's the world of finance."

Mike continued, "You're known to be a sore loser, so you started to date Cora Smothers. You'd learned of her emotional problems. She was flattered by your attention and mesmerized by your vast fortune. You used her. You made that poor impressionable insecure kid betray Tamara, by snooping around the Steele's premises.

"Then Cora backed you into a corner, threatening to go to Steele and confess to feeding you information regarding the Merrick Plan. You didn't expect her to campaign for the position of being your new bride. Jewelry, expensive trips and furs didn't do it for her. She wanted a diamond rock around the fourth finger of her left hand. She became obsessed, threatening to pay Mrs. Winthrop a visit and tell of your affair with her. You couldn't allow her to spoil everything, so you had her whacked."

"Why in the world would I bother killing a little tramp like that?"

"Reread the note, man! Cora threatened to ruin everything. There was no way your wife was going to give you a divorce without making you pay through the nose. When her Madison Avenue lawyer finished with you, you'd be lucky to afford lunch in the Department of General Service's cafeteria."

"Okay, Cora threatened me! But there was no way I was going to leave my wife for her."

"Sounds like a logical murder motive to me!" barked Mike.

Winthrop shrugged. "You can't prove anything."

"I beg to disagree with you." Mike clamped an internal lid on his emotions. "Regarding Cora there is enough to put you in the hot seat. I bet with some digging we will connect you with Tamara's murder as well."

"Ryan, you're reaching. I wouldn't waste my time with that Steele brat."

"Okay, let's put Tamara's murder on the back burner. I'm really here because I'm interested in locating my partner, Detective Margaret Younger."

"What does that have to do with me?"

"I have a sneaky suspicion you know the whereabouts of the detective."

"You're nuts. Here's what I think. The big brass is on your back for not solving this case and you're just on a fishing expedition."

Mike smiled and spread both of his hands on Winthrop's desk. "Why don't you go into the file I laid right there, and turn to the fourth page?"

Winthrop raised his eyebrows and then followed Mike's instructions. He stared at the file, and sat there stunned.

"You have nothing to say?" Mike felt heat rising up through his neck. "You hated that religious preacher. Her *idiot plan* might cause you to lose to your arch rival, Edmund Steele. With the Merrick Plan in his pocket, Steele won a round in your sick and perverted competition. You were so enraged by losing to Steele that you were driven to kill his daughter."

"Ryan, you're just blowing smoke." Winthrop's face looked pasty, but his hands no longer shook.

"Right now maybe I am," agreed Mike, eyes glinting. "But if I find one more link between you and the Tamara Steele case, you can bank on it that I'll be back."

Peggy woke up in excruciating pain. Her hands were stretched side to side and taped to the bedposts. From the golden light coming through the cellar window, she concluded that it was morning. Fear gripped her; she was too scared to pray.

It was an understatement to say that Rachel wasn't too concerned with her prisoner's needs, as evidenced by the growling of Peg's stomach and the dryness of her tongue. But the Voice demonstrated God's faithfulness. The Voice brought Peggy to the Ninety-First Psalm, and she remembered her heavenly Father's assurance:

> *Surely he will save you from the fowler's snare and from the deadly pestilence.*
>
> *He will cover you with his feathers, and under his wings you will find refuge.*
>
> *His faithfulness will be your shield and rampart.*

You will not fear the terror of the night nor the arrow that flies by day.

"Dear Lord," she began praying. "Please be patient with me. You have blessed me throughout my life. You are my shield and my heart dwells in your sacred heart. I trust You."

Her prayer was interrupted by the sound of footsteps. Rachel loomed over her, holding a half-empty martini glass.

"Hey, sister, how's the Lord treating you today?"

Peggy twisted her head to look at Rachel; she felt pity for her. "You know, Rachel, there was a time when I thought we were sisters in the Lord."

Rachel greedily downed the rest of her drink. "You're so phony and hypocritical. You and your precious friend, *Tamara*, wouldn't know what a true sister was if you tripped over one." Rachel's voice was thick and incoherent.

Peg heard new steps on the stairs. Fred came down "I've got some food."

He proceeded to set the contents of the bag on the seat of a chair near Peg's bed.

Fred released Peg's hands. Then he helped her into a sitting position.

Rachel's hate and jealousy overcame her. She staggered over to the chair with the food, shoved it against the wall, causing it to spill all over the cement floor.

"Rachel," gasped Fred, "why did you do that? This lady hasn't eaten!"

"Shut up and give me a drink."

"But, honey, we have to be a little human."

"Freddy boy, what are you getting, religion? Are you familiar with the little commandment on killing? We didn't exactly obey that one."

"Rachel!" Fred glanced nervously at Peggy. "You'd better keep your mouth shut. And for God's sake lay off the booze."

"How dare you order me around! Get me a drink!"

Fred's voice assumed a softer tone. "Honey, you've had enough."

"Never mind, I'll get it myself!" Rachel started for the stairway. Fred tried to help her but she violently shoved him away. Maneuvering hazily up the steps, she hit the rail on one side and the wall on the other. Fred was frightened that she would lose her balance and tumble down the stairs.

"Fred, tie her up," Rachel ordered as she disappeared.

"Okay," he yelled back. He motioned Peggy to keep quiet and muttered, "We'll wait thirty minutes. . . I bet she'll pass out on the couch."

"But I don't understand." Peggy was not ready to trust Fred.

Fred went to a small refrigerator, retrieving a cold bottle of water, which he handed to Peggy. She lunged for the bottle, drinking deeply.

"Easy, detective, easy, you haven't had any liquid since Friday, and it's Sunday morning. You don't want to get sick now." He took the water from her. Peggy's face had a pleading look. Fred told her, "Detective, I'll give you more water when I get back. I'll be back in two minutes with some more food."

Peggy watched him leave, praising God for his promises. Again she heard the Voice: "*I will never leave you nor forsake you.*"

After his interview with Winthrop on Monday morning, Mike called the Youngers. He prayed for good news. "Hello, Mrs. Younger. Mike Ryan here. Have you heard from Peg?"

"No, Mike, we haven't."

"Has Fran gotten in touch with her?" Mike knew it was a silly question.

"No. I'm really worried, Mike."

"I won't kid you, Mrs. Younger, you have reason to be worried. Do you have a key to Peg's house?"

"Why, yes, I do."

"Could you and Mr. Younger meet me there in ten minutes? Maybe we can find something that will give us a lead to Peggy's whereabouts."

"O Lord, please help her be all right," her mother wept.

Fred was as good as his word. He brought Peg some more food. She was so grateful that tears began to flow.

After she finished eating, he walked over and gently but insistently pushed her weakened frame prone again on the dilapidated bed. Then he took a roll of tape and ripped off two long pieces.

"I'm sorry, Detective, but I have to tie you up again." He spread her two arms out and loosely taped each on opposite bedposts. She groaned in pain

"Fred," she said as the young man bound her, "I have a sneaky suspicion that you were not really involved with Tamara Steele's murder."

"What makes you say that?" he asked, finishing his appointed task.

"Well, you seem to be a compassionate person from your treatment of me. If you were like Rachel, you wouldn't have given a thought to my hunger. Also, you're not the type to brutally slaughter a beautiful person like Tamara."

Fred's face reddened and he looked away. "Detective, you know as well as anybody that you can't tell a murderer by his looks."

Peg spoke firmly. "In your case, I can. You're not a murderer. Help me escape and I'll speak with the District Attorney. He could reduce your sentence."

Fred gazed at his hands "You're asking me to turn my back on Rachel. I can't do that. She's the only woman that ever cared for me."

Praying to herself, Peggy tried again. "I appreciate your loyalty. But she is a murderer. You have no future with her. She'll only ruin your life if you continue to support her."

Rachel's voice interrupted them from above. "Freddy, what's taking you so long?"

Fred jerked to his feet. "Be right up, honey." He turned to Peggy "Detective, I have to go."

"Please," Peggy pleaded.

"I can't," he answered.

After he left Winthrop, Mike decided to call John Paulson to meet him and the Youngers at Peggy's. They all arrived at the appointed time.

"Thanks for humoring me," Mike told them. "This could be a complete waste of time, but to tell you the truth I'm frustrated and maybe a little scared."

The three followed Mrs. Younger to Peggy's front door. She unlocked it and they all entered.

Peggy's rooms were immaculate; nothing seemed out of place, except for mail that had been pushed through the door slot. Not bothering to pick it up yet, Fran climbed the stairs to Peg's bedroom while the others looked through the kitchen, living room, and dining room. In a few minutes, Fran descended the stairs, joining the others as they finished their fruitless search. She breathed a frustrated sigh. "Well, folks, our Peg didn't leave for an extended vacation; all of her clothes are neatly arranged in her closet and her suitcase is empty."

"There isn't any sign of a struggle," observed Henry Younger.

Tears formed in her mother's eyes. "For all that is holy, where could she be?"

Fran sat on the couch, joining her mother. She put her arms around Mrs. Younger. “Mom, we’ve got to trust the Lord that Peg is safe.”

“Has anybody canvassed the neighborhood? Maybe she talked to someone. Margaret could have told someone where she was going,” Peg’s mother said, twisting her hands together.

“I spoke to her closest neighbors this afternoon. I didn’t come up with anything. I’m sorry, Mrs. Younger,” Mike volunteered sadly.

He joined everyone in the living room, sitting in a straight chair opposite them. He sighed; then slowly realized he was stepping on something. Moving his foot, he spotted a bracelet. He picked it up and read the inscription. “Look at this. Does Peg know anybody by the name of Rachel?”

“Well, there’s Rachel Giles.”

“Yeah, that’s right; we questioned both her and Julian Giles a few weeks ago. Does Peggy know anyone else by the name of Rachel?”

“Let me go into her address book and see.” Fran went to the telephone stand in the kitchen and came back with the address book.

“I can only find a Rachel Davis.”

Mrs. Younger stood and walked over to the mail scattered on the floor. She scooped up the various bills and junk mail and joined Mike and Fran. As she sat down, she dropped a postcard. Mike picked it up.

"Ladies, look at this!" he said. "It's from a Rachel Davis." He massaged his chin. "The card is from Ghana." He started reading the postcard aloud. '"I'm having a wonderful experience serving and praying with these brave children of God. Wish you were here with me to share this special time. Love, your sister in Christ, Rachel.'" Mike shook his head. "Not exactly a suspect."

"That leaves Rachel Giles," John concluded.

Mike shook his head, puzzled. "It was very obvious at our interview with Rachel and Julian that Rachel and Peg were never close."

"So it's safe to say that Rachel wouldn't stop by for coffee," said Fran.

"Hardly," said Mike.

"Then," questioned Mrs. Younger, "why would Rachel Giles visit Margaret?"

Everyone had their eyes on Mike. He remained very quiet, almost pensive.

Winthrop, Rachel Giles, Tamara and Edmund Steele, the Merrick deal. All were pieces of a puzzle floating around in Mike Ryan's head.

Chapter 45

George Winthrop summoned his administrative assistant as soon as Mike left.

"Sara, send for that idiot, Banning." Within a half hour, Banning arrived.

Sara questioned her motives for continuing to work for George Winthrop. He was always in a foul mood and he was self-centered, rude, selfish and manipulative. Was it the money? Surely she could get another job. Maybe she was letting herself be intimidated by him.

She led Detective Carl Banning into the lion's den. She left him feeling sorry that she had placed the defenseless detective in Winthrop's grip.

"Good morning, Mr. Winthrop, how are you doing today?"

Winthrop grunted, "How am I, you ask? You're really concerned about my frame of mind, are you?"

Banning began perspiring. "Of course I am, sir. I greatly admire and respect you."

"If you are so concerned with my disposition, then maybe you'll tell me why I had to endure Ryan's barging into my office a half hour ago harassing me and asking me pointed questions."

Banning felt his stomach churn.

"But, sir, I haven't seen Ryan in days. You have to give me more time."

Winthrop's face reddened. "While you're fiddling with your Gameboy I found out what has been occupying his time. His ex-partner is missing and he's devoting all his energy trying to find her. His search landed him at my doorstep."

"Younger is missing?"

"Detective Banning, are you deaf as well as dumb? Ryan's been a thorn in my side much too long. He's a cancer that has to be removed. He could ruin our plans for Nassau County. *I want him taken care of and I'm not very interested in how – I want him stopped now!*" Winthrop seized Banning's shirt front, yanked him to his feet, shoved him out of his office, and slammed the door.

Banning's knees were shaking. He had to put Ryan out of commission somehow.

Chapter 46

Hours later, Peg floated toward wakefulness. She felt anxious and nauseated. Peg thought she had reached Fred, encouraging him to think rationally about Rachel, convincing him that she was in fact mentally ill. But Fred's infatuation with Rachel clouded his judgment.

Peg dozed off again. Sleep provided some welcome relief. For a long time she wasn't conscious of the pain in her arms and legs caused by the tape binding her wrists to the bedposts.

When Peg woke from her deep sleep, her arms ached even more and there was Rachel standing next to the bed.

"Well, good morning, sleepyhead. Your lights were out for a very long time."

Rachel's voice sounded more hostile than ever.

"Where's Fred?" murmured Peg.

"Why? Are you hungry or something? I sent Fred on a little errand. You and he got too chummy. Your budding relationship made me a little jealous."

Peg tried to pray but she had difficulty focusing. She became frightened, very frightened. What degree of violence would Rachel inflict on her to relieve her madness?

She watched Rachel heading for a door at the opposite end of the basement. Rachel opened the closet and lugged out something very cumbersome. When she approached, Peg recognized the object.

Oh my Lord, it's a blow torch!

"It's amazing," commented Rachel in an oddly conversational tone. "You and your late friend display identical tactics. Tamara steals my husband, and then you try to lure my boyfriend from me." She fiddled with the blowtorch controls.

"Rachel," tremored Peg, "in heaven's name, what are you doing?"

"I'm going to do every woman a favor. You know your hair is beautiful. Maybe that's one of the reasons why men find you so attractive. For the benefit of all womankind, I'm going to give it a little tease."

"Rachel, you're *mad!*"

Rachel's fingers kept up their work. "I guess you're right, Peg," she said, "but maybe I have a reason. I get a little crazy when I stand by watching women who I trusted rob me of my men."

Rachel moved toward Peggy with the blow torch. She ignited it. The basement was hot already and the flame intensified the heat. Rachel brought the torch close enough for Peg to sense heat from the flame. Peg thought of the martyrs who were burned at the stake for their belief in God.

O Father, grant me the same courage as St. Joan of Arc.

The burning flame was inching closer and closer to Peg's forehead.

Mike's face was pensive as he fingered the bracelet with the name Rachel on it. "I'm going over to the Giles place to see if the man of the house has heard from his wife recently."

"Hey, Mike, how about some company?" John asked.

"Okay, let's roll!"

Mike and John arrived at Julian Giles' house. Mike rang the doorbell and two minutes later Giles himself opened the door. They must have interrupted his reading, for he held a half-read book under his arm.

“Gentleman,” he said calmly, “I was about to call you.”

Although John waited to be invited into the house, Mike barged in.

“Where is your wife?” he demanded.

“As I say, I was about to call the police. She’s been missing for three days.”

“Wow, you’re really concerned for your wife’s safety. It took you three days to report her absence.” Mike now was in Giles’ face. John subtly maneuvered his way between Mike and Giles.

“Reverend Giles,” John interjected, “allow me to get a little personal here. Are you and your wife having marital problems lately?”

“I resent your implication. Rachel and I have been married for twenty years. We have a good solid union.”

“I can’t believe your sanctimonious attitude,” snapped Mike. “Everyone knows your track record with women. It looks to me as though your extra-curricular marital activities could have driven Mrs. Giles to the edge.”

"How dare you accuse me of duplicity?" Giles raised his chin and fought for composure. "I have a spotless reputation as a promoter and defender of the faith."

Mike felt his chest tighten. His every thought was focused on Peggy. He began to soften his tone, still speaking through his teeth. "Reverend Giles, it has been not even two weeks since I accepted Jesus as my Lord and Savior, so I'm not yet accustomed to practicing the Beatitudes and His message of love. I'm still grappling over the idea of turning the other cheek. All I know is that my friend is missing and I'm frustrated that I can't find her."

John, who knew Mike's temperament well and was afraid he would lose control, took over the questioning. He reached into his pocket and pulled out a piece of jewelry.

"Reverend," he said, "do you recognize this bracelet?" Giles turned to John.

"Where did you find that?" Then, feeling intimidated by John, he decided to change his tact. He stood motionless, staring at the bracelet.

"I'm losing my patience. Is it or is it not Rachel's bracelet?" Mike broke in.

Giles seemed about to speak, but thought better of it and remained silent.

"If you have any idea where your wife is, you'd better tell us now," Mike warned.

Giles walked around in circles, wiping his forehead and wringing his hands. He stopped and looked at both detectives. "We have a summer home in New Hampshire. She could be there."

"Where in New Hampshire?" John stepped in again to handle the rest of the investigation. He didn't want Mike to lose it and risk police brutality.

"The summer home is outside of Manchester."

"Reverend, I'd advise you not to go on any extended trips. The jury is still out on you."

Giles scribbled the address of the summer home on a piece of paper and handed to John.

The detectives left, walking briskly towards Mike's car.

"John, I'm going back to the precinct. I left a file on my desk that I want to look at."

"Okay, brother, could you drop me at my car?"

When they arrived at the precinct's parking lot Mike dropped John at his car, and then parked his own.

As John placed the key in the ignition, he turned around to guide his car out of the parking space. Glancing at the back seat he noticed he was missing something. *Darn, I must have left my laptop on my desk.*

He parked his car again, got out, and headed toward the parking lot entrance. He thought he saw Mike behind the wheel of his car and walked over, saying, as he approached the passenger side, "Wow, man, you're fast. You got what you needed already?"

There was no response. At first John thought Mike hadn't heard him so he walked over to the driver's side. Then he realized the person inside was much shorter than Mike and was sitting in the driver's seat, fiddling with the steering wheel.

"Hey, you," barked John, "what do you think you're doing?"

The stranger turned and John saw an iron rod in the stranger's hand. . . coming at him. He grabbed the man's hand and twisted his arm. John pulled him from the car and the two men wrestled each other to the ground.

"What the heck is going on here?" Mike yelled, running towards them. He pulled the shorter man off John.

"Banning! John! What's with you guys?"

John picked himself up, trying to catch his breath. "He broke into your car."

"Banning, what did you want?" Perspiration poured from Banning's forehead. Stunned, he didn't answer Mike.

"Mike, when I walked up to your car, I saw him reaching under the steering wheel."

Mike looked into the car and came out with a cellophane bag.

"John, look. What do we have here?"

"If memory serves me right," said John, glaring at Banning, "I would have to say that it looks like a bag of *snow*."

"You are correct, my *learned* detective," replied Mike. "Why don't we three men go in the squad room where we can be comfortable?"

Peg shook with fear as Rachel approached her with the blow torch. She tried valiantly to maintain her composure. The heat of the flame enveloped her. Light smoke invaded her lungs.

But the Voice remained faithful.

I will not leave you as orphans.

I will come to you.

Both women heard footsteps on the stairs. If Peggy hadn't been in such a weakened condition she would have yelled *hallelujah*. Agitated, Rachel extinguished the flame and sped to the opposite side of the room, lugging the blowtorch. She shoved the blow torch out of sight in the back of the closet. Her eyes threw darts of anger toward her victim.

Fred walked down the stairs.

"Hey, Rach, you look terrible. Have you been drinking again?"

"First you tell me," shrieked Rachel, "what are you doing here? I thought I told you to go to Long Island and get my documents."

"I did go," Fred explained, "but when I was on the New England Thruway, I stopped at a rest area to order lunch and I didn't have my wallet."

"Well, go get your stupid wallet, and get back on the road!"

Fred cocked his sandy head, eyeing Rachel. "You're not even happy to see me."

"Give me a break!" Rachel's balance wavered slightly, but she regained it and tightened her limbs into a solid stance. "What are you — a wimp who needs his mother to tuck him in at night? I have little patience for this kind of nonsense."

Fred's voice was flat, his head still cocked to one side. "I thought we were in love, Rachel. I stood by and watched you kill Tamara!"

Rachel's response was to run to another closet, from which she retrieved a bottle of bourbon that was practically empty. Rachel gulped from the bottle, and then turned to Fred.

"I bet you were in love with Tamara like everyone else," she shouted.

"No! I love you, Rachel. But I just don't understand how you could have so viciously murdered Tamara. Wasn't she your friend?"

"You don't understand." Rachel raised the bottle again. "Let me try to make it simple so that even an ignoramus like you can understand.

"Tamara Steele stole the only man I ever loved!"

Rachel staggered over to Fred and squeezed his facial cheeks. "I keep you around because you're so cute."

He came suddenly alive and sneered, leaning away.

"Oops," giggled Rachel, "no more drinky. The bottle is empty. Let me go upstairs and get another one."

Fred waited until he heard the clanging of glasses upstairs.

"Man, she's really wasted. How are you doing?"

Peg raised her eyebrows and smiled. "Aside from aching wrists, being practically fried and not having anything to eat since you left I guess I don't have anything to complain about."

"Nothing to eat? I left food for you with Rachel. And what do you mean, practically fried?"

"She almost torched me with a blow torch. You left food? I didn't get any."

Fred wore a confused and worried look. "She's really losing it, isn't she?"

Peg had compassion for the man. He seemed to be truly under Rachel's spell.

"She does seem to be intoxicated all the time," said Peg tentatively.

He looked at her strangely. "Yeah, lately," he said. "But I can't believe that she's so over the top that she'd take a blow torch to you. Come on you're probably so weak from lack of food that you're hallucinating."

"If you doubt me, look in that closet."

Peg watched him as he crossed the room and opened the closet. The next time he came into view he was carrying the blow torch. "This thing is still warm. What in the world was she doing with a blow torch?"

He came next to the bed and stared at the instrument in his hands. "I don't know what to do anymore. She's shocks me."

"When I came into Miss Steele's room and found Rachel standing over the mutilated body with that knife in her hand, I was horrified."

"Wait a minute, Fred!" Peg's eyes widened. "You told me that you aided in Tamara's murder."

"I don't know." Fred got up abruptly and set the blow torch out of sight at the foot of the bed. "Maybe I thought the law would go easy on her if I incriminated myself, too."

"That was very foolish. I know you're very devoted to Rachel, but you can see how disturbed she is. Can't you? Untie me; please get me out of here. I told you before; I will try to help you."

"What are you two talking about?" Rachel shouted from the stairwell.

Fred's eyes popped wide. His hand dove into his pocket and came out bearing a pocket knife.

"I'll be right up, Rachel," he called.

Peggy's heart thumped. Rachel was stumbling down the stairs, apparently resting after each step. Fred didn't turn to look. He started cutting Peggy's taped hands free and kept cutting while Rachel's lurching footfalls grew louder. There was just enough time for Fred to slide the knife back into his pocket before Rachel would see.

When she appeared at the bottom of the steps, Rachel was waving an XP-100 pistol. She was now so drunk that she was weaving from side to side.

"Peg," she said, "I thought you were stealing my boyfriend. Can't you get a man of your own? Don't you have a thing for this Mike Ryan?"

"Honey," said Fred cautiously, "you have to put the gun down. Someone could get hurt."

He slowly moved toward Rachel. She continued to wave the gun in the air.

"Ah, this is touching." Rachel gave the gun a kiss on the barrel and waved it again. "You're worrying about your new girlfriend. I wish I could rearrange her pretty face."

Peg wondered if Rachel had been drunk when she killed Tamara. It seemed the alcohol had taken over her mind. Her face was contorted with hate.

Fred moved tentatively closer to Rachel. She didn't seem to notice him; she had raised the pistol into firing position and was trying to aim at Peg. With sudden quick steps, Fred grabbed Rachel's arm. She pulled away hard; they struggled; the next thing Peg heard was the deafening firing of a gun, followed by a thud.

The two detectives brought Carl Banning to the interrogation room. Mike forcefully threw him down on a folding chair.

"Carl," said Mike sweetly, "I believe you've got a lot of information to share with us, don't you?"

Banning turned to John. "You'd better keep that maniac off me! I've experienced his temper before, and I really don't want to go there again."

"Look, Banning," said John reasonably, "the people you answer to are all going down; it's only a matter of time. We know about George Winthrop and the Merrick Plan, about Tamara Steele and how she got caught in the cross-fire, and was subsequently murdered."

"I don't know what you're talking about," Banning squirmed. "Then why did you break into Mike's car?"

"John, I left my wallet in his car."

Mike said gruffly, "You know, man, I'm losing my patience. You broke into my car. . ."

"Your car was unlocked," Banning said weakly.

First of all, I always lock my car. Second of all, being such a skillful cop, you forgot to retrieve your Z tool. I noticed that you heaved it over the back seat."

John spoke, "Make it easy on yourself. Where did you score the coke that you tried to plant in Mike's car?"

"What coke?"

"You know," sighed John, "I'm a very patient guy. But as you and I both know, Mike isn't. Since my patience isn't leading us anywhere, I should leave you with him. Maybe he can persuade you to tell the truth."

Banning ran his fingers through his hair. "Please don't."

John shrugged. "Well?"

"Okay, okay," gushed Banning. "Shoot, I don't owe Winthrop anything. Why am I kidding myself? He's not going to do a thing for me."

Banning sang like a canary. He told them that Winthrop feared Mike was getting too close to finding out Winthrop's relationship with the County Executive. Banning had learned that the County Executive used threats and bribes to force some legislators to support Winthrop & Company's bid for the contract for the Merrick Plan. Banning wasn't sure who actually murdered Tamara, but he was certain that George Winthrop had played a major role.

George Winthrop sat in his office fondling his cigar. He thought about that punk Ryan, and the nerve he had busting into his office. *Did he know who he was dealing with? Years ago I could have taken his limbs and twisted them so he'd look like a pretzel.*

His thoughts traveled to his goals for himself and the county. Why didn't people share his vision for the island? The people surrounding him couldn't even conceive the amount of money to be generated by the Merrick Plan. Some NFL owners would sprint to Nassau County if they knew that a super-stadium was provided for them with a gambling casino just two hundred feet from the field. This superstructure would rival the Giants and the Jets to such a degree that they'd be in the red overnight.

But now this grand scheme of his could come crashing down on him because of idiots who were too yellow to see their individual assignments through. *I guess if you want a job done correctly you have to do it yourself.*

If he really was honest with himself he would have to admit his insatiable appetites were also to blame for the stalling of the Merrick Plan. If only he had stayed focused and had not gotten involved with Cora Smothers. She couldn't just be satisfied with a brief affair. No, she wanted to marry him. She had become such a liability that he had to whack her.

All is not lost, he thought. When Banning finished framing Ryan, a major obstacle would be eliminated, and Winthrop's dreams would gain new life.

"You know, Mike, this could be under the jurisdiction of the FBI," John said, sipping his coffee as they drove to George Winthrop's office. Mike hoped Winthrop would be in.

"Yeah," he responded to John's comment, "maybe they don't think I can handle the case myself. I'm just grateful you're helping me in your spare time."

John frowned. "Mike, this is a complex case. Prominent people in the County seem to have their hands in the cookie jar. You can't do it alone."

"All I care about is finding Peggy."

"I don't want to alarm you, but I believe that Tamara's murderer knows Peggy's whereabouts."

Mike pulled up at Winthrop's office.

"Here we are. Maybe Winthrop will be more cooperative once he finds out that his scam to frame me fell apart."

The two men made their way to his office. The office manager, remembering Mike's persuasiveness, ushered the two detectives in to Winthrop without a single protest.

When Winthrop lifted his head and saw Mike he turned white.

"Surprised to see me, Mr. Winthrop? I bet you expected me to be in handcuffs."

"I don't know what you mean," Winthrop stammered.

"Your plan didn't work. I'm shocked and a little disappointed. I thought you were devious, but now my view of you has really changed, sending out a bungler like Banning to plant a kilo of coke under the dashboard of my car. How amateurish can you get?"

"I don't know what you're talking about, Ryan. Who the h—l is Banning? I never heard the name before."

Mike rolled his eyes. "Give it up, Winthrop. You're done. My ex-partner sang like a nightingale, sharing a tale of conspiracy and double dealing. He also suggested that either you personally murdered Tamara or you were an accessory."

"I'm going to call my lawyer."

"You'd better have a team of lawyers. It's fortunate that you and your family command big bucks; you're going to use most of your estate for your defense."

Winthrop was visibly shaken. He held the receiver in his hand and then decided to put the phone back on its hook.

"Ryan, could we make a deal?"

"Oh, interested in making a deal, are you? What can you offer?" Mike said sarcastically.

Winthrop nervously massaged his chin.

"I could tell you who murdered Tamara Steele and Cora Smothers."

"Go on," John calmly encouraged.

"But what assurance do I have," hesitated Winthrop, "that the District Attorney would bargain with me?"

Mike heaved a frustrated sigh. "Forget about it. We are in no position to make you any deal. We don't even know whether or not the feds will take over the investigation. But this much we do know. It's only a matter of time before we solve this case. . . with or without your help. By refusing to help us now you'll be left without a bargaining chip. You could spend your remaining days rotting in some federal pen with no hope of parole."

Winthrop began silently to ponder his options. Finally, he flopped into his swivel chair. "Okay, what do you want to know?"

"Who killed Tamara Steele and why?"

"Rachel Giles plunged the shiv into her."

"You can't be serious. I don't feel that cooperation you promised. Feels more like you're just blowing smoke. You expect us to believe a gentle, unassuming person like Rachel Giles brutally stabbed Tamara Steele."

"Look, Detective Ryan, you got me. Now I'm desperate, and I will use any method available to me to lighten my sentence. From my vantage point, lying to you is not an option."

Mike paused; he had to agree with Winthrop.

"I'm curious. What motive did Rachel have for wasting Tamara Steele?" Mike wondered aloud.

"I can tell you," said Winthrop, "in two words: *Julian Giles*. She viewed him as a god. My guess is with *preacher* Giles's history of womanizing, Rachel lost all control and sense of reality. The Steele woman became an imaginary target of Rachel's madness." Personally, I was indebted to Rachel for getting rid of Miss Evangelist because, at the time, Tamara Steele was ruining our plan to make this island the playground of the world. Our county could rival Monte Carlo. But all that is lost now. Still, if you gentlemen want to forget this conversation, I can make it worth your while."

"John, do you believe this guy?" Mike and John exchanged disgusted glances. Then Mike turned to Winthrop and said, "You want to add bribery to the list of crimes that you've already committed? Do you, Winthrop? Let's get on with this nightmare. How about Cora Smothers? Did you kill her?"

Winthrop became reckless. "I only wish I had. These stupid people under me can't even stage a simple suicide. Naturally when I learned that my crazy cousin bumped off Steele, no matter how remote, I couldn't afford any further scandal connected to our family. I typed the suicide note on Cora's laptop."

"What about Howard Carey?"

"Oh, that simpleton! Of all the cases he bungled, he had to get the Steele case right. We had to get rid of him." Winthrop said it as if yet another murder was only logical.

Mike pressed further. "Is there anybody in this administration tied into the Merrick Plan?" Winthrop sat silently for some time, considering his position. He didn't want to be known as a rat. But really, what did he owe anyone? He'd bet if his cronies were in his shoes they would give him up without blinking an eye.

"Sam Bower, he took a large piece of the pie."

"Could you be more specific?" asked Mike when Winthrop hesitated.

"When I approached Bower about my vision of the Merrick Plan he went for it as a longshoreman would go for a porterhouse steak. He salivated when he thought of his political influence and the fresh coin that would line his pockets."

"Was he involved in the murders?"

"No, Sam wanted to keep his hands clean. He did, however, twist numerous arms in the legislature to vote for the Merrick Plan. He threatened careers, bribed some legislators, and promised exposure of personal corruption if they failed to march in line."

John clicked the off button on his mini recorder.

Winthrop became flustered. "Who said you could record our conversion? This is a complete outrage! It's entrapment; I've been framed!"

Mike looked at John. "I can't believe this guy." Mike stared at Winthrop and laughed, "Man, I've got to hand it to you. After all your double dealing, and after being caught and having your confession on tape, you're still acting like a big shot, like you still have all the moves."

"Mr. Winthrop," said John gently, "the FBI will contact you in a few hours. You're now under the jurisdiction of the Attorney General."

"FBI, what are you talking about?"

"Since the county had accepted funds from the federal government, and you and Bower had misappropriated these said funds, then the case is turned over to the U.S. Attorney General."

Winthrop's eyes widened and a vein stood out on his broad forehead. "You promised if I cooperated you'd put in a good word for me."

"Oh, sure," said John. "Mike and I will each pray that you will ask God's forgiveness, and once you have, that He will indeed forgive you."

"Hey, what the h—l are you talking about?"

"We're talking about your relationship with Jesus Christ."

"Are you two on drugs or something? All I care about is my relationship with the Attorney General."

"With all your crimes," John warned, "we can't possibly convince the judge to lesson one second of your sentence."

"John," said Mike, "we have a missing policewoman to find. George, you'll be in our prayers. God speed."

"John," said Mike as the two of them reached the precinct building, "I don't know why, but I get the feeling that if we find Peggy, Rachel won't be far behind."

"I hear New Hampshire is great this time of year. Ready for a drive, Mike?"

"You don't have to ask me twice. Let's go."

Upon calling their families, and shoving clothes into bags, the two detectives headed for the New England Thruway.

Rachel stared at Fred's fallen body. Even in her drunken state, she realized that she must have killed the only person in the entire world that really cared for her. This realization forced her to weep bitterly.

Peg, though her hands were free, sat motionless on the bed, keeping her hands stretched to touch the bedposts. Since the pistol sat at Rachel's side and Rachel was in a volatile state, Peg didn't want to give her the slightest excuse to kill again.

Rachel finally passed out, collapsing on Fred's motionless body. Evening had now invaded the cellar, adding to Peg's disorientation. Hunger and pain continued to plague her, but regardless of these obstacles, she summoned all the strength she had left to escape.

She struggled to sit up, swinging her legs to the side of the bed. Ignoring the excruciating pain, she forced herself to stand. Her feet finally obeyed her will, and with miniature steps in the darkness, she found and reached the cellar wall. Soon after, she stumbled onto the cellar steps. Her legs felt like ten-ton weights as she mounted them. At one point she screamed with agony, then clamped her lips shut. She was afraid that her outburst would awaken Rachel. Thankfully, she only heard Rachel's heavy breathing.

She finally conquered the stairs and praised God that her prison was now a heinous memory. She shuffled around the living room, searching for lamps or a light switch. She fumbled and almost knocked over one lamp, but managed to illuminate the room with another one.

If I could only find my bag and Rachel's car keys. . .

She hurriedly searched for Rachel's keys. Her mission was interrupted by a blast of thunder and with it the fierce pounding of the rain attacking the roof.

Suddenly she heard Rachel stirring in the cellar.

Oh, my Lord, why can't I find anything?

She heard the sound of her footsteps on the cellar stairs.

"Oh Peggy, Peggy, where are you?" Rachel's voice floated pleadingly upward. "Fred is not getting up. You can't leave me all by myself. We can be friends again. You'll see, I'll be a good girl; just stay with me."

Peg knew that if she ever wanted to see Michael again she would have to make a run for it. She didn't have time to look for her bag, or anything else for that matter. She limped outside and despite the pain she moved as fast as she could.

But the rain and the night tested her resolve. A fierce wind developed, causing the rain to act like a whip, slapping her across the face with each step. Since she had been blindfolded when she was brought to the area, it was impossible for her to have any frame of reference, and she suspected she might be traveling in circles. The fierce wind was so powerful that she was constantly losing her balance and falling.

She must have been struggling along for hours because she felt exhausted.

She couldn't tell whether she had made any progress or not. She staggered through the mud and it was so dark that she couldn't see a foot in front of her. Suddenly her forehead struck a low lying branch and she tumbled into a ditch. She lay unconscious for how long she didn't know.

When she awakened she heard the sound of two men hovering over her.

"Hey, Charlie, look what we have here."

"Yeah, bro, maybe we'll party after all!"

Chapter 47

Ten-year-old Charlie Stokes gripped his six-year-old brother Jerry's hand as they waited for the orphanage to open. Their mother had given them each a shopping bag containing a jelly sandwich, clean underwear, and a favorite action figure. She kissed both of them on the forehead, took her new boyfriend's hand, and headed for a fleabag hotel at the end of town.

From that moment on, Charlie and Jerry were always in trouble. At age eight, Jerry grabbed a wallet from another resident's locker. The owner complained to the headmaster. Naturally Jerry was sent to his office, where he was forced to stay in detention for a week.

When Charlie learned that his younger brother had been punished because of another boy in the orphanage, he became so intensely enraged that he ambushed the boy with a lead pipe, and succeeded in breaking his arm and then howled with laughter at his victim's agony.

The orphanage eventually turned Charlie over to juvenile court, where he was found to be psychopathic with extreme sadistic tendencies. At the age of fourteen he was sentenced to a juvenile correctional facility in Binghamton, New York; he remained incarcerated until his twenty-first birthday.

Even though Jerry didn't see his brother for four years, he had always idolized Charlie and desperately sought his approval. Consequently, at age fourteen, Jerry lifted a gun from a retired police officer for whom he was doing small errands; he then tried to knock over a liquor store.

"Hey, old man, empty the cash register and hand over what's in it," he ordered.

The proprietor was a Vietnam veteran and he was sick and tired of young punks running roughshod over the peaceful neighborhood he once knew as a kid.

"You little creep! If you think I'm giving you one red cent you're smoking too much of those funny cigarettes."

The boy began to tremble. He remembered his brother describing knocking over a liquor store as "easy as snatching a pocketbook from an old lady."

"Man," he babbled, "I have a gun and if you don't give me the cash, I'm going to blow you away."

"Look at you, you dumb kid. Why don't you put the piece down? You're just a stupid punk who's trying to act like a big shot; you're really just a chicken hearted. . ."

The man's mocking attitude got to him. Jerry suddenly developed new resolve. Though his hand trembled, he managed to pull the trigger. The gun faithfully obeyed, and the bullet found its target.

The man's body slumped over the counter; both his shock and his breathing ended.

Jerry's fear then turned to a new bravado. He thought of Charlie and the new pride he would have for his little brother. Jerry began to jump up and down excitedly. He ran to the cash register to claim his prize, pushing the body off the counter as if it was merely a sack of potatoes. He couldn't open the drawer so he went to the back of the store looking for a tool.

Jerry wasn't aware that the storeowner had pressed the alarm that notified the nearest precinct of a crime being committed. He busied himself searching for something to open the cash drawer, and when he finally appeared from the back of the store, he was surprised by two patrolmen. They wrestled him to the ground and handcuffed him.

Jerry was granted his wish, joining his hero brother by being remanded to seven years at Binghamton. Meanwhile Charlie, having more street smarts than his younger brother, gained in stature with the inmates. By the time of his release, he left Binghamton with the knowledge of a vast network of thieves, dealers and pushers.

With the aid of his network he made certain that his baby brother's experience in the reform school was a positive one. Jerry's sentence was reduced. After serving five years, he then joined his brother in drug distribution. Under Charlie's tutelage, Jerry became a huge success by making a deal with a supplier of pure cocaine with a street value of five million dollars.

Charlie, bursting with pride over his little brother's success, decided to celebrate with a week of drinking, inhaling, and a little romance at a rented cabin located in New Hampshire. The two wasted little time starting their vacation. Cocaine mixed with Jack Daniels made the trip on the New England Thruway feel like a trip on a magic carpet ride.

However, the back roads of New Hampshire were not as kind as the thruway. The combination of drugs and alcohol made Jerry feel invincible. Driving the car at sixty miles an hour amid the fog and rain forced the Jaguar to careen off the dirt road and wrap itself around a tree.

The famous duo suffered only minor scrapes and bruises, but managed to retain their drunken euphoria.

"Hey bro, where the h—l are we?"

"How the h—l should I know," Charlie snapped. "You got us in this mess."

"Come on, bro, I was only having a little fun."

"Better call our little honeys and tell them we'll be late. Where the h—l is the cell phone?" They both staggered. Charlie grabbed the bottle of Jack from his brother, held it to his lips and greedily took a healthy swig.

WELLCOME TO SCENIC NEW HAMPHIRE said the sign that Mike and John passed as they crossed the state line on Route 787. Suddenly Mike heard a clanging noise coming from the radiator. He released a mournful groan. He always took special care of this old relic, but recently he had neglected the attention it needed to stay drivable. Now, as he saw smoke bursting from the car's hood, he knew that he and John were in trouble.

He got off at the next ramp and headed for the nearest town, a burg called Ridgeville. It turned out to be a typical one-horse town, a New England hamlet that could be described in a Stephen King novel. It consisted of one general store, a dilapidated hotel, and a seedy bar and grill. Law enforcement was relegated to a sheriff who also happened to be the town's mayor as well as proprietor of the general store. There was only one filling pump and that too was located at the general store.

Mike parked the car by the store. Once inside, Mike and John saw that they carried everything a town like Ridgeville could ever want or need. He and John greeted the owner, a skinny man with a balding head and a little belly who was wearing a sheriff's badge and examining papers fastened on a clipboard.

"Hi," said Mike. "I think there's a hole in my car radiator. Is there someone who can help us?"

The man raised an eyebrow, but didn't look up and took a few minutes to answer.

"Where are you fellows from?" he said at last, still perusing his clipboard.

"Long Island," said John.

"No, there's nothing we can do." The man's eyes remained down.

Mike started to breathe heavily. "Look," he said, "you don't understand. We are detectives from Nassau County in New York and we're in your neck of the woods on a case."

At that, the proprietor/sheriff raised his head and stared at Mike and then John. He scanned each of them with suspicion. Then he went back to checking his inventory, Mike looked at John and raised his arms, expressing bewilderment.

"Excuse me," he tried again, "but I don't think you understand. My car is in need of serious repair, and a fellow detective could be in grave danger if we don't do something *now*."

The proprietor picked up his head, speaking slowly with an obvious New England accent.

"I don't know how many times I need to tell you that we can't help you," he said, his voice increasing in intensity on the last several words. Again he returned to his clipboard.

Mike was about to lose control. He didn't understand the reason this man apparently refused to support a brother law enforcer. Finally, his temper got the best of him. Mike grabbed the proprietor's tie, yanking him across the counter.

"Sheriff," he said just as slowly, "a woman police detective has been abducted by a deranged killer and *it is very possible that she could lose her life*."

A few police officers wandered into the store, and seeing their boss being manhandled by a perfect stranger, drew their guns.

"Hold on there, mister, you had better let go of our sheriff, or you'll have to answer to us," shouted the younger one.

"Guys," cried Mike, "we're on the job. Your sheriff refuses to cooperate in a police matter."

"Sam, Ned," snapped the proprietor, "arrest these two city big shots who threatened me."

"You don't know what you're doing," warned Mike. "If anything happens to our friend, Detective Younger, you guys will be in serious trouble."

Mike's protest was ignored, and as the officers placed handcuffs on he and John, Mike silently prayed: *Lord, please watch over her.*

"Charlie, look who we got here," Jerry grinned, still high from the coke and the Jack. Peg looked up from what seemed to be a gigantic hole created by neighborhood hunters to catch and trap bears.

"Yeah, little bro, and I saw a place a little ways from here where we three can relax and have a little fun."

Peg wondered what she was doing here. In fact, she was confused about a lot of things, starting with her name. She did know two hard facts: she was hungry and she was cold.

"Jere, I want you to get a couple of things from the car."

"Do I have to? It's pitch black out there."

"Don't tell me I have a wimpy brother on my hands? I thought we were out for some fun."

"Sure we want to have fun with her," whined Jerry, "but she has to get out of the dumb hole for us to have a good time."

"So we need a rope to pull her out of the ditch, and since the rope is in the trunk somebody has to get it, and I elect you." Charlie punched his brother's arm.

"Why do I have to do all the dirty work?" complained Jerry.

"Well, maybe since I have to do all the thinking around here, I need to save all my strength to come up with good ideas."

Jerry was suddenly confused. Maybe it was all the drugs and the booze, but matters were becoming a little too complicated for him. "Charlie, I'm sorry." He watched as his little brother staggered into the brush to get to the car.

I hope he makes it. That guy has been a real liability ever since he was born. He's so stupid — he *gets in his own way*. Charlie looked down on Peg and reflected on how what started out to be a boring week now had some promise.

Ten minutes passed and Jerry wandered back through the mud with the rope slung over his shoulder.

"Hey, Charlie, I brought a couple of bottles of Jack."

"Good thinking. We'll need it for the party."

Rachel Giles was now somewhat clear-headed. She knew that if she was going to find Peggy and get rid of her, she needed to lay off the bourbon. She wondered, herself, why she drank so heavily.

Looking out the window she saw the sweeping rain. She went to the closet, changed into a warm sweat suit, and found a heavy water-repellent raincoat.

She thought about the damage that her drinking had done. Her tongue had become too loose. After all, Peggy didn't have to know that she had murdered Tamara or the reasons she killed her. Rachel had lost her grip. She didn't know what drove her to shoot Fred. He would have done anything for her. Killing Peggy would bring out every law enforcer in the area, and Fred's assistance would have been invaluable. But as her Granny would have said: *No use crying over spilled milk.*

Rachel reached up to a shelf in the basement closet and found her Grandfather's hunting rifle. She opened a box, and placed two shells in each chamber.

I guess it's time for some hunting.

Peggy had no memory of anything about herself. She realized she needed help. Therefore, when Charlie threw down the rope, ordering her to loop part of it around her waist, she agreed. As the brothers pulled her up, she cooperated by methodically working her feet up the side of the ditch.

When she reached level ground she was greeted by yellowed teeth and foul-smelling odors.

"Well, you're some looker."

"Jerry, give the lady some elbow room."

Now Peggy was afraid. But since she had lost her memory, and therefore had no reference point for where to go for help, she had to trust these people.

Charlie took her arm on the pretext of steadying her.

"What's your name?" he asked.

Peggy paused and forced herself to say something.

"Diane. . . yes, my name is Diane."

Both men gave her a strange look.

"How long have you been out in this crazy weather?"

Again she paused. She knew she was acting peculiar and something told her to tread carefully. "I think about two hours."

"Look," said Jerry, "we'd better get some shelter or one of us may catch pneumonia. There's a farm-house over to our right."

They walked about a thousand feet and came upon an old-fashioned farmhouse. Jerry knocked on the door and was greeted by a man of about seventy. Although it was ten o'clock at night the man of the house wasn't afraid.

"Good evening, folks. What can I do for you?"

Charlie acted as spokesman.

"Sir, my brother Jerry here and my wife Diane and I had a car accident and we were wondering if we can stay in your barn just to get dried off."

"No, not on your life. What kind of God-fearing people would we be if we made you sleep in a cold damp barn? No, you three will sleep in our cozy house where you'll be warm by the fire."

"Seth, who is it?" called a voice from an inside room.

"Woman, set three more places for dinner."

In a short while, Alma, Seth's wife, had the home cooked meal prepared and ready for consumption. Peggy devoured the food in a matter of minutes.

"Land's sakes, child, you must not have eaten in days!" exclaimed Alma. Peggy gave the lady of the house a quick smile and hoped the she wouldn't ask her any questions.

After dinner, Seth suggested they all retire to the living room for coffee and cake. When Alma poured the coffee, Jerry reached into his breast pocket, pulled out a pint of Jack, and added some to his coffee.

"Excuse me," said Seth, "but we don't allow liquor in this house."

Charlie took a Luger pistol from his pocket. "Don't get in our way, old folks! Diane, Jerry and I are going to party, so you just sit down and keep your mouth shut."

Charlie made sure that his party wasn't going to be interrupted by placing the couple in another room and binding them. Then the real party began. Jerry found an unsophisticated CD player. From his coat pocket he pulled out a battered CD and shoved it in the slot. Rap music reverberated off the walls and Jerry passed the bottle of Jack to Peggy, who shook her head.

"Don't you want to drink?"

"No, I don't think I drink."

"I don't get it. You don't think you drink. I mean either you drink or you don't," Jerry said, frowning.

"I'm sorry; I mean; I never drink alcohol."

Peggy watched as the brothers consumed the bottle of Jack Daniels. She became frightened as they began to snort the cocaine. The music became louder and more threatening. The combination of Jack Daniels and cocaine put Charlie in an amorous mood. He stared at Peg, and even though she had been disheveled by four days of captivity, in his eyes it didn't diminish her physical appeal.

He didn't have to worry about any rivalry from his brother, Jerry had passed out. Charlie went over to Peg's chair. He kept looking her up and down, making her shiver.

"Hey, baby doll," he leered, "I saw you watching me. You know that you and I have some sort of chemistry. Let's find us a place where we can be alone."

Perspiration began to form above Peggy's upper lip. She knew in her gut that whatever she was before her memory loss, she didn't deal in one-night stands. For some strange reason she had the urge to call out to someone or something to protect and save her from this evil onslaught. She communicated to the Benign Being.

I don't know who you are, but I sense that we have met before, that you are greater, more powerful than this man. I come to you weak and defenseless, begging you to protect me from this man.

Peggy found herself looking up at a gigantic figure with a chest span of four feet, who hovered over Charlie. The man commanded awe and radiated mighty power. He had sweeping light golden hair and his face was radiant with love.

When Charlie yelled, Jerry lurched from his stupor onto his feet. Both of them saw him; they had no idea where he came from. They frantically ran out of the house, screaming as if possessed. The massive figure vanished as mysteriously as it had appeared.

Peggy rushed into the bedroom, where she untied the old couple. As she comforted them, her memory began to return. Praising God, she asked Seth whether she could use the phone. He directed her to it. She immediately called Mike's cell…no answer. She then called Mike's house. Mrs. Ryan was so happy to hear Peg's voice that she didn't give her a chance to speak. Finally, she told her that Mike and John were driving to New England in search of her.

Peggy opened the front door and there was a familiar woman standing on the front porch aiming a rifle at her face.

Mike was too hot under the collar to deal with anything, much less the jail; consequently wisdom dictated that John would handle any negotiations that would aid in their release and ultimately in finding Peggy.

"Guard," said John, "could I make a phone call?"

"You know that a perp has to be arraigned before a judge," Mike put in nastily.

John grabbed Mike by the lapel and dragged him to the opposite corner of the cell. "Mike, you're not helping Peg or our cause by mouthing off at the guard. He's just following orders."

Mike already knew he'd acted foolishly. "Yeah, man, I guess I'm not acting very professional."

"Brother, pray, and just let me handle the guard." John walked back to the front of the cell.

"Guard, could I have a word with you?"

Reluctantly, the guard came to the cell, and said resentfully, "Yeah, what do you want now, to give me more insults? You cops from New York think you're such big deals and you look down on us. We do have serious crimes in Ridgeville, you know."

"Officer, no matter what region of the country, police work is one huge headache," John agreed, placating the officer. "Look, wherever you come from, we're still brothers."

The guard appeared mollified. He unlocked the cell and held the door open just enough for one man to pass. "You," he said, motioning to John, "follow me."

Complying, John followed him to the front desk.

"Here," said the guard. "Make your call. I'm going for a smoke. I'll be finished in a few minutes. Tell the sheriff and I'll just deny it."

John quickly made the call to Lieutenant Dunbar and filled him in about the sheriff and the need to rescue Peg. Dunbar became furious.

"Those stupid hicks! How dare they try to put a monkey wrench in an investigation? You tell whoever is in charge of a rinky-dinky town like Ridgeville that if they don't release my detectives and give them every courtesy, the feds will wreak havoc in that one-horse dump."

Seth came to the door behind Peggy and was shocked to see a woman facing them with a high-powered rifle.

Rachel pointed the gun at him. "Get inside before you get hurt."

The old man stumbled back, almost falling. He was saved thanks to Peggy's sturdy hand. Peggy looked at Rachel.

"These are innocent people. All you want is me. I'm willing to go with you if you'll leave them alone."

Rachel looked at Peggy and started to laugh in an eerie way. "There you go again, ordering people around, just like Tamara. You just think you're superior to everyone."

Peg prayed silently: *Dear heavenly Father, please give me words that won't ignite Rachel. Give her a compassionate heart for Seth and Alma.*

"You two get out of here, if you know what's good for you," Rachel ordered, pointing toward the front door.

"This is our home; we have nowhere else to go," Alma cried.

Peggy saw Rachel's rising reaction of anger. The elderly lady didn't know who she was dealing with.

"Alma," said Peggy, "please do what she says. There has to be a neighbor you can run to."

Clutching each other, the elderly couple left reluctantly, disappearing into the rain.

The two women found themselves alone. Rachel spoke first.

"You thought that you outsmarted me. But here I am again. I vow that in a few minutes you'll be down like all the others who have tried to ruin my life. Don't bother trying to talk me out of killing you."

Peg knew there was no use reasoning with Rachel. In spite of the odds being stacked against her, Peg experienced an indescribable peace. Her only option was prayer.

O dear Father, I have a lot to live for. I have always thought your plan for me was to serve you and bring others to you. What about Michael and Jamie? I 'm confused. But Your ways are not my ways and being engulfed in Your love for the rest of eternity is good enough for me.

"Margaret Younger." Rachel's voice took on an oddly conciliatory note. "This is going to be smooth and painless; I'm doing you a favor which you don't deserve."

Rachel aimed the rifle at Peggy's forehead. Her finger caressed the trigger, and as she began to squeeze, Peggy saw the awesome figure again. The heavenly guard lifted up the rifle as Rachel pressed the trigger, forcing its fiery explosion to deposit the shell in the ceiling. Peg, stunned, had the presence of mind to run out the door into the rain-soaked woods. Recovering from the shock, Rachel ran after her prey.

Flying in a Nassau County Helicopter, Lieutenant Dunbar listened as Agent Rogers mapped out the strategy for the rescue of Detective Younger.

"Tell me, Lieutenant Dunbar," said Rogers, "are Detectives Mike Ryan and John Paulson all right?"

"Yeah, I told that tinhorn of a sheriff to release my men or I'd put his head in a sling," said Dunbar.

The agent snorted. "I guess he stood up and took notice."

"Mike and John are on their way to Rachel Giles' place with four officers and six FBI agents with bloodhounds."

The agent nodded. "I hope we're not too late."

"Yeah, the time worries me too. I don't know much about this dame Rachel Giles. We've learned she's responsible for two murders. I'm worried that she believes killing one more won't make a difference."

The chopper hovered over Rachel Giles' vacation home.

Mike and John, with the agents and the Ridgeville officers, crouched and slowly moved across the lawn toward the Giles' house. Mike led the detail and, with his revolver cocked, kicked in the door. The men entered, gripping their guns with both hands, opening doors and checking closets. The first floor of the house was empty.

In the basement they found Fred sprawled on the floor. Mike went over to the motionless body and shook it.

"This guy is finished," he sighed.

A Ridgeville officer found Charlie, and brought him to Mike and John.

"Detectives, I found this guy wondering in the area. He has a fantastic story.

"Who the heck are you?" John asked.

Charlie wore a crazed looked and was trembling.

"Never mind about who I am, there's a crazed beast out there." He tried to describe what he saw.

The detail officers looked at him, and one of the agents remarked. "Look friend you have to lay off the drugs; it's starting to fry your brain."

"Was there a woman with you?"

He described Peg, her color hair, eyes and figure.

"Oh yeah, Diane, she was with us."

"Look pal, either you're an insane pot head, or you're playing games; and if you're not going to be straight up, we're going to rearrange your face."

"Detective, all she told me was her name was Diane. But, I'm telling all of you, there's a monster out there.

"John, I haven't the time for this; I want to find Peggy. Take him away." Mike looked at John pleadingly.

"Where is Peg? We've got to find her John; she's my whole life now."

"Brother, I know it looks dim, but you must trust in the Lord." John continued to survey the room, praying for much-needed clues. He saw a shag rug that was disturbed and noticed that various closet doors were left opened.

"Looks like there's been a struggle," he commented.

"Yeah, said Mike, "whoever was mixing it up must have run outside."

John joined the four officers searching the upstairs for a few minutes, then came down again, while Mike kept searching the living room. “Mike,” said John, “I figure this is Rachel Giles’ shirt. Hopefully, the dogs will sniff it and lead us to Rachel — and ultimately to Peggy.”

“Okay, guys,” said Mike, “what are we waiting for?”

The heavy rain started again, and Peggy kept running through the dense trees, though slowly. The resurgence of rain became more ferocious than before, blinding her with each step. She came to a clearing and was relieved when the fierce rain subsided. Suddenly, she felt something menacing between her shoulder blades. Peggy turned around and found herself once again staring down the barrel of Rachel’s gun. Although Rachel was smiling, she looked at her victim with venom and hate.

“I’m tired of hunting all over for you. I don’t know where you’re going after I pull the trigger, but your destiny is irrelevant to me.”

Rachel began to squeeze the trigger, but stopped when she heard the sound of an engine. The sound rapidly became more pronounced. Headlights invaded the darkness and a helicopter hovered over Peg and Rachel.

Then they heard the scattered voices of men and the yelping of hounds. Lights approached from the woods all around the clearing. Radios crackled. Suddenly a loudspeaker emitted a deafening voice from the helicopter.

"Rachel Giles, this is the FBI! We order you to drop your firearm and put your hands over your head."

Frightened, yet full of resolve, Rachel forced Peg to her knees, aiming the gun at the back of her head.

"Rachel!" This time the voice came from the edge of the clearing. "Rachel, this is Mike Ryan. You've done enough harm! Now put the gun down and back away from Detective Younger."

Rachel continued to ignore the order and started to press the trigger, but Mike jumped between the two women. Shocked and startled, Rachel aimed the rifle in Mike's direction and fired. He hit the ground. Officers leaped forward and wrestled Rachel to the ground, quickly cuffing her wrists. Peggy, seeing Michael down, hurried over to him, grabbed a jacket from an agent and covered his body. He reached up and caressed her face, telling her he wasn't badly hurt, the bullet had only grazed his shoulder. She covered his forehead with kisses crying and laughing at the same time, knowing eventually that he was going to be all right.

Rachael Giles cursed and screamed at the law officers who were escorting her to a waiting squad car.

Margaret Younger was thankful, joyful that the horrendous ordeal she experienced at the hands of Rachel Giles was finally over. Though she regretted having to leave Michael in a New Hampshire hospital, she felt their brief separation was a mixed blessing. She needed time to digest the experience and events spawned by the death of her dear friend, Tamara Steele.

Today she was rejoicing for the man she dearly loved. He was going to be released from the hospital at one o'clock. Jamie begged Peg and Mrs. Ryan to let him skip school to surprise Mike. Naturally, both women conceded.

Peg laughed as she turned onto Mike's block to pick up his mother and son, knowing that he would initially be angry at both of them and for allowing Jamie to miss school. They were familiar with Mike's rigid sense of responsibility, and they would apologize for their *reckless action*. But they also knew that Mike would be thrilled to see his son.

On the ride from Long Island back up to New Hampshire, while Jamie fidgeted with the car radio trying to find a Christian rap station, Peggy's mind returned to her ordeal as a captive. She recalled the tremendous fear that enveloped her, and the torture Rachel inflicted. She shivered at the memory of Rachel's voice trying to rob her of her faith. She marveled at her brief encounter with amnesia. Just the fact that she had survived, despite Rachel's insanity was a miracle; and Mike and John's untiring commitment to finding her touched her spirit. Peg felt a wave of humility come over her as she thought of God's intense love.

Peg looked at Jamie and smiled, as he was keeping time with the music.

Mike sat in a wheelchair waiting for Peggy and his mother to rescue him from this torture.

He had to agree with the hospital staff: he was an impossible patient. He complained about the food, the pain in his shoulder, the other patient in the room, and his attending physician, whom he harassed daily about getting him an earlier discharge. The only saving grace about his confinement was being able to see John, who, after returning to Long Island for a short visit with his wife, had decided to drive back to Ridgeville to tie up loose ends. He brought with him a copy of The *Long Island Newsday.*

"Well, brother," he said to Mike, "we made the papers." John handed him the copy of *Newsday*, and Mike read the headlines:

> *Nassau County Elite Indicted*
>
> *Corruption and conspiracy traced to the highest office in Nassau County involving the brutal murder of famed evangelist Tamara Steele. Officials await arraignment in Nassau County Courthouse Today.*

Mike continued to read down the column.

> *George Winthrop, son of Kenneth Winthrop, if found guilty, is expected to serve fifteen years to life for his part in the murders of Cora Smothers and Howard Carey, plus another twenty years for bribery and extortion involving the Merrick Plan in which Samuel Bower, Nassau County Executive is directly implicated.*

Bower has resigned his office. When pressed for comment, Bower's lawyer shouted NO COMMENT to the journalists surrounding the former County Executive.

In a related story, the lawyers of Rachel Giles, wife of former televangelist Julian Giles, have made a deal with the District Attorney. She has confessed to the murder of Tamara Steele and Fred Barnes. She stands to spend the remainder of her life in an institution for the criminally insane.

Mike put the paper on a tray. "Well, I guess justice is served."

"Yes, brother," said John, "and if justice hadn't been served, the guilty involved would still have to face a *Righteous Judge*."

Mike looked at this wonderful man of God and said, "Amen, brother, amen."

Epilogue

Weeks after the Steele case was brought to trial the whole country was focused on the determined efforts of the first African-American U.S. president to enact health care reform. Michael glanced at an article on the topic and tossed the newspaper onto his desk. How could he be interested in something so remote and foreign to his life? Nothing and no one could take precedence over God's precious gifts to Him: knowing Jesus as Lord, and being loved by Margaret Younger.

He and Peggy had agreed not to be partners. They concluded that working together would be too complicated. John Paulson became Mike's full-time partner. They would meet a half a hour before work each day and pray together, and once a week they had a Bible study. Life was exciting.

Dunbar had been strangely courteous lately, which made Mike wary. But Dunbar no longer had the power to hinder Mike's joy and his peace.

Mike thanked the Lord for his new relationship with his son Jamie. After weeks of regularly praying with Cops for Christ, Mike remembered when Jamie was born the pediatrician told him and Katie that Jamie had cerebral palsy and would probably not have a "normal" life. He would have to attend special schools and undergo various therapies. He realized that deep down he was ashamed of Jamie's disability. Katie loved and cherished her wounded infant son.

No matter how Mike tried to be joyous over his newborn son, he grieved for the child and for himself. He didn't know the implications of Jamie's disability. Questions continued to haunt him. Could he function like *normal* kids? Could he be proud of him? Or, would he be ashamed of him? He shared his sorrow with Katie and she condemned him. He agreed he was acting like a creep, and so he began stuffing his feelings.

He was counseled by some brothers in Cops for Christ and now truly believes that the Heavenly Father understood and had forgiven him. They also advised him to share his secret with Jamie, which he did.

He asked Jamie's forgiveness. Jamie hugged his dad, telling him that a Deacon at church prepared him for this possibility. He had known of his father's shame for some time.

"Son, you never told me. Why?"

"Pop, I knew you would be hurt. I didn't want that."

"Jamie, you're some kid."

They both hugged and wept, holding one another.

Ever since Mike had made Jesus the Lord of his life, the Carpenter from Nazareth never ceased to amaze him. This was especially true when Lieutenant Dunbar called him into his office one dreary Monday morning.

Mike looked at John after the call came through, raised his eyes skyward, and trudged through Dunbar's door.

"Good morning Detective. How's Jamie?" Dunbar asked, pacing slowly in front of his desk.

"Okay," said Mike.

"And your shoulder has it healed?"

"Lieutenant, I sure hope so; it's been three months since I was shot."

"Oh, yeah, of course. . . Did you know that the sergeant's test is being offered in a couple of weeks?"

"Yes, I know," said Mike. "The notice is on the bulletin board. Lieutenant, was there something special you wanted to talk to me about?"

"Oh yes. I'm sorry. I don't know how to begin. But I've heard that you're a member of Cops for Christ, and I wonder if you could tell me something about the group."

Dunbar walked to the door, checking to see whether anyone in the squad room was listening. He shut the door firmly, came back and sat opposite Mike. Then the lieutenant opened up. He talked about his wife filing for divorce, and said with genuine grief that his children had been acting cold and distant towards him. Shocked, Mike, who was filled with the Holy Spirit, spoke of the heavenly Father's profound love for Dunbar, and explained that a personal relationship with Jesus supersedes any earthly one.

After leaving the Lieutenant's office, Mike rejoiced that Jesus had chosen him to be His instrument.

Although Peggy's days were filled with joy because of Michael's love for her and his deep commitment to the Lord, she was somewhat subdued. In some respects, the Steele murder had wreaked havoc on her emotions, and she had much to process. Tamara Steele's murder presented many doubts, doubts she never experienced before. She couldn't perceive a person like Rachel could hate her so much to torture and plan her death.

Michael added to her confusion. Lately, he had been pressuring her to marry him. Only a few weeks ago she would have rejoiced and praised God at the prospect of being Mrs. Michael Ryan. But she knew as long as Katie's murder wasn't solved, and her killer remained free, Mike would continue to be haunted by guilt.

However, God had fulfilled a part of her heart's desire. She knew that Michael loved her and would always be there. Jesus' greatest gift to her was revealing Himself to Michael. For this, she was grateful.

Breinigsville, PA USA
19 May 2010
238373BV00001BA/1/P